REVOLUTION

An Anthology

Caroline A. Gill
Christina Benjamin
Desira Fuqua
Jessie Campbell
Kelly Risser
Nooce Miller
Raye Wagner
Tricia Zoeller

Fragile Peace

War Brides

Vagabond by

Collette

Foreword by Janet Wallace & Carlyle Labuschagne

Compiled by Katie M. John
Sponsored by Little Bird Publishing House

Cover Design by Philip Benjamin of Benjamin
Designs.

Caroline A. Gill. *All The Good In The World*

Christina Benjamin. *Wings of Liberty*

Desira Fuqua. *Rebellion*

Jessie Campbell. *Sacrifice*

Kelly Risser. *Rise From The Ashes*

Nooce Miller. *Shattering Glass*

Raye Wagner. *Narcos*

Tricia Zoeller. *The Last Thunderbird*

Cover Designed & Copyrighted by Philip Benjamin of Benjamin Design.

Used with permission.

ptbenjamin@gmail.com

"SOMETIMES WE MUST BE BRAVE
ENOUGH TO GO IT ALONE, DESPITE THOSE
WHO DOUBT US, SO THOSE FIRST STEPS
ON THE DARK AND ROCKY PATH BECOME
BLAZING TRAILS FOR OTHERS TO FOLLOW
– AND SO THAT EACH OF US CAN FIND
OUR WAY TO EACH OTHER, THAT WE
MAY GATHER AT THE BONFIRE OF OUR
DREAMS."

Janet Wallace

FOREWORD

By Janet Wallace
Founder of UTOPiA Con

Katie M. John, author and founder of Little Bird Publishing House, sponsor of the #UTOPiA2016 Revolution Anthology, asked me to write a foreword for the book that includes eight fictional short stories that, at their core, center around change, sacrifice, rebellion, and hope, in the many different forms those virtues come in.

How does one write a foreword to a revolution? You don't, at least not a traditional one. When faced with revolutionary ideas, dreams, or even a li'l anthology project, it's good to make a break from tradition. You let the stories and heroes speak for themselves, stand for what they believe in…on their own.

What I can do, though, is talk about how very proud I am to be a part of an anthology and a community that, at every turn, whether it's on social media, or through everyday business pursuits and interactions, shows me the kind of person I want to be. A community that shows me not only what is possible, but what is actually taking place all around us — in the writing caves, at the cons, and over the airwaves — true collaboration in the spirit of adventure and betterment for all.

The three main tenets of UTOPiAcon are education, inspiration, and collaboration. These three words are mantras I repeat daily to keep me on track, to make sure I am doing and giving my best for and to this community. And from the concept of the anthology, to the partnership between Little Bird and UTOPiAcon, to the cover design contest, to the contribution to Help Build A Library in South Africa, to introducing readers to new authors, to marketing with bloggers, to the stories themselves, this project has represented the heart of those three tenets, beating out a rhythm of a tribe dedicated to leading dreams to success.

One of the most exciting things about this anthology is how global in nature it is. UTOPiA is based in Nashville, TN. Little Bird Publishing House has its home in London. And Help Build a Library in South Africa is located in Johannesburg. In addition, the authors all reside in different states. This project has shown me the positive and far-reaching influence that UTOPiA has had on the global writing and reading community, as well as how many of us think and dream and live and thrive beyond borders, highlighting our similarities — our struggles and desires.

It's inspiring to see how we are drawn together like magnets to our destinies. How like minds and like hearts can outshine negativity and fear. How together we are stronger than when we stand alone. But sometimes, we must be brave enough to go it alone, despite those who doubt us, so those first steps on the dark and rocky path become blazing trails for others to follow – and so that each of us can find our way to each other, that we may gather at the bonfire of our dreams. There we will stand on the ruins of our pasts, and roast marshmallows over the dancing flames, celebrating each battle, each scar, and each victory.

As you read the short stories housed within the pages of the anthology, or any story you read really, I hope you'll remember that behind each is a journey of vulnerability and courage... the author's, the mother's, the daughter's, the sister's. Perhaps the story or the story maker will inspire and motivate you to pursue your own truth, whatever that may be for you.

Janet Wallace
Founder of UTOPiA Con

ABOUT

HELP BUILD A LIBRARY IN SOUTH AFRICA FOUNDATION

By CARLYLE LABUSCHAGNE

I was totally blown away, to say the least, when I was contacted by both Janet Wallace (Founder of UTOPiA) and Katie M. John (Founder of Little Bird Publishing) about the anthology, 'Revolution' and how they wished for the profits to be given to my library project back in South Africa.

Books and their authors have the power to make real change, not just to an individual, but on a wider social scale. When I deliver books to underprivileged kids, my heart swells no end to see the impact that these stories have on them.

The money made as part of this project is going to make a real difference; it's going to allow me to move the project to the next level, paying for books and shipping costs (not cheap with the worrying South African inflation issues) and allowing me to raise the profile of the foundation.

Of course I have to say a very huge thank you to each of the authors; Raye Wagner, Christina Benjamin, Kelly Risser, Desira Fuqua, Caroline A. Gill, Tricia Zoeller, Nooce Miller, and Jessie Campbell who participated in the anthology, the cover designer, Paul Benjamin, the team at Little Bird Publishing House, and the UTOPiA team.

Katie and Janet hold a special place in my heart for my author journey wouldn't be what it is without their influence and support. In becoming an author, I was able to find the courage and inspiration to do that for others, especially to those who don't have the means or knowledge of what reading and writing is all about. This anthology can help me help the youth of South Africa realize there is a future in reading and writing in our country!

I followed UTOPiA con since year one, only dreaming I would one day be able to be there with my author heroes who pushed me and taught me so much. They inspired me to understand where I could be and what I could do for myself and others. The impossible came true in 2014 when I attended my first UTOPiA. I was so overwhelmed by the people, and the event in general was something I lived with each breath.

Without UTOPiA, I would never have realized that dreams are what we make, and that even the odd ones like me have a place in the world. I gained impossible confidence after attending and became someone who got the blessed life of going after what I wanted: it totally changed me into who I am. It's not something I can easily put in words – only tears – as most UTOPiANS know me! It's an event every creative person should attend.

Thank you to you, the reader of this book, for contributing and shaping young lives in South Africa.

Carlyle Labuschagne
Founder of Help Build A Library In South Africa Foundation &
Author of The Broken Destiny Series
www.carlylelabuschagne.com

CONTENTS

NARCOS

By
Raye Wagner

ABOUT

Raye Wagner grew up just outside of Seattle, Washington. As the second of eight children, she was surrounded by monsters, demons, and her sometimes mortal family. She read heaps while locked away in her room.

Raye studied the art of medicine long before she had an interest in the Gods or Mount Olympus, and still practices part-time as a nurse practitioner. One sunny afternoon, the myth of the Sphinx dropped into Raye's mind, and she started scribbling the outline of the story after her sister confirmed it was worth telling.

She writes young adult fiction for teens and adults.

Raye enjoys Tae Kwon Do, baking, and spending time with family. She and her husband live in the suburbs of Nashville, Tennessee with their three children, a dog, and room full of reptiles.

www.rayewagner.com

Prologue

"This is not what we agreed," Sef hissed. Fear clenched his stomach, and he wished they'd never come back to Mexico.

The smell of Teloloapan wafted through the open doorway. The stench of garbage and overripe fruit hung in the warm humid air, but the sour odor of unwashed humanity standing in front of him made him cringe. This was the second time this month the terms of their arrangement had changed. Not that the underling in front of him would know. And not that he'd care, either.

Just last week, Duarte had told Sef the price had gone up. He just didn't want to believe it.

As if in acknowledgement, the man shrugged. His once white tank was stained with dark flecks splattered along the hem.

"It's your life. If you want our protection for you and your family, this is what it costs." He tapped a crusted fingernail on the doorframe. "Right now."

Sef pursed his lips. If he paid, he'd effectually be agreeing to the new terms. But if he didn't pay… Was he willing to take that risk? No, he wasn't. "Just a moment." He swallowed back the frustration at his own impotence. Where were the police?

Even he knew the answer.

"You have five minutes," the Narcos replied. He turned and nodded out to the street.

Five young men leaned against a shiny black sedan. Their filthy clothing was stained and ill-fitting. The nod signaled something, and two of the boys ducked into the car.

Sef closed the door and rushed down the tiled hall to the small bedroom. He'd almost taken his meager earnings from the *tienda* to the bank this morning. Now, he was glad he hadn't. He dropped to his knees and reached under the bed.

"Sef?" Mariela came around the corner, cradling her swollen belly. Her petite body looked ready to burst with their first child.

"Hey, baby, I was going to clean the…"

Sef stood, a large coffee can in one hand, a fist-full of bills in the other.

Mariela frowned. "What are you doing?" Her confusion spread between them, a testament to her naivety. "What's going on?"

"No time to explain, Mari." He brushed by, the urgency of the situation more pressing than his wife's consternation. He could tell her later, when he had time to find words that wouldn't scare her. Let her continue to believe she was safe.

This horror. . . She wouldn't understand. Even though she'd been born in Mexico, she was raised in the Estados Unidos, a nation sheltered from the rampant evil of the drug trade. Narcos were a rumor there, a story told by politicians to scare their constituents. Nothing like the reality; a poison that permeated the populace of the southern country; a threat that oozed fear and trepidation into the very air they breathed.

"No, Sef." Her grip stopped his rapid retreat. "What are you doing with our money?"

He pulled her hand from his sleeve, cursed her stubbornness, and sent a plea heavenward. "Protection. It is for our protection." How else could he explain? Without waiting for a further response, Sef hurried to the front of the house. He flung the door open and jerked to a stop.

The swarthy man now stood just off the left side of the porch, far away from the front door. He faced the street and the young men, his dark, oiled hair reflecting the sunlight. There was no shift in his posture as he continued counting,

"…three, two, one." He finished, and without even looking back, he waved his hand. At the signal, three young men raised automatic rifles to their shoulders and pointed at the entrance to Sef's home.

Sef lurched forward, extending his hands, begging them to take the money.

Peppered shots punctured the air. Sharp heat ripped through Sef's abdomen, pushing him back on the porch. Blinding pain pulsed through his chest, then his legs, and he collapsed on the rough wood. Blood saturated his torn shirt, and his life dripped down the front of him.

All the while, his gaze fixed across the patch of concrete at the boys ending his life. He opened his mouth to beg, but the words wouldn't come. His hand stretched, reached, holding out his offering.

The smell of copper drowned out every other scent. His vision tunneled, and he could hear someone screaming.

His last thoughts were not of his beautiful young wife or their unborn son. He didn't question the injustice of the violence that was ending his existence. And contrary to popular belief, his life did not flash before his eyes.

His last thoughts were simply...

But here is your money.

Chapter 1

"Mom!" Rai slammed the door shut with his foot. "Mom, I'm home." He dropped his backpack on the floor and walked the twelve feet from the front door to the kitchen. One glance was all it took to see his mother wasn't there. Only a few more strides to check the two bedrooms, the bathroom, and...Nope. She wasn't home.

He went back into the kitchen and scanned the meager offerings. Hopefully, she was at the market. He grabbed a banana from the fruit bowl and saw the note on the table.

Dr. J called and needed help. I will be back by 5 *with groceries!* *Do your homework before you go* *play! Love, M x*

Gah! He wadded up the paper and threw it in the trash with his banana peel. It was too hot to do homework. He flopped on the couch and flung his arm over his eyes. It was too hot to do anything. The birds outside chirped and sang, and the distant sound of the river teased him. But his mom would flip if she came home and he was at the water. A soft rap at the kitchen door interrupted his peace, and he rolled to the side with a groan.

"Go away, Adan." His mumble was lost in the upholstery of the cushions.

The knock came again, this time harder.

"I said," he stood and with three strides crossed the floor and flung open the door, "go away..."— his voice dropped to just above a whisper —"Aden." His skin flushed as he looked down, not at his best friend, but Aden's sister, Izel. "I'm sorry. I thought you were –"

"Aden. Yeah, I got that." She laughed. Her dark hair hung loose over her shoulders, and her hazel eyes were a bright contrast to her warm russet skin.

The small sound tickled his heart. "Um, want to come in?" He swallowed the nervous lump that blocked his throat. When had she gotten so pretty?

She shook her head. "Mateo and Aden want you to come to the river. I'm just here because they wanted a head start."

More like wanted to make sure he'd come. Aden knew about Rai's homework, Rai told him about the hours it would take to get it all done while they sat next to each other on the bus. He also knew how Rai felt about Izel. Irritation with his friend swirled with his own conflicting wants and responsibilities. No, Izel would be there.

"Okay, let me change," he told her. Leaving the door open in case she wanted to come in. He walked back to his room.

"Can I have a banana?" Her voice carried down the short hall and in through his open door.

"Of course." He threw his school uniform on the bed, and came out in cut-off jeans that he'd outgrown last year. His arms tangled in his green t-shirt as he struggle to pull it over his head.

Izel laughed again. "Seriously? You can't get your shirt on?" She pulled the bottom hem loose from the sleeve it was tangled in.

His head popped through the opening at the top, and his eyebrows pulled down.

"Oh, come on now." She poked him in the stomach. "Don't be a baby. You know I'm just kidding."

"Don't call me a baby."

Her eyes widened, and her lips curled up slowly. "Baby." She giggled. "Baby. Baby. Baby!" She leaped away and ran out the kitchen door still holding her banana and ran down the worn pathway. "Baby!"

It took him seconds to catch her and throw her over his shoulder. "Who's the baby now?"

"Stop," she shrieked.

As if carrying a sack of limes, she jostled and bounced against his shoulder as he ran down the path.

Her giggles made it difficult to finish her sentences. "Stop...You'll smash...my...banana!"

But he couldn't stop. His momentum combined with her extra weight propelled them forward as he practically slid down the slope to the river.

Three steps in and it was deep enough that Rai let his legs give out and the two of them collapsed into the cool water.

Izel's black hair fanned out between them. He allowed himself a moment to enjoy the simple pleasure of their interaction, perfect and uncomplicated... and then suddenly her hair disappeared.

Rough hands forced him under. Rai struggled for air, his lungs already short of breath from the run. He turned, his eyes and hands reaching for his tormentor, but the silt and sand obscured his view. He flailed, kicking his legs out. Muffled sounds came from above the water, the splashing of his hands as he struggled, and he kicked again and again. Finally, he connected, the weight released him, and his head popped up in time to hear Mateo cursing.

"¡Punta!" Mateo rubbed his shin. His classically handsome features marred with a scowl.

Rai sputtered and tried to catch his breath. "What's wrong with you?" He stood in the shallow water, his hands on his knees, and he looked up into Mateo's dark eyes. "What was that for?"

Mateo shrugged. "I was just messing around."

The temperature climbed despite the fact Rai was still in the water. Time seemed to stand still and Rai's eyes travelled from Mateo, to Izel, to Aden. Aden cocked a brow at him as if to say, 'Well?'

"Right." Rai reached out his hand to Mateo.

Mateo took his hand and pulled Rai in for a chest bump. "Yeah, whatever. You should apologize to Izzy, not me."

Rai looked at Izel. Her hair hung straight and wet, her clothes clung to her skin. He blushed and looked away. "Sorry, Iz. I shouldn't have dumped you in the river."

"Whatever," Izel huffed. "I thought that's why we came down here... to get wet. You didn't do anything wrong." Her eyes hardened as they turned to Mateo.

But Mateo wasn't looking at them anymore. He was halfway up the bank headed towards the rope that hung over the water. "Come on, *cabrones*! Last one in the water has to pay for lunch tomorrow!"

"Then you'll be buying, idiot." Rai's voice chased after Mateo.

Aden's gaze went to his sister. "You all right?"

She rolled her eyes. "I already said I was fine, stupid. Come on." Cupping her hand she splashed at her brother.

Seconds later, there was a shout overhead, and Mateo swung out over the water.

Several hours later, Rai and his mother sat at the table, finishing dinner.

"Did you get your homework done?" Mari's voice was soft, but Rai could hear the iron behind his mother's words.

"Almost," he lied. "I'll go finish it up after I get the dishes done." Rai stood and cleared their places.

His mom laughed. "Nice try." She smiled, and there was no trace of anger on her features. "Did you even start it before Aden and Izzy dragged you off?"

He couldn't help the blush that crept up his neck and blossomed on his cheeks. He cursed his fair skin, a gift from his father's European heritage, for betraying him. "I—"

"No, don't try and explain." She stood and took the remaining dishes and followed him into the kitchen. "It wasn't so long ago that I don't remember what it was like to have friends."

"How did you know it was Iz?"

His mother pointed to the door, and there on the floor were

her sandals. She must have taken them off when she came inside to wait for him, and were left behind when he chased her out of the door.

She grabbed another towel. "How was school?"

He shrugged. "Fine. Same old, same old."

She nodded. "And your grades?"

"Mom." He rolled his eyes. "I'm doing well."

"Good, good. I just want you to be able to go to a good college. College is so important."

He laughed. He'd been hearing this lecture since he could remember. "I'll go to college. Maybe I'll become a doctor, like Dr. J."

"If I could be so lucky." She leaned over and kissed him on the cheek. "Now go do your homework."

Serenity descended over their home. The warm air smelled faintly of ripe fruit, and the splashing of the river carried on the breeze. Rai opened his algebra book and stared at the complex equations. The numbers and letters swam in front of his eyes. With a deep breath he shut out the world and forced himself to concentrate.

Hours later, his eyes burned with fatigue. He finished math, history, and his speech for debate. It was dark out, but the glow from Xtepal rose through the trees. He stared at the golden haze that rose above the trees and thought of Izel. It would be best if he could forget about her. If she were just the annoying sister of his best friend, but somewhere in the last year she'd started to change. Or maybe he had.

A flash of white lit up the night sky. Seconds later a boom echoed up the hillside, and a blast of heat pushed through the air. Billowing black curled through an orange haze where the golden glow of Xtepal had been minutes before.

"*Dios!*" His mother's voice carried from her room. Moments later she opened his door. "They are here, Rai. The Narcos are in Xtepal."

Chapter 2

"Do you remember when the Narcos first came?" Izel's eyes slid to the well-groomed man at the back of the bus. His oiled hair and new clothes were a stark contrast to the other riders.

She leaned over the aisle to whisper to him, as if that would draw less attention. As if every male occupant wasn't completely aware of her. "Do you remember?"

Rai nodded. It had been six years ago. The memory of that day at the river, his conversation with his mom, all of it burned in his memory with the blast of destruction that had occurred that night. "When they bombed the police station?"

Izzy grimaced. "No. When they started visiting the shop and demanding money."

This was something she'd never told him. Even Aden had never said anything about this. It sounded too much like how his father died. "They ask you for money?"

She shrugged, and her tank top slid off her shoulder with the movement.

Rai's fingers itched to push it up and cover the hot pink bra strap. His gaze darted around the bus and met the dark eyes of the slime-ball in the back. The jerk had the nerve to smirk. Rai narrowed his eyes and shifted so he was facing Izel. "Do they ask you for money?"

"Not me, just Aden and Papa. But not anymore. Aden said they stopped a while ago. Did they ever ask you for money?" She pushed the tank's thick strap back on to her shoulder.

The tension in his chest released a little. He contemplated her question. Had they ever asked his mom? She'd never stand for it. Would she? He shook his head. "Why did they stop?" Change couldn't be good; there were more Narcos now than ever before.

"No idea. That's what I was going to ask, if you know what's changed? Mateo said—"

"Iz, you got to stay away from him." Something had happened to Mateo in the last year. The anger that simmered just under the surface was bubbling over more and more. But more than that, he'd shown up last week with new shoes. Nike shoes.

Izel rolled her eyes. "I'm not with him anymore. We were just hanging out."

The people jostled and bumped as the bus drove over the rough road.

Rai knew they'd broken up. Aden told him that Izel had made him be there in the house when she ended it. No matter how caviler she seemed now, she'd been afraid.

Someone yelled. A rapid pop of gunfire broke through the noise of the bus. Someone screamed, and the bus lurched as the driver slammed on the brakes.

Terror, sharp and hot ran through Rai's veins. He stood and swayed with the movement of the bus before crashing into Izel. "Scoot—" He fell into her, and shoved her next to the window as he took the outside seat.

Her hands braced against his body, even as she shifted over. "What are you—"

The bus skidded to a stop.

"Don't leave my side," Rai warned. This was wrong. Somehow his mind refused to believe this was happening. It couldn't be happening. It was the risk they took anytime they left their homes.

"Everybody up!" The oily man stood, his hand reached behind him, and then he brandished a handgun. "Get. UP!" He scanned the occupants of the bus.

Rai's stomach dropped.

The man swung the gun, and pointed it toward the front.

Rai covered Izel, his body draped over her, smashing her into the vinyl seat. He ducked his head into her back.

A small whimper escaped her lips, and Rai's heart contracted.

The gun popped.

A hush fell, followed by a piercing scream that turned into a heart-wrenching wail.

"Don't look," Rai whispered. He felt her nod against his chest.

"Get off the bus!" the Narco yelled.

Cold metal pressed into Rai's back, and his heart stopped.

"Do you need a personal invitation, pretty boy?"

Rai sat up, and pulled Izel up with him. "No, sir," he choked out. Pain exploded in across the top of his head, and his vision swam. He only knew he wasn't shot because the gun hadn't gone off again.

"Get off the bus then."

The Narco yanked him away from Izel and shoved him forward. Rai lost his footing and stumbled to the floor. He struggled to right himself, his vision still blurry, and his head throbbing. His hands gripped the tops of the seats as he guided his way down the aisle. Agony blasted through his back and he tumbled down the stairs landing in the dirt. Another detonation of pain, and Rai curled up into a ball.

"Stupid."

"Line them up," a familiar voice filtered through the haze of pain.

Rai lifted his head, only to be met with another kick.

"Keep your head down if you want to live, pretty boy." The Narco from the bus punctuated his statement with another kick, and then another.

He couldn't breathe. Rai sucked in short breaths, each one felt like a knife in his chest. There was something wrong. Tears leaked through his closed eyes. This couldn't be happening.

"No!" Izel screamed.

"Izzy!" Rai sat up, the world spun, and he tried to find her in the crowded mass.

"Rai!" Panic laced his name.

"I said stay down," Oily man said as he gripped Rai's shirt.

Rai refused to even look at him. His gaze scanned over the people, trying to find…

They'd separated the women and the men. No, the young women.

"No!" Rai struggled to stand. Nausea gripped his stomach, the sharp pain in his side pulsed, and his vision swam.

Something hard smashed into his face, and Rai doubled over. Another hit, and darkness rushed to claim him.

As Rai slumped to the ground, his vision tunneled.

The girls were being herded into vehicles.

The last thing he saw before darkness claimed him, was a pair of new Nike shoes.

He started with the police.

"The *camellos* took them all." Rai stood at the counter in the small police station, and eyed the heavy man in front of him. He'd told him everything that had happened, even described the oily man who'd been at the back of the bus.

Deputy Simon nodded his head and scratched something on a piece of paper. "All the girls?"

"Yes. No. But most of them." It was the third day he'd been to the police station, and the third deputy. He looked around at the other officers. Where were the other two he'd spoken to?

"Mm-hmm." The fat man scratched something else on the paper. "And they were kidnapped?"

Rai glared at the obese officer in his rumpled uniform. "Yes," he bit out. "Herded them into cars or something."

"Or something?" He raised his eyebrows. "How many were there?"

"How many what? Women? Narcos?" Rai glanced at the paper the police officer was writing on. *Santa Maria!* He was doodling? There were no notes, not a single thing about the oily man, the cars, the new shoes. None of it. Rai balled his hand into a fist. "Why aren't you writing this down?" He pushed his anger to the side. "How are you going to catch them, if you don't know who they are, or what they look like?"

"Look, son—"

Something deep within him snapped. "I am not your son." Rai leaned forward into the man's space and glared at him. "They are kidnapping our girls, and you are drawing—"

The officer took a step back, and let out a slow deep breath. "How long has she been gone?"

His tirade was cut, just like that. Rai wanted to cry, and storm, and yell, but his heart was pierced and bleeding. "I didn't tell you—"

"Listen, this isn't my first bull-fight. Someone took off, either your girlfriend, your sister, or maybe even your mother. I get it. It's not the first time this has happened. But don't come in and spread stories trying to get help." The man straightened. He crumpled the paper in his meaty fist, and threw it in the garbage. "Don't you think if a bunch of women were kidnapped, we'd be doing something? Don't you think we'd have a line of people in here, not just one sad teenage boy?" He shook his head. "Go home. She'll come back, or she won't. But don't waste our time with your drama."

Rai's mouth gaped open. "But the Narcos—"

"Get. Out!" He punctuated his command with a fist to the countertop.

How could this be happening? How could no one have come forward?

Silence descended over the small office. His gaze darted to the other officers. Four other men stared at him darkly.

When the policeman swore, and started around the counter, Rai knew he'd get nothing from him. Nothing from any of them.

Rai turned and ran.

Chapter 3

"What do they do with the girls?" Rai asked. He shifted from foot to foot refusing to sit down on one of the plastic chairs.

Everyone else had come and gone. Rai had sat through the meeting barely listening to the angry muttering of his neighbors. He'd ignored Dr. Javier's plans. Shut out every explanation, every question, every answer. All that mattered was this.

"Does your mother know you're here?" Dr. Javier straightened the chairs in the cramped waiting room, further scuffing the grayed tile.

Rai gritted his teeth. "What do they do with the girls?"

Dr. Javier flinched and faced the young man with a grimace. "What do you think they do with them?" He blew out a long breath. "I'm sorry, Rai."

Rai froze. "What do you mean?"

"You want me to spell it out? They keep them in animal pens. The camellos use them, rape them, beat them. If Izel is lucky, it will only be one man. Sometimes when they are done, they let them go. Sometimes they kill them."

"No," Rai whispered. "You must be joking."

Dr. Javier slammed a chair on the ground. "Does it look like I'm joking? Do you think we're meeting at four in the morning as a joke? There is nothing funny about this Rai. Mari has done her best to keep you sheltered, but those dead bodies in the square are the people of Xtepal. They're the ones that got caught rebelling against the Narcos."

Rai shook his head, as he backed away from Dr. J. "No."

"Someday you will have to decide what you stand for, Rai."

Rai opened the door, and the cool air of Xtepal flowed into the stuffy room. The smells of sunshine and dirt, the smells of home called to him. "No."

"Say hello to Mari for me," Dr. Javier said. He straightened the last chair in the waiting room and then walked to the back of his office.

Rai fled.

*

"She's been gone for two months," Aden said. His shoe traced circles in the dirt. His eyes fixed on the ground.

The two young men stood in the patch of earth outside the Moreras' tienda. At one point Aden's mother had planted flowers there in that spot of dirt. Rai remembered orange blooms on a vibrant green bush. That was back when the store got a fresh coat of paint every year. Back before Mr. Moreras started drinking. Before Mrs. Moreras ran away.

"She didn't run away."

Aden's words brought Rai back to the present, and his thoughts went to Izel. "I know. I was there." It had taken six weeks before he could take a deep breath. He'd had two fractured ribs, and there was a new bump to his nose where it had been broken. Self-consciously, his hand went to the bump.

"Not Izzy. My mom."

Wait… "What?" How had Aden known Rai was thinking about her?

"Mom didn't run away." Aden looked up, his face ravaged with a grief. "She was going to Catepec to visit her family. The Narcos got her. Just like Izzy." His eyes were swollen and red with unshed tears.

Oh, no. No, no, no. An ache blossomed in Rai's chest. The pain he forced away from his heart broke through the dam and flooded him. "Santa Maria," he swore.

"But Izzy's still alive." Aden's jaw hardened, and he kicked a rock, sending it skidding across the alley.

Rai wished it were true. Sometime in the last four years he went from tolerating his best friend's sister, to loving her. Not that he'd ever told her. At first it was because she'd chosen to be with Mateo. And then it was because... He couldn't even remember anymore. Had he been to shy? Was that all? Such a stupid reason.

But after what Dr. Javier had told him, he wasn't sure if it was better for her to be alive or not. Selfishly, he hoped she was.

"How do you know?" What he expected was for Aden to tell him something about how he would know, because Izel was his sister. Something about their sibling connection. Something about the love they had for each other.

"Mateo told me."

Shock clenched his throat, and Rai spewed his drink, spraying Aden with sticky orange fluid. Words wouldn't come. He couldn't be... There was no way... "What the heck—"

Aden frowned, and wiped his face with the hem of his shirt. "Yesterday."

Rai hadn't seen Mateo for weeks, but then, he'd spent a while at home recuperating, and then he'd gone into Cordoba to register for classes. Not that he wanted to see Mateo. The memory of new sneakers made him doubly suspicious. "He's with them, isn't he?"

Aden pursed his lips until the skin blanched. The vein at the base of his neck pulsed, and his gaze filled with hate. He shifted and closed his eyes.

"If the Narcos have her..." Rai wasn't even sure what he was asking. Could they get her back? Would they let her go? Would Mateo help? Had he been the one at the bus?

"It doesn't matter, Rai." Another rock skittered across the dirt. "There's nothing we can do. Besides, you're going to school in the fall anyway."

Why did he sound bitter about it? "I thought... Aren't you coming?" They were going to room together. Rai's aunt knew someone close to campus, and had got them a room.

But one look at Aden told him the answer. His friends eyes dropped, and his jaw clenched.

"You know I can't. I need to stay and run the store. Dad…" He lifted his shirt hem and scrubbed his face. "There's no reason for me to go to University now."

"But, you were going to be a biologist. You're going to save all those lizards, and—"

"Stop!" Aden's yell carried over the noise of the alley, and an eerie silence fell.

The sounds came back gradually, the clinking of dishes, the chatter of women. But Aden's body was a coiled snake ready to strike.

"Don't you get it?" Aden seethed. "Not everyone has a mom that wants something better for them. Not everyone has your life, Rai. Some of us live in the real world, with real problems, and it sucks. So don't ask me why. Just don't."

It was a sucker punch. Of course, Aden had to stay home now. Who else would care for his father? Who else would care for the store? There was no one left.

"I'm sorry." The words felt so inadequate, like such a measly offering.

"I don't want your pity." Aden clenched his fists. "I don't need it."

"No, of course… not." Santa Maria! He couldn't say anything right. "What about—"

Aden shook his head. "I have to go. There is… something I have to do." For the first time that afternoon, he met Rai's gaze. "I'm being a jackass, but…" He barked a laugh, but it rang false of humor, and when his gaze came back to Rai, his eyes were filled with tears. "You were my best friend." He held out his fist, and it trembled in the space between them.

Rai bumped fists in their childhood fashion. Up. Down. Straight on. The fist-bumps predated the horror of their lives. It predated the Narcos. It even predated Mateo.

"We should—"

"I've got to go. For real, man." Aden drew his shoulders back, and fixed a smile on his face. "I'll catch ya' later, bro."

Two days later, Aden had on a new pair of sneakers.

*

He'd lost everyone.

Rai sat on his bed staring at the stucco ceiling. The yellow paint above had chipped away, revealing previous green and blue coats, and in places gray concrete. The warm air hung heavy with lazy sunshine, and a fly buzzed teasing the silence.

Rai held a picture of Aden, Izel, and himself to his chest. It had been taken only a couple of years ago, but life had still sprawled ahead of them unencumbered with worry. The *camellos* were a concern for the adults back then, and they'd gone to the river every day that summer and played in too cool water. The siblings' wide smiles captured their unfettered joy, and their teeth a bright white contrast to their russet skin. Rai's glance had fallen to Izel, and in truth that was the summer he'd first noticed her as more than his best friend's sister.

Izel. He growled his frustration, and in a swift movement he stood and slammed the picture down on the dresser.

How could Aden join them? After they took his sister? It made him want to punch his friend in the face. As if that would knock some sense into him. No, it didn't matter. He wouldn't let it matter. He was leaving soon, and he would put it all behind him. But the words from Dr. Javier nagged like a sliver, irritating his conscience. He could never joint the Narcos. Never. But if he did nothing, was that just as bad? Could he really fight his friends?

And like a punch to the gut, he felt the certainty of his thoughts. If they were Narcos, they weren't his friends. Not anymore. And could he stand by and let them take any more girls? What if they came after his mother?

The sun started its descent behind the mountains, and the air started to cool. His mother should be home—

"Rai!" Mari's voice beat her through the door, her panic rolling through the house. "Rai?"

He rushed out of the bedroom. "I'm here mama."

Relief washed over her face. "You are okay?" She set her bag on the floor and crossed the room. Her gaze studied him, searching for something.

A deep sense of foreboding clawed at him, and he shoved his fear down. The only thing left to lose was standing safely in front of him. "Yes. I've been here all day."

She nodded and moved past him into the kitchen. The clanking of pots announced that dinner would be early. "Dr. Javier said he saw you last week."

He grunted, as he collapsed on the couch. If there was a way to un-know what Dr. J had told him about Izel and the other girls, he would gladly do it. His hand absently went to his nose.

"Are you going to join him?"

The six words stopped his heart. He sat up. Was she for real? "You want me to join them? *Auto defensa?*" That's what he'd heard they were calling themselves. A nod to self-defense, a resistance fighting against the corruption of the government, and the poison of the drug trade.

The veil that had covered his eyes had shattered. Xtepal was not the same. The people were not the same. Fear ruled them. Fear and the traffickers. At some point, he would have to stand for something. Even if he left like he planned, and went to school, he would eventually want to come back. At least to visit his mom. Could he leave his mom in Xtepal?

Not like it was.

And that was his decision made. "Yes. I'm going to join them."

Mari frowned, and sat next to him sinking into the worn couch. The citrusy smell of her perfume hugged him. She ruffled his hair. "You are cautious, just like him." Tears leaked from the corner of her eyes, a trickle sliding down her cheeks. "He would be so proud of the man you are becoming."

Chapter 4

The early morning dark was sprinkled with fading stars, the moon hung low and heavy. Rai pulled on the door to Dr. Javier's clinic, but it refused to open. The office was locked, and Rai checked his watch again. He was a little early, but the closed door and the silence behind it told him of his ignorance. If they were not meeting here, where could they be?

The buildings of Xtepal ran through his mind. The school had a large gymnasium, but it wouldn't be open this early. Nothing was open, except Mr. Moreras's little store, and he'd walked past it on his way here. Much like Mr. Moreras, the light was on, but no one was there.

So, had the *Auto Defensa* abandoned their ideas? No. Dr. J would never give up.

The church bell rang through the valley. One clang after another rode through the darkness calling parishioners in for worship and confession. Those that needed it most were likely only just going to bed, or passing out.

He would have to stop by Dr. J's later and find out when and where they were meeting.

Rai started back through Xtepal, dragging his shoes on the broken concrete of the roads. The buildings sagged as if weighed down with the worries of their occupants and owners. All around him were signs of the disease rotting them from the inside out. He'd heard that in some towns the Narcos actually built schools, paved roads, and helped the community live better. These were likely stories told to build false hope. How could something evil, build something good? The last dong from the church bell swept out of the valley on the breeze.

As Rai walked past the church doors, he heard the rumble of voices from within. Without pausing to consider who they might belong to, Rai bounded up the two steps and yanked open the door.

The voices stopped.

Dr. Javier crossed the worn wood floor with a smile on his face.

"Rai! You've decided to join us?" It wasn't really a question, as the little doctor pulled Rai into the chapel. "Come, come and see."

But Rai could already see. He could see the defeat written on the faces of the dozen or so men standing around the pews. Anger and defeat. He already had enough of the one, and he refused to give into the other.

"When are we planning to strike?" His only concern was the when and the how – because now that he'd decided, he refuse to do nothing. As he met the gaze of Pedro, Sal, and Michael, they glanced away. Fear snaked its way through his chest, and he faced Dr. Javier. "We are planning on doing something, right?"

Dr. J frowned. "Of course we are." He shifted his slight weight from one foot to the other. "Only we haven't decided what."

That was the easy part.

"We kick them out!" Rai seethed.

"How?" Sal zeroed in on Rai, his thick mustache twitching. "How are you going to do that? They have the guns, they have the power. How are you going to take that away?"

Silence descended. Rai contemplated Sal's point. It wasn't going to be enough to punch or kick. They would have to be willing to fight fire with fire, which meant they needed weapons.

"I have gone to the police—"

Dr. Javier shook his head, then interrupted. "The police have been bought. So has Mr. Santos. I wrote to the *Federales*. They were here last week, and said their investigation turned up nothing."

Something about the worn wood chapel was warm and comforting despite the horror of what was being said. That Mr.

Santos, the governor, and the police were paid off wasn't too surprising. Everyone knew it. But corruption all the way up to the federal government meant there was no legal recourse to the problem of the *camellos*.

"We need to take Xtepal back ourselves," Dr. Javier said. He sat as if his words meant he would have to carry the burden alone.

The other men shifted, and Rai fought the urge to do the same. What Dr. Javier was implying would be illegal. They would be vigilantes.

"What about the police?" Sal asked.

Sal's oldest daughter had been one of the first to disappear years ago. His youngest had been on the bus with Rai and Izzy. Benita. She was only fourteen.

"We will have to kick them out as well." The deep baritone was filled with challenge.

Rai turned toward the voice and saw Raul, a deceptively small man, glaring at Dr. Javier. His dark gaze dared anyone to contradict him.

Raul looked weak with scrawny arms and a narrow waist, and certainly much younger than his twenty two years. But Rai had seen more than one bully humiliated when the slight Raul beat the crap out of them.

"If they are not with us, they are against us," Raul continued. "*We* will need to make Xtepal safe again. No one else will do it."

No one said anything.

Rai's heart thundered in his chest. His thoughts went to Aden, Mateo, and then Izel. Izel. Always Izel.

"I'm in." Hearing it from his own lips solidified his resolve. He was still scared, his palms sweating and his stomach churning, but if it meant even the slightest chance of getting Izel back, he would do it.

A chorus of, "Me, too" and, "All right" rang through the chapel. Rai looked from one face to another. Each mirrored his own fear and conviction with wide eyes, grim smiles, and squared shoulders.

The click of the clock was followed by the gears winding up for the bell to toll.

"We will meet again tomorrow," Dr. Javier said. The solid clang of the bell punctuated his directive as it reverberated through each man's chest. "Think of your best ideas. We will need to get weapons to get the Narcos out and keep them out."

"Or we just kill them all," Raul said.

The idea of shooting someone was terrifying and exciting. Rai wondered if he would be required to do it? Would he have to kill someone? Would he be able to pull the trigger? What if it was Mateo? Or Aden? He hoped it would never come to that.

The sliver of pale light from the new moon kept him intent on the path ahead. Rai shuffled up the narrow dirt road to home thinking about the meeting yesterday morning. Just as it had been all week when they gathered in the early hours between night and day, no one had any ideas how to kick the Narcos out of Xtepal.

The feelings of impotence and frustration built, and he kicked at a loose rock in his path.

As a child, he'd hated living so far out of Xtepal, away from everyone. Now, he actually appreciated his mother's wisdom in keeping them away from what she feared would come. He thought of how it must have been for her to lose her husband to the senseless killing of the Narcos before Rai was even born. If the heavy emptiness in his heart about Izel was anything like what his mother felt, he wondered how she hadn't gone crazy. His morose thoughts were as dark as the night, and the chill of the breeze carried with it a sense of foreboding.

The snap of a twig made him freeze, and his heart sprinted in his chest, begging him to run.

His eyes scanned the darkness, even as he contemplated if he should run to or away from his home. But the thick pitch of night obscured his vision, and his feet refused to move until he could see the threat.

A soft whimper tickled his ears, and his heart stopped. It was human . . . and female.

"Izzy?" Hope blossomed in his chest, and for the first time in four months his heart felt tethered to his ribs. Could it be?

The brush rustled, and more whimpering followed. Rai stepped toward the foliage spilling from the forest. Another cry of pain came through the dark space, this one louder, closer. Desperate.

"Izel!" He crashed into the forest. Panic and fear pounded through his veins. Had she escaped? Or was it some other—

"'Rai?" His name was only a sigh on the wind.

She stumbled into him, and he caught the waif of a girl that once was. Her emaciated frame sunk into him, her ribs pressing into his side.

Rai stepped back, but she avoided his gaze and ducked her head. Even in the dim light he could see the swollen disfigurement of her cheek just below her eye. Her hair was matted and clumped, and her threadbare rags smelled of urine and body odor.

"Hey." He instinctively slid his arm around her shoulder.

Izel flinched away from the contact. She straightened, and a hiss escaped her lips as she hunched over. Without looking at him she stepped around him and on to the road toward his home.

He stared after the broken girl, and the words of Dr. Javier ran through his mind. Hot anger gripped him, and he clenched his teeth as he balled his hands into fists.

Izel tripped, and fell with another cry of pain.

Running to her, the anger inside him screamed for justice.

The thin girl struggled to stand, but before taking another step, she collapsed back into the dirt sobbing. It felt as if his heart was being shredded. He scooped her up in his arms, and pulled her close. Izel pushed at him with arms far too weak to cause damage. Too weak to even push him back. A strangled cry broke from her lips, making his heart hurt even more. As if that were even possible.

"Shh," he soothed. "Let me take you home."

She continued to shake, and pitiful mewling sounds filled the space between her face and his chest. Her tears soaked the thin cotton of his shirt. The stench of abuse was so much stronger up close, and Rai turned his head to the side and breathed through his mouth.

Rage filled him, burning lava spilling from his heart and dripping down to his toes. All of his doubt evaporated. It didn't matter who stood in his way, or why. The Narcos would be stopped.

He kicked at the front door with his foot, and then cradled Izel closer when she winced with the movement. Another whimper floated on the air, and Rai wanted to scream. He wanted to assure her she would be safe, but the words would be vain and foolish promises. Mari cracked the door, and then swung it wide.

"*Santa madre*! Is that Izzy?" Mari backed into the house to make room for them to pass. "Put her in my room."

Rai crossed into the larger bedroom and set Izel on the faded patchwork quilt. As he reached out to touch her head, Izel flinched. Pulling away, she scooted to the opposite edge, and turned toward the wall giving him only her back.

"Iz?" He wanted so much to comfort her. But he didn't know what to do, or what to say.

"Rai, honey," Mari said, as she came in the room carrying towels and clean clothes. "Why don't you go see if Aden is home?"

What she meant was leave, as was evident by her sharp look and pointed finger motioning toward the door.

"Are you—"

"Izzy needs a bath."

Right. He blushed at the thought, and then looked at the girl he still loved. Her sickly, undernourished frame still faced the wall, and Rai noticed sores and abrasions he'd missed before in the dark. His anger surged again, and he recognized the wisdom in his absence.

"I'll be back." He wanted the words to be reassurance, but he wasn't sure Izel even heard him. Or maybe she didn't care. And that thought incensed him more.

Chapter 5

Aden wasn't home. It was probably good he wasn't either, Rai thought as he strode through Xtepal. More than anything he wanted to hit someone, and Aden, the betrayer, would have been a satisfying target.

"Rai!"

He turned and saw Raul striding toward him.

"Have you heard?" Raul asked. "Something is happening with the Narcos."

That moment solidified a sense of mutual purposefulness. "What do you mean?" Rai jogged over to his compatriot.

"Over at the Santos's home. They were keeping the girls there, in the barn. A whole bunch of them got out." Raul grinned.

Izel wasn't the only one that escaped, which filled Rai with hope.

"Want to come with me?" Raul asked.

Rai nodded. Maybe he could help those other girls. Maybe he could strike out at the Narcos. Maybe he could *finally* do something that mattered.

They snuck through the quiet town. Years ago there would have been people chatting outside the Moreras' small store, or the Canva's restaurant that was more bar than restaurant. Canva's was still open, but it had become a place for the Narcos after eight o'clock. Oddly, it was quiet, as had been the Moreras' tienda. Eerily, quiet. Where were they?

The Santos's home overlooked the town. It was by far the nicest home of Xtepal, bordering on a mansion in size.

As Rai and Raul got closer, acrid smoke singed the air. The darkness grew hazy. The two young men looked at each other and without words, both picked up their pace until they were running toward the governor's residence.

Someone was screaming. A sharp burst of gunfire pierced the

air and the scream was silenced. Rai dropped to the ground and noticed Raul had instinctively done the same. With a wave, Raul urged them forward. Crouching they inched their way to the outskirts of the sprawling property.

Two men with machine guns stood at the gate guarding the entrance. A crumpled body lay on the road in front of them. Raul pulled Rai into the thick brush that spilled from the jungle toward civilization.

"If we come at them from the side, we stand the best chance of taking them down," Raul whispered in Rai's ear.

It wasn't much of a chance Rai's rational side told him, but one thought of Izel, beaten and bruised, and his fear burned away.

He nodded at Raul, and then darted across the road.

Every step increased his heart rate, until if felt as if it would beat through his chest. The croaking of frogs and buzz of the night insects would never be enough to hide the noise as he crept through the outskirts of the forest.

As he drew closer, he could hear their voices, angry mutterings that cursed a betrayer of their group.

"He'll get what he deserves come morning for sure. Escobar won't stand for it. They weren't his girls to release."

Rai let the words roll off him and into the mulch at his feet. He now stood just behind the guy on the right. He crept to the edge of the trees and looked to see Raul exactly opposite him. With a nod of his head, Raul threw something onto the road and started to charge.

Time slowed.

The men swung their guns first to the road, and then started to turn as someone screamed in rage. Rai hit the Narco and they both crashed to the ground. Every bit of his anger flowed, and he punched over and over with all of his energy. Again and again and again. Moisture covered his hands, and still he struck out. This man could have been the one to hit Izel. He could have raped her. Another punch and another.

"Rai!"

His narrow focus broke, and Rai looked up to Raul, now wearing an automatic rifle slung over his shoulder, and a handgun tucked into the waist of his pants.

"I think you've got him, man."

Raul pulled on Rai's sleeve, and he stood.

Something in him, the rational part, thought he should be sick about the bloody heap of a man unconscious at his feet. But the image of Izel scooting away from him brought the anger to the surface again, and he kicked the prone figure.

"Get his guns," Raul instructed.

Rai reigned in his emotions, pushing them all, the good and the bad, to the back of his mind, as he pulled the rifle from the Narco. He patted the figure down, finding two handguns and a spare clip. The evil man also had a knife tucked in his boot.

"Now shoot him," Raul said. "One shot, here." He pointed at his temple, and then his heart. "Or here."

And a sliver of humanity burst through Rai's heart. He didn't want to kill anyone. He shook his head. "I can't."

"Can't? No, Rai. You can. Get over whatever misconception you have. There is nothing good in the devil at your feet. If you don't kill him, he will come back to reign more terror upon those we love."

Raul grabbed Rai's hand and shoved his own weapon into it. Rai knew what he was doing and was powerless to stop it. Raul held Rai's hand with the loaded weapon to the man's chest.

"Pull the trigger."

But he couldn't. It was wrong. Murder was wrong.

"Pull the trigger, Rai, or he will kill your mom."

His finger twitched. He tugged at the cold metal, but then released as soon as he met resistance. This was wrong, but there was nothing left but to meet evil with evil. He closed his eyes, and prayed that God would forgive him. With a deep breath, he thought of Izel laughing, as she had all those years ago, all those carefree times before the Narcos came. Time compressed, his memories sped forward to the crumpled girl he'd picked up on the road tonight, and his finger jerked past the resistance.

The shot rang out, and Rai jumped away from the body, dropping the gun.

Raul grabbed him and pointed at the weapon in the dirt. "Pick it up. We've got to go. And next time, don't scream. It gives them too much warning."

Rai gulped down a spark of shame, and then shook it off. They were alive and they had weapons. So far, they'd met their objectives.

"Now the fun will really start. Let's go pick them off like the *cabras* they are." Raul's smile gleamed in the silver moonlight.

It was the only way. Fight fire with fire.

And they snuck through the gate into the Santos's lush grounds. The smell of smoke grew stronger. Fire licked the stables. Men shouted and their shadowy shapes ran back and forth to the well in a frenzy. Others ran to the barn only a few yards away from the burning stable.

"One at a time. Isolate and kill." Raul's instructions were cold and calculated.

Each time Rai pulled the trigger, he told himself that the man he shot could've hit Izel, could have even violated her, and he left his guilt and shame in the dirt in the rivulets of blood that oozed from the victims of his vengeance. By the time the Narcos noticed their numbers dwindling, the fire was out, and the few left were almost too easy to pick off.

When the grounds were clear, Rai and Raul snuck toward the house. The impressive structure's doors gaped an open invitation to enter. Shouting and shooting rang from within.

"Do we go in?" Rai asked from the shadows of the trees lining the stairway up to the gigantic house.

Raul frowned. "We don't know how many are there, and we

won't have any cover. Let's go to the barn and see if there are any girls left to set free."

There weren't, but they found something almost as good. The weapon stash tucked at the back of the barn would arm the entire town for weeks. And without it, the Narcos would lose their advantage. The boys grinned at each other.

"We'll have to hurry. We don't know when they'll send someone out."

"Dump them in the woods. We can have the rest of the group help us move them in the morning," Rai suggested as he pulled a wooden box out of the barn. Raul helped him lift it and together they headed toward the back of the property where woods lined the lush green lawn.

"Good idea."

They worked in silence, running back and forth. After the third trip they heard voices crossing from the house in the smoky darkness. Two, no three men. And there were two more caches of weapons. They could leave now, but then they would effectively leave the Narcos armed to retaliate. Rai nodded at Raul and pulled the weapon from his shoulders. They would have to do this. *One more time*, Rai told himself, and he changed the clip of the rifle.

The voices grew louder.

"He will have his balls and his head chopped off tomorrow."

"It is no less than he deserves. I hope Escobar makes him suffer. All of our girls, gone."

Deep breath in. Rai brought the gun to his shoulder. Breathe out.

"We'll get them back. No one in this town even cares about those bit—"

Shots pierced the darkness. One of the men screamed but the noise ended in a gurgle, and all three of them dropped onto the grass.

"We need to hurry. More will come."

As if Rai needed to be told. The two of them ran, adrenaline pushing them to go faster. The last wooden crate held ammunition, and even with both of them, they couldn't lift it. A voice crackled outside the door, and Rai reached for a gun. It was the sound of a walkie talkie. They had only minutes before the Narcos in the house would know something was wrong.

"Take as much as you can," Raul said.

Rai nodded. He pulled out box after box of bullets, and then his heart stopped. He dropped them all to the floor and held up an oval object with a smile.

They couldn't take all the ammunition with them, but they could make sure the Narcos didn't get either.

Raul nodded in understanding.

"I think you just pull that and then you'll have to run like the devil is chasing you. I don't know how long you'll have before it blows."

Raul grabbed a couple more boxes, and then ran to the door. Rai's palms were slick with sweat. He grabbed the thin metal ring and pulled out the pin. He dropped it into the cache of weapons and ran. He plowed through the door and into a warm body. Someone cursed, but he pulled from their grasp and continued to run. Their shouts faded as Rai pumped his arms and raced into the darkness.

The seconds ticked into eternity, and then the explosion of the grenade rippled through the ammunition turning the night sky orange. The force lifted Rai from his feet. He flew through the air and crashed into the darkness. Someone pulled on his arm, but something was wrong with his vision. All he could see was black. It was then that he noticed the only sound he could hear was a high pitch ringing. Whoever had a firm grip on his arm continued to yank him forward. Rai stumbled after his guide. He hoped it was Raul, and when he was still alive after counting to a hundred, he felt confident that it was. The blackness faded to gray and shadows danced in his vision.

"… do you think you were doing?"

The faint voice sounded as if it were coming through water, but it was possibly the best thing he'd ever heard.

"Raul?"

Silence was followed by a muffled whisper. Finally the voice rang clear.

"Can you hear me?"

Rai nodded. It felt as if his head were going to explode. "Barely. Why are you whispering? Are we still close to the Santos's?"

The force of Raul's clap to Rai's shoulder made him lurch forward.

"I'm yelling as loud as I can. Right in your ear," Raul said. "*Santa Maria*, what am I going to tell your mother?"

Rai shrugged. He was so glad to be alive, and the thought of hugging his mom again brought tears to his eyes.

"Don't cry, Rai. We did it." Raul pulled him forward again, and Rai tripped his way along the road. "Holy crap, I can't believe we did it!"

But they still needed to get the weapons out of the woods, and get the people of Xtepal behind the idea of protecting themselves. And Rai would be useless to help.

"I'll get Dr. Javier. It will be okay. And it won't be over tomorrow. This is only the beginning."

And Rai knew it was true.

Chapter 6

It had been two months.

The Narcos struck back, but their numbers were diminished and reinforcements hadn't been sent when the men tried to retaliate. By the time reinforcements came for the Narcos, Dr. Javier had secured Xtepal and set up roadblocks in and out of the town. Vehicles were combed through, and outsiders were searched at gun point before allowing entrance. The *Auto defense* had lost three people that first week at a roadblock, but the Narcos had been picked off within a few hours, and more men sent to secure the area again.

Rai had been surprised at the number of townspeople that stood up to defend and patrol, and when his vision returned he took up regular patrols, too.

Still Izel refused to speak to him, but she didn't run to hide anymore either. She had been raped more times than she could count, and was now pregnant as a result of one of the assaults. She would talk to Mari when Rai wasn't around, and Mari assured Rai that eventually Izel would find peace again. It was the hope he clung to.

And so he did what he could to keep her safe.

The ambush came from the right. The rapid fire of guns exploded into the night and Rai and Raul dropped to the ground with the rest of their men.

They had trained for this, and within minutes, the attackers became the victims, rounded up and secured.

Rai took a deep breath and leveled the gun at Mateo. "How many?" He asked Raul. He didn't take his eyes off his childhood friend.

"Five," Raul answered.

Five more he would have to answer to God for. Five less to

have to worry about attacking again.

"Do you really think you have the *cajones* to pull that trigger?" Mateo taunted.

He always taunted. When they were younger, Rai thought it made him tough, now it made him pitiable. A year ago he would've been right. The old Rai wouldn't have even thought about it. The Rai that swam in the river with Aden and Izel, or helped his mom bring in the groceries. The Rai that did nothing when Izzy disappeared, or when Aden joined the Narcos. But that Rai? He was dead.

The shot rang out, a loud echo in the silent night. As if the air held its breath, and then with its release came Mateo's scream. Rai cocked the gun again. "Bring me the youngest," he said to Raul.

"He will kill him. Whoever you send back. Escobar will torture him and kill him." Mateo panted through the pain while he pressed on his leg. Dark red seeped between his fingers. "Please, Rai..."

Rai motioned for Raul to watch over Mateo, and then turned his attention to their captives. Three men glared their hatred and defiance. Anger rolled off them in waves. Rai knew what was under that anger. But their fear would not change what they'd do if he let them go. As lead, he could ask someone else to do this for him. But he would not. Not now.

Each shot was a clean kill. One by one, the three slumped forward on the dirt, convulsing and gasping as their life bled out. A dark stain spread from each body, the blood, so much blood...

Rai forced his gaze to the young boy Raul held. His dark hair hung in shaggy clumps, his dingy clothes hung on his small frame, and his feet were filthy and bare. He couldn't be more than seven. Far too young to send back with a message. Hopefully, not too old to save.

"What is your name?" Rai asked.

The child trembled, but stuck his chin out. "Arturo." He

swallowed, and his pants darkened with moisture down the front.

And that decided Rai. "You will go with Raul." His gaze went to the young man, and Raul nodded his approval.

"What about me?" Mateo yelled, and then winced from the movement. "You can't leave me here, Rai." Panic laced his words.

Rai nodded to the rest of the team, urging them to follow Raul.

The coppery tang of blood hung in the humid air. Rai watched as his group walked back toward the checkpoint, and Raul guided the boy further down the road to town.

"If you leave me here, he'll kill me." Desperation dripped down Mateo's face.

Rai released a slow breath, pushing down his anger, tapping down his hurt. He couldn't even look at Mateo, or he'd never be able to ask. "Did you…" He swallowed the pain that threatened to bubble over. "Did you take Izel to Escobar?" he whispered.

The sudden silence was piercing, and Rai didn't need to look to see the guilt cross Mateo's face.

He turned to meet Mateo's eyes. "And what about Aden?"

Mateo froze. "I don't know what you're talking about."

What was he talking about? Both of them knew Aden had joined the Narcos. "Is he climbing the ranks as fast as you are? Are you helping him get his feet wet?" It hurt to think about.

"Aden's dead."

The two words were a knife to his gut, and he clenched the grip of the revolver in his hand. "How?" he asked as he turned to face Mateo. "How did he die?" He closed the gap between them and knelt so they were eye to eye.

Mateo shook. His arms, hands, body. Whether from the shock of the bullet lodged in his thigh, or from Rai's question, Rai couldn't tell.

"Will you take me with you?" Mateo's voice was filled with doubt. "If I tell you the truth…"

Could he? Mateo was not a youth. He'd known what he was getting mixed up with when he'd joined the Narcos.

"What happened?"

"They caught him. Sneaking around the pens where they keep the girls. He'd let a bunch of women go a couple months ago." His face was pale, and his eyes so haunted by the truth. "Escobar caught him. I didn't know... I didn't know it was him, though Rai. Why would he be so stupid?"

"So they killed him?"

Mateo's trembling got worse, and his teeth started to chatter. "Cut off his head." He wiped at his face and smeared blood across his cheeks. "I didn't know it was him."

The world stopped. The meaning of those six words was painfully clear.

Thoughts of Aden came unbidden. Memories of fishing in the river, playing house with Iz, stealing gum from his father's store. Aden, who played peacemaker, was generous to a fault, and who always, always, looked after his sister. Of course, he'd joined the Narcos.

"I won't take you with me." Rai stood. "It wouldn't be fair to the lives we're trying to protect." He released the cylinder and emptied out four shells and two bullets. He slid one bullet back into the gun and dropped the shells in the dirt. The cylinder closed with a click. "You're wrong Mateo. We will fight back. The Narcos are no longer welcome in Xtepal. *Auto Defensa* are kicking them out."

"You won't be able to stop us."

Rai tossed the gun in the dirt in front of Mateo, but just out of reach. "You don't get it." He nudged the gun back another six inches. "We just did."

Rai turned his back and started the walk back to the blockade. He ignored the pleas, the bitter swearing, and then the painful grunts as Mateo slid through the dirt. He was back on the road, enveloped in the dark when the final shot rang out. His steps halted, and he swallowed back the pain of his loss.

"Dr. J is calling for a full report, Rai." Carlos clapped him on the back as he entered the previous military checkpoint. "And he wants it live."

Of course. Someone would have told him that it was Mateo. Probably Carlos. "Now?"

Carlos nodded. "Your shift was to be over at six anyway."

Funny how hours could be seconds, or seconds hours. Time was strange like that.

"You're to be back at six again, though. No rest for the wicked, eh?" Carlos laughed, but the chortle was too hard, too forced.

"I guess not." He saw Mateo's blood pooling under his leg, and blinked the image away.

"Go get some rest, son," Dante said as he entered the base. "We'll need your eyes to be sharp again tonight. Escobar will retaliate when he finds his men dead."

But Escobar no longer had the advantage, and they knew it.

Rai pushed away the thoughts of Mateo. He pushed away the thoughts of Aden. Instead he focused on how he could fix the broken girl he still loved. The one waiting for him at home.

"I will see you at six." He looked at each man and hoped it were true. And then he walked down the cracked asphalt toward Xtepal.

WINGS OF LIBERTY

By
Christina Benjamin

ABOUT

Christina Benjamin is the Award-Winning Author of the Young Adult fantasy series *The Geneva Project.*

Benjamin's writing hooks fans of mega-hit YA fantasy fiction and offers them a new series to obsess over. She paints a vivid world where magic and imagination run wild in her epic tale of adventure, courage and friendship.

Benjamin resides in Florida. She's dedicated to giving back to the writing community. She speaks at schools to inspire creativity in young writers and has created Page-Burners.com, a site to promote fellow YA authors.

www.christinabenjaminauthor.com

Chapter 1 – Paul

Paul shivered as the cool mist settled over him. He considered himself a brave man, but there was something terrifying about being alone in the woods this far out of town. There were tales of witches and magic in these parts. He'd never really given them much thought, but on a night like tonight, he could see how easy it would be to let such thoughts invade his mind. Even with his lantern blazing, he could scarcely see past his horse's ears.

"Whoa, girl," he crooned trying to sooth the spooked mare. "There's nothing to fear. We've done this ride a hundred times." He patted her shoulder, encouraging his mount to press on.

It was true, Paul had taken this ride many times. As a courier for the Boston Committee, he was one of the few reliable riders bestowed with delivering important messages to the militia. But tonight was different. Tonight he rode for the Sons of Liberty. *More like Sons of Revolution*, Paul thought as he rode through the thick fog. The encrypted message in his pocket drove him on. *'This could change everything,'* John had said when handing Paul the letter that evening.

Hidden branches reached from the shadows without mercy. Paul wasn't making much headway and began to think he'd be safer on foot when he heard a loud caw, followed by a swoosh of wings. He looked up, but it wasn't soon enough. A large crow swooped down, screeching and clawing at his face. Paul's mare took off. It was all he could do to stay on and cover his head, trying to deflect the sharp talons that chased him. The horse weaved through the perilous darkness while Paul fought to regain control. He miraculously reined her in and dismounted. He wielded his lantern high with a shaking arm. When he was sure the crow wasn't near, he set it down.

Catching his breath, Paul blotted the blood from his cheek. The bird had got him just below his right eye. He winced at the touch of gaping flesh. He tried to get his bearings. Surely he'd passed the rendezvous point by now, but he could see no hint of his friends. Rustling in the trees behind him caused his hair to stand on end in warning.

"Joseph? Sam?" he whispered.

He was answered with more rustling. Heart pounding, Paul drew his weapon, a .54 caliber flintlock pistol. A twig snapped and his horse reared up, ripping the reins from his grasp. He dove to the ground, desperate to avoid the flailing hooves as the horse bolted into the darkness.

Paul climbed to his feet, wiping the earth and leaves from his sullied pants. "Great," he muttered picking up his lantern. He tried in vain to see through the eerie mist, but it was useless. Hanging the lantern from a branch in a nearby tree, he decided the best thing he could do was stay put with the hope Joseph and Sam would see the light and find him.

Chapter 2 – Cerra

"He's been marked, Cerra."

"Liza, look at him," Cerra pleaded. "He's not here to hunt us."

"You know the rules; he's been marked by the coven. He must be extinguished."

"I'm not so sure we can trust the coven's judgment. I've seen them take bribes from the Redcoats. How do you know we're on the right side?"

"We're on the side of the coven," Liza spat. "How can you have any compassion for these mortals? I'll gladly kill as many as I'm ordered to. They don't seem to have any problem killing our kind – or have you forgotten Salem?"

"I wish I could forget," Cerra whispered as visions of her ancestors being brutally murdered singed her clairvoyant mind.

Cerra stared down at the confused man from her perch in the tree. His horse had run off, leaving him stranded in the forest – not a safe place for a mortal. He held a pistol in his trembling hand. *Brave*, she thought. *Handsome, too.* Even with the gash, it was hard to ignore his beauty. His dark brown hair had come loose from its tie and now hung in curtains, blocking his sharp blue eyes from time to time. She watched intently as he removed his jacket and grabbed his ivory shirtsleeve at the shoulder, tearing it clean off in one motion. The arm underneath was strong, muscular. She guessed his work was of a physical nature by the definition of his muscles. Cerra bit down on her lip as she wondered what the rest of him looked like underneath all that fabric. He was breathtaking. How could she extinguish such a beautiful creature?

She watched him grit his teeth in pain as he bound the gashes on his hand with strips of fabric from his sleeve. He used another to press the deep cut under his eye. Curiously, he stuffed the rest of the fabric into his pocket except for one strip.

Chapter 3 – Paul

Paul was anxious with worry for his friends. They should've met him already. Perhaps they'd been ambushed. There were many against their cause. Thoughts and conversations whirled through his head. *Had he trusted someone he shouldn't? Had they been sold out?* The freedom of the nation was at stake. His nerves itched. He couldn't sit idly by and wait. He needed to get back to town and find out what'd gone wrong. Paul turned toward the tree and reached up, a strip of fabric fluttering in his hand. He was about to hook it around a branch, a message to his friends that he'd returned home, when something caught his attention. His heart shuddered. Two pairs of beady black eyes stared back at him. *Crows.*

He swore under his breath. They were the same vile crows that had chased him down, he was sure of it. Instinct licked his spine – his blood sang, *Danger! Run!*

Chapter 4 – Cerra

The man fumbled for his weapon.

"Now!" Liza called, leaping from her branch in a swirl of black feathers.

"Wait!" Cerra cried, but Liza was already transforming. She followed her sister, transforming as she leapt between Liza and the man. "No!"

In a clash of bodies, the three of them landed in a screeching heap on the damp earth. Liza drew her blade, wielding it high above her head. She screamed as she drove it toward the man's chest. Cerra leapt between them, deflecting the blade expertly with her own.

Liza's eyes glittered with wild rage. "Dare you defy us?"

A blast shook Cerra's mind, stealing her words before they left her mouth. A premonition ripped through her like a bolt of lightning. She shrieked knowing what was about to happen and hurried to defy it, hurling her blade at her sister. It lodged deep in Liza's shoulder and she fell just as the rifle blast Cerra had anticipated echoed through the forest.

Cerra squeezed her eyes shut, trying to stop the tears. The vision had been so real – she'd seen the man fire a clean shot through Liza's heart. She reacted without hesitation, and not a moment too soon. Liza was still alive. Cerra loosed a breath as a bittersweet joy flooded her heart. She'd used her premonition to alter fate – there would be a price. There was always a price. But Cerra hadn't had a choice, she couldn't let her sister die. Still, she knew by saving Liza, she had just sealed her own fate and exiled herself from her ruthless coven.

Liza crouched low, one hand clutching her shoulder where the blade had sunk, the other digging into the earth. Betrayal swam across her shocked face. She narrowed her eyes and growled, "I cast you out, Cerra!" Then, in a whirl of black mist she was gone, leaving Cerra and the man alone in the forest under a rainstorm of obsidian feathers, falling through the mist.

Chapter 5 – Paul

"Don't move!" Paul yelled. He'd scrambled as far away from the strange creature as his lantern would allow. He'd dropped it when they – she – whatever *it* was – descended upon him. Unsure what else could be lurking in the shadows, he wasn't eager to leave the fading ring of light. "I have you in my sights. You should leave while you have the chance," he warned, aiming his pistol.

The figure wilted to the forest floor. It looked like nothing more than a fragile woman, weeping and alone, but he knew he hadn't imagined the scene from moments ago. Paul shook his head to clear his mind. The girl was still there, in a puddle of black robes – her wild, black eyes fixed upon him. "This is your last warning. Get! I won't miss this time!"

"I can't," it replied.

"I mean it. Leave, before I change my mind," Paul bellowed. "Go back to whatever circle of hell you came from!" He cocked his weapon and leveled it at the figure.

"I can't go back. Not after what I have done." It stifled a sob. "I defied the coven and betrayed my sister to save you."

"Bloody hell," Paul cursed, "if that's what you call saving me, I don't need your help."

"No, you don't understand," it pleaded, inching toward him. "I just saved your life. You've been marked. I was under orders to kill you. Just because I defied the orders doesn't mean they've changed. We need to get out of here. Now!"

Paul laughed. "If you think I'm going anywhere with you, then you're even crazier than I guessed."

The creature shifted toward him and he countered, pointing the pistol directly at her chest. They were locked in a stand-off. Paul had been in many before. He knew it was all about eye contact. The minute the opponent dropped their gaze, it was time to fire. Paul stared at the girl in front of him. Her long black hair fell past her shoulders. It was damp and gnarled in a wild way. The skin under her shredded black robes was alabaster white. The sheer amount she was exposing made it hard for him to concentrate.

"My name is Cerra," she said. "I know you probably don't believe me, but if you want to live, I need you to trust me."

"You just tried to kill me."

"I didn't. I swear it. I was trying to save you. I'm tired of killing for him."

"For whom?" Paul asked, curiosity piquing his voice.

"The Redcoat General."

"Gage?" he whispered. "You work for Gage?"

"No – "

Paul didn't give her a chance to respond. He threw his pistol at her head, catching her off guard, he swept her legs and locked his arm around her throat.

"Who the hell sent you?" he hissed in her ear, grabbing at her flailing limbs. Despite what he'd seen, everything about the creature he held forcefully against him felt human, womanly – her body warm against his.

"Please, it's not like that. I want to explain, but we can't stay here; they'll come back."

"Good, then you can have a reunion," Paul said, dragging the girl back to the tree he'd found her in. He grabbed the rope from the lantern and tied her wrists with it, fastening her tight."

"Please don't leave me," she wailed. "They'll kill me. I betrayed the coven. I betrayed my sister… Please, I have no one."

The desperation in her voice was eating at him. *Could he really leave a girl alone in the woods? Especially one frightened for her life?* He walked a few paces away and then stopped, muttering profanities under his breath.

"What the hell am I doing? She tried to kill me." But he

couldn't leave her. He scrubbed his face in agitation and marched back to the tree. "Give me one good reason to help you."

"Because if it wasn't for me, you'd already be dead."

"Prove to me that's not a lie," Paul demanded, bringing his face dangerously close to hers.

She hung her head. "I can't."

Paul shook his head and was about to turn away when she spoke. "At least cut me down. I don't stand a chance like this."

Fighting his better judgment, Paul agreed. The moment her hands were free she wrapped them around his and fell to her knees. "Take me with you. Please. I have nowhere to go. I – " Her words choked mid-sentence, and Paul watched in horror as her black irises bled into the white until there was nothing left. She shuddered and opened her mouth to speak.

"They're on their way. Much closer than you've been led to believe. They've already set sail. The sea teems with red. Red, red, red – over the streets, soaking the earth. The colonies will fall to a crown of roses."

Paul fought the weakness in his knees when he heard her words. "How do you know that?" he demanded, shaking her and pulling her to her feet. "Who told you that?"

She was panting and the look of terror in her eyes haunted him. "I saw it. I saw them coming."

"Who?" Paul ordered.

"The British are coming!"

"How the hell do you know this?"

"I see things," she sobbed. "I saw you die. So many die."

The girl was shaking so much her teeth began to chatter. Paul slipped his long leather duster over her shoulders and set his jaw. "Come on. You're coming with me. Looks like you might be telling the truth after all."

Chapter 6 – Cerra

A boy near the city gates tipped his hat as they passed through. "Welcome back, Paul."

Paul. So that was his name. After the man from the forest agreed to take her with him, he hadn't uttered another word to her, despite her endless questioning. With Cerra's guidance, they'd made it out of the forest fairly quickly, and unscathed. They'd even come across the man's spooked horse, grazing in a meadow on the outskirts of town.

He'd insisted Cerra ride in front of him so he could keep an eye on her. She didn't fight him. Cerra wanted to get as far away from the reach of her coven as possible. On horseback, they reached town in no time. Boston. Cerra had never been there before. Riding through the streets under the cloak of darkness made the hulking buildings seem sinister. Long shadows bled into the orange glow of candlelight dotting the lanes. Cerra's head swiveled from side to side, taking in the strange sights – beggars, drunkards, prostitutes, soldiers. *And they're scared of the forest?* Cerra thought to herself.

As they rode deeper into town, Cerra could no longer ignore the putrid odor that filled the streets. She ducked her head inside the collar of the jacket trying to hide from it. She felt a soft chuckle come from the man seated closely behind her. "You'll never get used to the smell." He reined in the horse. "We're here."

Chapter 7 – Paul

"Have you gone mad, Paul? Bringing her here wasn't a good idea," Sam muttered through curled lips.

"Well, I didn't have much choice, did I? Seeing as you two left me out to dry in the woods."

"I told you, Gage issued a curfew. We couldn't get out. We're under lockdown." Sam argued.

"Since when do we listen to Gage?" Paul shot back.

Joseph put a calming hand on Sam's shoulder. "How about we all calm down. If what this girl of yours says is true, and the British are planning an attack, then she saved Paul's life – and maybe all of Boston if we have enough warning."

Sam snorted. "Say's her. How do we know she's not working for the bloody Redcoats? Giving us some bogus plan to throw us off."

"I'm telling you the truth." Three heads turned to Cerra, who until that moment had been nervously sitting in the corner of the dimly lit backroom.

Sam strode toward her. He grabbed her by the collar and pushed her up against the wall, making the illegal wine bottles clink. "Listen, I don't know what game you're playing, but you're messing with our lives here."

Her dark eyes dilated with fear, but she held her ground. "I'm not playing a game, but they are. I'm trying to save lives. We're on the same side."

Joseph, always levelheaded, slid between Cerra and Sam. "Miss, is there any way you can prove to us what you're saying is true?"

The frightened girl looked to Paul. Running a hand through his thick mop of dark hair, he let out a deep breath and nodded to her. "You can trust him, Cerra. Tell him how you know."

"I have a gift." She exhaled. "I'm a seer, clairvoyant. I can predict things right before they're about to happen, and I'm never wrong." She was met with silence. "When I touched Paul, I had a premonition. It was as clear as day. The British are already on their way."

Sam shook his head, clapping slowly. "Wow, you know how to pick 'em, Pauly. This just keeps getting better and better."

"Now wait a second," Joseph interrupted. "I've researched this in my medical training. There have been proven studies that this sort of intuitive sight exists."

"Well then, *Doctor*, what do you propose we do with her?" Sam asked sarcastically.

Paul finally joined the conversation. "Listen, you both know me. I'm not one to believe in this kind of stuff, but what I saw in the forest tonight... Let's just say, I've changed my mind. We at least owe it to the cause to check this out. Joseph, can you check with the men? Sam, see what you can dig up from Hancock. He always seems to catch wind of this kind of thing."

Both men nodded. "What about her?" Sam asked, jutting his chin in Cerra's direction.

All three of the men shifted their gaze toward her.

"Why doesn't she stay with you until we can verify this," Joseph suggested.

"Me?" Paul balked. "What am I supposed to do with her?"

"Well, I'm not keeping her," Sam sneered.

"Gentlemen," Joseph interrupted. "She's not an animal. She just needs somewhere safe to stay until we sort this out. I have too many patients to tend to, and Sam is already on Gage's most wanted list. That leaves you, Paul."

"Fine," Paul muttered.

"Keep her safe. If this turns out to be true, her gift might be exactly what we need to win this war," Joseph replied.

The three men clasped hands. "Sons," they said in unison.

Chapter 3 – Cerra

Cerra had to jog to keep up with Paul's brisk pace. *Some job at keeping me safe,* she grumbled to herself as she sloshed through the muddy streets of Boston. The hour was late and town was under curfew. Brigades of Redcoats marched about as Cerra and Paul picked their way through the shadows.

"In here," Paul whispered, ushering her down an alley. He disappeared through a door. She paused to the read the sign out front before following. *Revere's Silversmithe Shoppe.* Cerra's eyes wandered back to Paul's muscular arms. *That explains the muscles,* she thought.

Once inside, he lit a candle and headed up a narrow staircase at the back of the storefront. "Home sweet home," he quipped, setting the candle on a modest wooden table in the single room quarters. "It isn't much, but it's mine." His strong hands were on his hips as he looked around. "You're welcome to it," he said, smiling for the first time since she'd met him. He was quite handsome when he smiled. "Make yourself comfortable."

Cerra surveyed the humble room. There was a single bed with a worn patchwork quilt, a table with one chair, a chipped washbasin and well-used workbench. She watched Paul as he walked to the back wall where he hung his gun belt among the coats and other clothing. She felt her pulse quicken when he stripped off what was left of his tattered shirt. He moved to the washbasin and splashed water over his face, scrubbing his handsome features. When he turned back to face her, his chest was glistening. A soft laugh escaped him when he met her gaze. "Like what you see?"

Realizing she'd been gawking, Cerra snapped her mouth shut. "No, sorry – I didn't mean any disrespect."

"Take it easy. I was joking," he teased. "Listen, I already know you're not like most women and I don't have time for pretenses. I'm not sure if you realize it, but you got yourself wrapped up in a revolution."

"I know more of it than you might think," Cerra retorted.

Paul was silent for a moment taking in her sudden flare of temper. A mixture of fear and intrigue washed across his face. "I'm sorry if we got off on the wrong foot. Let's say we start over?"

"And how do you propose we do that?" Cerra asked.

"How about you tell me what you know about the Gage's plans?"

"And what do I get in return?"

"What do you want?"

Cerra thought for a moment. Her mind swam as another premonition rocked her to her knees. She clutched her head as images of her sister and the coven hunting her down seared her mind. When she came to, she was panting in Paul's arms. For a brief moment of disorientation she fought the arms that caged her. "It's just me. Cerra, it's me. It's Paul. I'm not going to hurt you."

When her breath slowed, she stared into his deep blue eyes. They looked honest and kind and full of life. He looked as though he was genuinely worried for her. She'd never known anyone to look at her like that, like a person, rather than a tool to be used for her gift. That's what she'd wanted her whole life, to have a chance to be normal. A chance for happiness.

"Freedom," she whispered. "I want freedom."

Chapter 9 – Paul

Paul breathed a sigh of relief when Cerra stopped shaking and finally opened her eyes again. Spellbound by her unnatural beauty, he couldn't help but stare. Her pale skin was flushed, and there was so much of it exposed. He was used to the modest dresses of the colonial women, but Cerra was certainly not a normal woman. Her bust heaved against the tightness of her tattered black corset, and he felt his own skin prickle with heat. Paul hadn't held a woman in his arms in a very long time. Cerra's thick, black hair felt like silk on his bare chest, and he shivered against it. Her eyes were as black as night, but when she gazed up at him, he saw so much hope in them.

She'd frightened the hell out of him in the forest, but the more time he spent with her, the more he began to realize that she was the one who was frightened. Whether he believed in her ability to foresee the future or not, the poor girl was definitely tormented by something. Her voice broke his gaze. "Freedom," she whispered. "I want freedom."

"Then it seems we're in agreement." Paul grinned.

He helped her to her feet and led her over to his bed so she could sit down while he scavenged around his shabby home.

"Here," he said tossing her an extra shirt.

"What's this for?" she asked.

"You."

"I'm quite comfortable in this," Cerra said looking insulted.

"Well I'm not. Women don't dress like that around here. You need to blend in."

"But we're in your home. Who's going to see me?"

"I am. And I'm not used to seeing that much of a woman, so if you wouldn't mind... It'd be a bit easier to concentrate if you weren't wearing that," he said pointing to Cerra's revealing black dress.

"Oh," she said, biting her lip to hide a smile. "I see. Turn around then."

Paul obliged and worked on getting a fire going in his wood-burning stove.

"Okay," Cerra called. "Is this better?"

When Paul turned back around he nearly choked. Cerra was standing in the center of the room wearing nothing but his cotton shirt. She looked like a seductive angel in the glow of the firelight with the hem of the ivory fabric barely reaching the middle of her slender thighs.

"What's wrong?" Cerra asked seeing Paul's eyes bulge.

"I meant for you to put the shirt on over your dress."

"Well you didn't say that," she fumed, putting her hands on her hips.

Paul's hand immediately rose. "Don't!"

"What now?"

"Please don't do that," he replied turning away but pointing to the rising hem of her garment.

Cerra took a deep breath, exhaling dramatically as she sat down on the bed crossing her legs. "Better?" she asked.

"Much," Paul said when he turned around.

"You sure have a lot of rules around here."

He laughed. "You have no idea."

"Well, why don't you fill me in?"

Paul flipped his chair around and sat on it so he could face her. "The rules are what we're trying to change."

"Who's we?"

Paul studied her warily.

"You can trust me, you know?"

"There's still a lot I don't know about you."

"Then ask," she begged. The pleading look in her eyes went straight through him. He never ignored his gut, and right now it was telling him that he could trust the gorgeous mystery woman in front of him.

71

"Alright," he nodded, racking his brain with where to start first. "What's your full name?"

"Cerra Bonafae."

"What are you?"

"That's complicated."

"Are you... human?"

"No."

Paul stared at her at a loss for words.

"Your people call me a witch, but that's not entirely true. I'm a seer of the Night Shadow coven. My father sold me to the coven when he learned about my gifts. Our leader recently made a deal with General Gage."

"Gage?" Paul interrupted.

Cerra nodded. "He pays for my premonitions."

"And what do you predict?"

"Outcomes to his courses of action and those who might stand in his way."

"Like me?"

She nodded again.

"That's why you said I was marked?"

"Yes, and you really need to let me treat that wound. If Gage sees you with the mark he'll wonder why you're not dead. He might think I was wrong."

"Wrong about what?"

"I told you I'm never wrong," Cerra replied.

Paul met her gaze. "What weren't you wrong about?"

"That you're going to be the reason he fails."

Chapter 10 – Cerra

"I have questions too, you know?"

"It's getting late," Paul replied as he stood from his chair.

Cerra crossed her arms and angrily shook her head. "I guess I can be wrong after all."

"About what?" Paul asked taking the bait.

"I expected you to be different than Gage."

"I'm nothing like him," Paul ground out.

"Really? He wouldn't answer my questions either. All he's good at is giving execution orders. You know you're supposed to be dead right now and I'm the only reason you're not."

"And why, pray tell, did you decided to change your mind and let me live?"

"Because, I'm tired of all this senseless killing."

"How the hell do you expect me to trust you? How many innocent people have you killed for Gage? You can't just flip sides whenever you want, Cerra. This isn't a game."

"That's exactly what this is. It's a giant chess match. But Gage has been cheating. He knew your moves before you made them."

"Yes, thanks to you, no doubt."

"Not just me. He's been using seers his entire career. Haven't you ever wondered how he achieved such a swift rise to power?"

Paul glared at her. "Seems like you two had a good thing going. Why change sides now?"

"Listen, no one ever asked me what side I wanted to be on," she fired back. "I was being used as a weapon against my will. I didn't have a choice, and if you know anything about Gage, you know that's true. He made me believe you were the enemy. But when I saw your face I knew..."

"Knew what?"

"In my premonition, I saw you. Your face, your flag is the

one that offers salvation. You're going to bring about a powerful change for the future." She was on her feet now, walking closer to Paul. "You're a hero, Paul. You save people. You save a whole country. You made me see Gage for what he truly is, a power hungry tyrant. There was no choice after that. I've been on your side since the vision. I just had to wait for the right moment to act."

"You really saw all that?" he asked.

Cerra nodded.

"Fine," he said pulling his chair over again. He nodded for her to move back to the bed. "You get five questions."

Cerra grinned and trotted back to the bed.

"What's your full name?" she asked mimicking his first question.

"Paul Revere," he replied crossing his muscular arms over his chest. "Don't waste your questions. I was serious. You're down to four now."

"Fine." She thought for a moment. "Why were you tying pieces of your shirt to the tree in the forest?"

"Breadcrumbs," he replied.

"Breadcrumbs?"

"Yes. I was going to leave a trail so I wouldn't get lost."

"Oh," she said, smirking. "I don't have that problem."

"Some of us are human," Paul countered, the easiness leaving his voice.

Cerra narrowed her onyx eyes. "What's your agenda?"

"Agenda?" Paul asked.

"Yes, I want confirmation that I'm on the right side, and that you're not doing all this for your own personal gain. What is this cause you and your friends are fighting for?"

"We're showing those loyalist bastards that we can't be strong-armed into silent suffrage. We're fighting for equality, freedom, justice. We know we'll never get that under the crown. We want a new independent country."

"Do you think there'd be freedom for someone like me in this new country?"

"I don't know," he replied. Cerra's heart sank a little but she appreciated his honesty and continued.

"Sons… That's what you and your friends said earlier. What does it mean?"

"It's a code word. We call ourselves Sons of Liberty. It's a name to identify those who are friends to the cause."

"Do you trust them? Sam and Joseph? The rest of the Sons?"

"With my life."

"Sam didn't seem too fond of me. You don't think he'd turn me over to Gage, do you?"

Paul's mouth quirked into a quick grin. "Nah, that's just Sam. He's not too fond of anybody. But he trusts me, and if I say I trust you, then you're safe."

Cerra gazed into Paul's earnest blue eyes. She could tell they'd seen much sadness, yet it hadn't taken the fight and determination from him. When he said she was safe with him, she truly felt it. It wasn't a feeling she was accustomed to. "Thank you," she whispered.

"For what?" he asked.

"For seeing who I am and not running away. For listening to me. For bringing me here," she gestured around the room, "and offering me safety."

"You saved my life. We're even now."

Cerra nodded, making a mental note that Paul wasn't one for compliments.

"Who is she?" Cerra asked, her eyes settling on a portrait on the wall opposite her.

Paul glanced over his shoulder. When he turned back to Cerra again the softness had left his face. He stood and put the chair back in its proper place. "I think you used up your five questions. It's getting late. We need to get some rest. I have a feeling tomorrow is going to be an eventful day."

"But you haven't let me fix your face," Cerra said standing to meet him.

"It's fine," he argued.

"No, it's not. Besides, it does nothing to enhance your features," she said, trying to lighten the mood.

"I don't care what I look like," Paul grumbled.

Cerra reached out and caught his arm. "I don't either, but Gage will. If he sees you with the mark he'll come after me. And when he doesn't find me, it'll be my family who pays for my sins."

"Your family? The ones who sold you to a coven of witches?"

"They're all I have," she whispered. Liza flashed in her mind again, features washed in betrayal. "Don't you have anyone you care about? That you'd do anything for?"

"Fine. Let's just get this over with," Paul said.

Chapter 11 – Paul

Paul sat on the bed apprehensively watching Cerra approach him. She'd warned him it would hurt, but that stitching his wound was necessary. After ordering him to sit on the bed and handing him a piece of clean damp cloth to press to his cheek, she started preparing the needle and thread. She walked over to him, her bare legs parting his so she could get closer. His breath caught in his throat. She was beautiful in the most bewildering way. Her untamed onyx hair, her sparkling black eyes, her skin, so flawless and white. Paul had never encountered anyone like her. Everything about Cerra begged him to touch her, yet warned him doing so could be fatal. Being this close to her was impossible.

"Lean your head back," she commanded.

Paul complied and tilted his head so he was staring directly at her striking face. His eyes locked with hers, both searching for something unknown in the other. As soon as her slender fingertips made contact with his cheek, Paul saw fear flash across her face like a bolt of lightening. Her black pupils swallowed the whites of her eyes again, leaving nothing but blackness to reflect Paul's frightened expression. Cerra's body went rigid. Paul grabbed her face, pulling her forehead to his, wanting to comfort her somehow. "Breathe," he whispered. But as their foreheads met, it was Paul who found himself breathless.

Painful images that he'd spent years burying seared his mind. He saw the only woman he ever loved smiling at him. That smile splintered his heart. All he'd ever wanted to do was protect her, but he wasn't there for her when she needed him. He saw her wrapped in his arms cold and dead. He saw her meager headstone in a field among many others. "No!" he cried, squeezing his eyes shut tighter, but the images just kept coming, like a waterfall of tears that's he'd never allowed himself to shed.

"Addie!"

It was Cerra who pulled herself from the vision first. Panting and covered in sweat, she laid Paul back onto the bed, stroking his face and whispering calming words.

"Shhh… Breathe Paul. Shhh… Don't fight it. Let it pass."

When he finally opened his eyes, they were stained with tears. He shook his head and tried to get up, muttering excuses but Cerra's firm hand on his chest stopped him.

"Paul, that's never happened before. I've never shared a vision with someone."

Paul stared into Cerra's eager glossy eyes and painfully shook his head. He couldn't deny what had happened between them, but he couldn't find the right words to say either.

"She was your wife," Cerra stated.

Paul nodded, still unable to speak.

"I'm sorry," she replied, gently squeezing his hand.

Paul let out a deep, shivering breath.

"Lie down," Cerra said. She grabbed a blanket from the foot of the bed and covered him. "It'll pass. You just need to rest. The visions can take a lot out of you. Especially when you're not used to them."

Paul didn't argue. He let Cerra fuss over him and cover him with the heavy wool blanket, but he couldn't get warm. The visions of his dead wife had seeped deep within him, stealing away all the warmth he'd had in his heart.

Chapter 12 – Cerra

Cerra was at a loss. Mortals were so fragile. She'd always known that. But she'd never fathomed that she would share a vision with one. From Paul's constant shivers, she began to worry that humans weren't built to withstand the aftermath of such power. Cerra didn't know what Paul was going through, but she couldn't stand to see him suffer. Especially not when it was her fault he'd somehow gotten sucked into her vision.

Against her better judgment, she climbed into the tiny bed with him. She slipped under the covers until her warm body was pressed firmly against him. He felt like ice. Cerra rubbed her hands up and down his arms to try to bring warmth back to them. She wrapped her arm across his chest and pressed her cheek to his. "Paul," she whispered. "You are stronger than this. I've seen it. The Sons need you. The new nation needs you."

Paul opened his eyes and stared at her. He looked so forlorn it made her heart twist painfully.

"I'm so sorry for your suffering. I didn't mean to make it worse," Cerra replied.

"You didn't."

It was good to hear him speak again. *At least I didn't fry his brain*, Cerra thought.

"In a way I'm grateful. I haven't seen Addie like that in a very long time. She was so real, so alive. I guess it was just a bit of a shock."

"That's her?" Cerra asked, nodding to the portrait of the fair-haired woman on the opposite wall.

"Yes."

"How long were you married?"

"Only a few months before I joined the war. By the time I got word she was stricken with fever, it was too late. I rode for two days straight but still didn't arrive until hours after she'd passed."

Paul shuddered. "I should've been there. I didn't even know she was pregnant. No one told me. But when I saw her body, there was no denying it. I couldn't save her. I lost her and the baby." A groan racked Paul's chilled body. "I did it to her. I killed her."

"Paul. Small Pox killed them. There was nothing you could have done."

"I wish it had been me. Addie didn't deserve to die that way, riddled with disease."

"I'm sorry, Paul," Cerra whispered. "But if you'd been with her then you'd be dead too. You have an opportunity to make them proud. I keep trying to tell you that you serve a greater purpose. I've seen it. And after what happened tonight, it might be possible for you to see it too."

Paul closed his eyes and took a deep breath.

"But for now, sleep. Tomorrow we can take up the fight."

Cerra stoked Paul's hair soothingly until his breathing became slow and regular. When she was sure he was asleep, she allowed herself to study him. He was handsome, even with the mark etched deep in his cheek. Her heart ached having witnessed the family and love he'd lost. It was no wonder he was hell bent on fighting for liberty. She knew the feeling, having lost her mother to a hunter before she'd learned to hone her power of premonition. She blamed herself for not seeing him coming, and that agony drove her to use her powers for good – hoping it would somehow erase the pain from not being able to protect her mother.

Cerra found herself admiring Paul. He looked younger when he slept – closer to her own age than she'd originally thought. The worry and pain he normally wore melted away when he slept. She continued to run her fingers through his thick brown hair. It was coarse, yet soft at the same time – just like him. It smelled of leather and metal – just like him. She closed her eyes and sent up a silent prayer, hoping she could help this man achieve the success she'd seen so it might ease some of the pain in his heart.

Cerra leaned over him and kissed his cheek. She still needed to do something about his mark. She squeezed her eyes closed, concentrating on pulling the immense pain from Paul's subconscious. It lay heavy in her heart and made it easy to shed a tear on his behalf. She caught the single tear on her fingertip and dripped it into the wound on his cheek. She watched with satisfaction as the X-shaped tear in his skin magically stitched itself back together. She'd never used her power to regenerate on a mortal before and was excited to see it worked.

"Now Gage won't even see you coming," she purred as she laid her head next to Paul's.

Chapter 13 – Paul

A thunderous pounding on the door startled Paul from his sleep. For a split second he opened his eyes to the most beautifully bewitching face he'd ever seen. *Cerra. I'm in bed with Cerra!*

Paul's mind snapped to attention as the events of the past evening crashed through his groggy mind. Before either of them could utter a word, the incessant pounding interrupted them again and Paul's door burst open.

"Paul! What the devil are you doing in bed? Haven't you heard the bells?"

Paul was on his feet in an instant. "John? What are you doing here?" he asked looking around in bewilderment. Cerra had vanished.

"Come quickly. Sam's about to get himself killed. Gage just ordered the most brutal flogging I've ever witnessed in the square as a warning for anyone caught conspiring against the crown, and Sam's gone ballistic."

Paul scrubbed the sleep from his face and looked around the room in utter confusion. *Where on earth had she gone?*

"Paul!" John called, pulling him from his thoughts. "Didn't you hear me? Sam needs us. We need to go talk some sense into my cousin or he's going to get himself killed. He's threatening to march on Gage this instant! I need your help. He won't listen to me."

"Of course," Paul replied grabbing his jacket and gun belt from the wall. "Let's go."

As they made their way to the door, movement near the window caught Paul's eye. He looked over just in time to see a large crow taking flight from his windowsill.

"What the bloody hell is wrong with you today?" John called from the doorway. "Let's go."

Paul trudged after John into the muddy Boston morning. The crisp air carried an energy charged with revolt. He'd felt it building for the past few months. But after the public flogging in the square, the hate was palpable. Boston was a powder keg of tension and it would only take one spark to set the whole town aflame. John was right to worry that his cousin; Sam would be that spark. Sam was the mouthpiece of the Sons of Liberty and after something like this, everyone would be looking to him for a reaction.

Paul followed John to the square, where a small crowd milled about. There was fresh blood on the street, and Joseph knelt over a heap of rags and flesh. As they approached, Joseph shook his head stopping their advance. He was flanked by trigger-happy Redcoats who watched as he tried to treat the afflicted man in the filthy street. Sam was nowhere in sight, which Paul took as a good sign. They followed Joseph's eyes down an alley off the square. Recognizing Joseph's meaning, they changed direction and headed for the familiar passageway.

Paul heard a low caw and looked up to see a large black crow gliding above him. He smiled and trailed John to the warehouse, leaving the door slightly ajar behind him. John slipped behind the false wall and Paul followed suit. There, being restrained against his will, was Sam and about a dozen Sons of Liberty.

"Thank heaven," Hancock said when Paul and John entered the room. "Can one of you please make him see reason? He's hell bent on making himself a martyr."

Paul walked over to Sam, motioning for the burly man holding him to release him. "They're right, mate. Going after Gage now will only get you killed. And that won't accomplish anything."

"Then what will, Paul?" Sam yelled. He was seething mad. "I can't sit here and watch innocent people treated this way. That man was one of our own. If we don't stand up for ourselves, no one will. We have to retaliate. If the colonists think this can happen to them at any time they'll lose their nerve to fight; we have to strike back while we still can."

"We will. And I think I have just the weapon."

Everyone in the room was silent, eager to hear what Paul was proposing.

"You can come in now," he called.

Chapter 14 – Cerra

Cerra stood on the other side of the false wall listening to Paul's voice. Everything went quiet for a moment, and then she heard his voice boom. "You can come in now."

She slowly pushed the wall and timidly entered the dimly lit room. She felt every eye shift to stare at her. She was dressed in a drab gray colonial dress she'd stolen from a clothesline near Paul's apartment in hopes of blending in. The amount of suspicious stares directed at her made Cerra second-guess her choice. She glanced down at her outfit, wondering if she was wearing it wrong. *Maybe I'll never be able to fit in*, she thought nervously as she moved soundlessly toward Paul.

She breathed a sigh of relief when he put his hand out encouraging her to join him and Sam.

"Not this again," she heard Sam growl.

"Just hear her out," Paul countered. "If you don't think she can help the cause I won't bring it up again."

"Who the hell is this?" John asked.

"We're about to find out, aren't we?" Sam replied staring at Cerra.

Cerra pulled herself to her full height and raised her chin as she turned to face John and the crowd of men in the room. She glanced at Paul, who nodded for her to continue. "My name is Cerra Bonafae and I've been working for General Gage. I have inside knowledge of his plans, and I want to share them with you so you can stop him, but we don't have much time."

A hushed murmur rushed through the crowded room. Cerra waited for it to quiet down before she continued.

"He knows about your store of weapons in Concord. It's enough to warrant the King's approval for aggressive measures. He's sent 700 men to Boston. They're authorized to use lethal force on all colonist deemed a threat to the crown. He's also approved a warrant for Sam Adams and John Hancock. Gage knows you're driving the rebellion," Cerra said looking at Sam. "And that you're funding it," she directed at Hancock.

The room was silent. Sam glared at Cerra and paced back and forth, while his friends glanced nervously at each other.

"What would you have us do?" Hancock asked.

"You need to leave Boston immediately," Cerra replied.

"That's not going to happen," Sam said. "Gage is not going to run me out of my home."

"Sam, if you don't leave you won't have a home," his cousin interjected. "You're the head of this thing, and if you die then the revolution dies with you."

"Make no mistake," Cerra added. "The warrant isn't for your arrest. It's for your head. Gage means to have you killed."

"And how do you propose we get out of Boston?" Sam asked snidely. "Gage has Redcoats stationed on every road in and out of the city. Plus the curfew; he has us locked down."

"I can get you out," Cerra said matter-of-factly. "All of you."

"Where would you have us go?" Paul asked.

"Concord. You need to gather as many of your men as you can and get them to your weapons store if you want a chance to defeat Gage's army."

"So you'd have us all go to a place known to Gage? Where his army can surround and ambush us?" Sam laughed. "You must think we're fools."

"No," interrupted a voice from the back of the room. "She's right." Every head swiveled to look at Joseph. He stumbled into the room wearing a white shirt stained in blood and a determined look upon his face as he marched up to Cerra and Sam. "Sam, you and Hancock need to leave Boston immediately. The man that Gage ordered to be flogged was one of our messengers. He managed to give me his message with his dying breath."

Stillness fell over the room as everyone observed a moment of silence for their fallen comrade.

"What was the message?" Sam asked.

"A friend in Philadelphia got you an audience with Washington," Joseph continued.

"General Washington?" Hancock asked.

"The one and only," Joseph said somberly. "He's sympathetic to our cause, but he wants to meet you and Hancock."

"Why?" Sam asked.

"Because you both represent the revolution – the mouthpiece and the money."

"Where does he want to meet?" Hancock asked.

"You're to go to a safe house in Lexington and await word of a secure meeting place."

"But I can't abandon the men – not if what this girl says is true, and we're on the brink of war."

"I'll lead the men while you go get Washington on our side," Paul interjected.

Sam stared him down.

John pulled his cousin aside. "Sam, no one will see this as you abandoning them. If you can get Washington and his army on our side, they'll see it as a victory. We'll gain some credibility as well," John urged.

"Will you come with me, cousin? I could use your advisement," Sam asked.

John nodded.

"It's settled," Sam replied. "We'll gather everyone we can and leave tonight at nightfall. Hancock, John and myself for Lexington, the rest of you for Concord."

"Someone needs to stay here," Cerra interjected. The men snapped their attention back to her, as if they'd forgotten her already. "Gage will be sending men to Concord – of that I'm sure. But we need someone here to signal us when they're coming and by which route."

Paul pulled Cerra aside. "You don't know which way he's coming?" he whispered.

"No, he hasn't decided yet. By now he must know I've fled the coven. He might suspect that I'm working with you since your body never showed up dead as he requested."

Paul shivered but nodded to Cerra and rejoined the group.

Joseph smiled warmly at Cerra. "I'll stay. I can set a signal in the Old North Church bell tower to let you know when the Redcoats are coming."

"That will work," Cerra said. "Light one candle if they come by land, two if by sea. It'll give us fair warning of their approach."

Joseph nodded.

"You're sure about this?" Sam asked Joseph. "I'd feel better if you were with us."

"Yes. I'll be of more help here," Joseph replied. "Besides, I'm the only doctor in town. It would look suspicious if I left."

The men nodded and shook hands with Joseph, conveying their appreciation for his bravery.

"Which route should we take?" Paul asked.

"North wall?" Joseph suggested.

As Sam was nodding, Cerra interrupted. "No. They'll expect that."

"The North wall is the least guarded," Sam argued.

"Precisely," Cerra relied. "That's exactly what Gage expects you'll do. He's set a hundred men beyond the North wall to stop you. You won't make it out that way."

"Then where? Every known exit is blocked." Paul asked.

Cerra grinned. "Let me take care of the exit."

Chapter 15 – Paul

"You're sure this will work, Cerra?" Paul asked for the hundredth time as they huddled in his shop room with all the men they could gather.

"Paul, we've been over the plan. Now it comes down to if you trust me or not. Do you trust me?"

He nodded.

"Then yes, it will work. Just do exactly what we discussed."

Paul tucked the loose strands of his hair back in place – a nervous habit. "But the river is being watched as well. Half the Royal Navy is in the harbor as we speak."

Cerra reached up and steadied his hand, tucking the last stray hair in place. "Yes and even more ships are sailing, getting closer with each moment we delay," she replied with a steely gaze.

"Fine," Paul muttered. "Our lives are in your hands. Remember that."

"I will," Cerra said. "Paul, I promise I'll get you out of Boston safely. All of you."

He met her onyx stare and felt her conviction. He had to look away after a moment, scared that staring at her untamed beauty for too long could convince him of anything.

Sam joined them. "Are we ready?" he asked gruffly.

"Yes," Cerra replied. She pulled up the dark hood of her borrowed cloak, concealing her porcelain face in shadows. "Wait for my signal," she said.

Paul and the men watched Cerra slip out into the night. When the door creaked closed behind her, an icy dread crept into Paul's heart.

"She'll be fine," Joseph offered quietly.

"Paul," Sam warned. "Don't be a fool. There's no place for your heart in war. And make no mistake, what we're doing tonight will incite a war."

"I'm not a fool, Sam. I just happen to appreciate when someone risks their neck to save mine."

"Just make sure that's all you're appreciating," Sam advised.

"What the hell are you insinuating?" Paul barked.

Sam moved closer to Paul so no one else could hear them. "I'm saying, I will not jeopardize the fate of a nation on the whims of a weak-hearted man."

"Weak-hearted?" Paul bellowed.

"Do you think we don't see how you look at her? You're lonely, I get it. I lost my wife too, Paul. But I'm not going to risk the lives of these men by bedding a turncoat."

"I didn't bed her!" Paul growled. "Everything I told you about her is true. She saved my life and is offering to save all of us by risking her neck because Gage has been enslaving her too. She's helping us without being coerced because she believes in our cause. Is that not what we're fighting for, Sam? Honor, freedom, life, liberty?"

Sam studied Paul's face in silence before responding. "I don't give respect easily, Paul. But if the girl is true to her word then she'll have it. But it remains to be seen if she delivers us to freedom or death." With that he mashed his hat on and sauntered away into the group of silent men.

Chapter 16 – Cerra

Cerra slipped into the cold night air as silently as a shadow. She clung to the darkness of the alley until she was almost to the street. A street-light loomed ahead of her, burning brightly. She focused her gaze, lifting her hand toward it. The light began to flicker wildly. Cerra closed her fist, and the defenseless flame was snuffed out. A slow smile crept across her perfect lips.

She strolled out into the street and lifted both arms above her, relishing in the power coursing through her. The coven never allowed her to use her true powers. Since she was their most gifted clairvoyant, they demanded she focus all her energy on her premonitions. Especially once they found that General Gage was willing to pay handsomely for her services. Thinking of his smug face as he gave execution orders fueled Cerra's drive. She quickly clapped her hands to her sides and all the lights in Boston went out.

The hurried footsteps and shouts from the patrolling Redcoats echoed around her, but Cerra found her confidence building. She dropped her cloak and stalked toward the river. She shed articles of clothing as she went – a glove, a ribbon, a shoe, a garter, a corset – until she stood naked in the thick blackness she created. She reached the water's edge and stepped in. The water welcomed her like a cool satin gown. She waded out until the water enveloped her to her chest. Again, she raised her arms to the sky and called to the elements. A crack of lightening illuminated the sky, and the winds picked up. Cerra felt electrified with the elements responding to her call. She lowered her arms, letting her hands hover just above the water's surface as she called the fog to her. It rolled in, blanketing the darkened streets of Boston in a disorienting mist.

Cerra smiled. *Step one, complete.* She leapt from the water, shaking the beading droplets from her obsidian wings. She glided over the silent streets heading back toward Paul's shop. She circled the block before giving the signal that all was clear.

Chapter 17 – Paul

Paul jumped as a loud caw broke the silence – Cerra's signal. It was time to go. He had made up his mind that he trusted her completely while arguing with Sam. He gazed around his shop, taking it in for what he knew would be the last time. He looked at the nervous faces of the forty-six men waiting for his order. They were the hope of the nation, the Sons of Liberty. He set his shoulders and faced them. "Liberty or death."

"Liberty or death," they replied.

Opening the door, Paul motioned for the men to follow him into the alley. It was just as Cerra had promised. The streets were deserted and cloaked in darkness. He ordered the men to link arms and led them by instinct toward the river. He stumbled on something in the street. He groped around and picked up a dark cloak – Cerra's. Paul grinned knowing she'd left him her own version of breadcrumbs to follow. After finding a trail of discarded clothing, he knew his hunch was right.

The fog and darkness made their progress slow, but unimpeded by the enemy. They finally reached the river and four rowboats awaited them, just as Cerra promised. Paul looked at Sam smugly as he climbed into the boat with him, Hancock and John.

"We're not out of the woods yet," Sam chided.

Paul grinned as he picked up his paddle.

"Where is she, by the way?" Sam asked.

"Waiting for us in Charlestown."

"With an army of Redcoats?"

"With horses to get you to your meeting with Washington."

"We'll see."

John laughed and tossed Sam an oar. "Shut up and row, cousin."

After slicing through the eerie fog in silence for nearly an hour, it began to dissipate enough to make out the shoreline of Charlestown. Paul searched the bank for Cerra, but she was nowhere in sight. They stowed the boats in a thicket of reeds and waded to shore. The frigid night air clung to their damp clothes. Paul and Sam encouraged the men to keep moving to fight the freezing conditions. When they reached their rendezvous point and Cerra was still missing, Paul's pulse began to race.

"Something must be wrong. She was supposed to meet us right here."

Sam glanced around. They were at the edge of a farm on the outskirts of Charlestown. Six horses were saddled and hitched to the fence, just as Cerra promised. "We can't afford to wait, Paul," Sam said as he ducked under the fence rail.

"She got us this far. I'm not going to abandon her," Paul argued.

"Look, I apologize for what I said earlier. You were right. She made good on her word and delivered us safely from Boston. If something happened to her, the best way we can honor her is to carry out this plan. You need to get these men to Concord."

Paul fought his heart and nodded. "You're right. And you three need to get to Lexington. Get Washington on our side."

"I won't give him any other option," Sam said extending his hand to Paul who shook it earnestly.

Sam mounted his horse and waited for John and Hancock to do the same. "Godspeed, gentlemen," he called to Paul and the men.

"Godspeed."

Paul unhitched the remaining horses and led them over to the men, where his old friend Will Dawes was waiting. Paul had been the one to recruit Will to the Son's of Liberty. Will helped secure weapons for the Sons from his position with the Massachusetts Artillery Company. He and Paul had fought together in the war ages ago, and Paul trusted Will with his life. *Nothing quite bonds a friendship like combat,* he thought as he handed the reins to Will. Paul was glad to have him by his side to lead the men to Concord.

"What's the plan?" Will asked.

Paul glanced at the waxing moon for a moment. "We give Cerra a few more moments to rendezvous, and then we head to Concord."

Will nodded and relayed the message to the men. They moved to the edge of the forest to camouflage themselves and wait.

Paul's nerves were getting to his horse. The brown mare stamped and snorted. "Whoa, girl," he murmured trying to soothe her. He knew he'd already waited too long for Cerra. It had to be close to midnight. The moon was arcing in the night sky, and he could feel the men growing restless.

"Paul, I don't think we can wait much longer," Will whispered.

Just as Paul was about to suggest they go on without him, he heard a twig snap. Both men whirled loaded muskets in the direction of the sound and found themselves with their barrels aimed at a pale naked figure at the edge of the forest. Her hands went up and Paul called for everyone to lower their weapons.

"Cerra," he whispered as he ran toward her. He barely got his arms around her before she collapsed.

Chapter 13 — Cerra

"You waited," Cerra said breathlessly. "You shouldn't have waited."

"I couldn't leave without knowing you were okay. What happened?" Paul questioned. He took off his jacket and wrapped it around her. Cerra watched him pale as he noticed blood on his hands. "Cerra? You're bleeding. What happened?" he asked again.

"The coven," she wheezed. "I was trying to make sure the route through the forest was clear and they found me. Liza…" she trailed off, her eyes clouding with painful memories. "Gage put a price on my head. I can't go back in the forest, Paul. They'll kill me. I barely escaped with my life."

"What do we do?" Paul asked, panic edging his voice.

"Go. You'll make it to Concord. Gage doesn't suspect you've left yet and I've taken care of the few Redcoat checkpoints he had stationed on the route."

"Okay." Paul hoisted her up and she moaned in pain.

"No, Paul. I can't go with you. You need to leave me here."

"Cerra, I'm not leaving you."

Cerra looked pleadingly into Paul's deep blue eyes. "Paul, I can't go; I'll endanger you all. The coven will come after you if I'm with you."

"You're injured, Cerra. I'm not going to leave you here to die. Not after what you've done for us."

"I'll be fine. I can regenerate. I just need to rest," Cerra said softly. She placed a delicate hand on Paul's cheek, caressing the now flawless spot where his mark had been. She smiled sadly as she closed her eyes.

Paul scooped her up and carried her into the tall grass of the field where they'd been hiding. He gently laid her on the ground and kissed her forehead before retreating toward the men.

Cerra felt a tear slide down her cheek, but it wasn't from the pain of her injuries, it was from watching the only man who'd ever made her feel safe walk away. She closed her eyes tighter, wishing for the shadows of sleep to carry her away so she might escape the pain of her heart, which far surpassed the injuries of the flesh.

Chapter 19 – Paul

Paul stood in the shadows until the last of his men disappeared into the forest. He knew they were in good hands with Will. He'd been to the farm in Concord a number of times already, and Paul had no doubt he could get the men there safely. Especially after Cerra had risked her life to clear the path of Redcoats for them. He hitched his horse back to the fence and made his way to where he'd left Cerra.

She looked so still. Too still. His heart thundered in his chest as he stared at her searching for signs of life. His breath caught in chest until he detected the subtle rise of hers. She was so motionless he'd feared the worst. He let out a relieved breath and sunk to his knees next to her. He couldn't help himself from gazing at her peaceful beauty. It was almost painful to be so close and have such strong feelings for her. She had no idea that over the last few days he'd become spellbound by her. The brave woman that lay before him had risked her life twice for him, and he felt useless to repay her. All he'd done was drag her into his dangerous web of revolution. *And now look at her. She's hurt. Bleeding at your feet, and you don't know what to do.* Paul gently reached down to smooth back her damp black hair. It was as soft as corn silk. He was surprised that someone so fierce and strong could possess such a delicate feature.

"Please don't let her die, Lord. Don't steal another woman from my heart," he begged looking up at the stars.

When he looked back down at Cerra, her glossy onyx eyes stared back at him. "Paul?" she whispered. "Am I dreaming?"

"Cerra," he murmured lowering himself to lie next to her. Face to face, their bodies were nearly touching. "You're not dreaming. I'm here with you. You need to rest," he said gently stroking her face.

She reached her hand out to touch him, as if not believing he were real. "Paul…" she groaned. "Why did you stay?"

"It's my turn to save your life."

"But this isn't what I saw happen. This wasn't part of the plan."

Paul tried to suppress a light laugh. "Neither were you," he said. "I never saw you coming." He laced his fingers with hers and kissed her hand.

She shivered and inched closer to him. Being so close to her was intoxicating. He knew he should pull away but he couldn't seem to force his body to listen to reason. It was acting on its own. Cerra's rushed breath was hot against his neck, and her bare chest pushed against his. With a shaking hand, Paul reached up to caress her face. His rough thumb brushed over her full lips. She parted them and exhaled his name, making every ounce of his being want her.

"Cerra," he whispered against her lips.

Her answer was lost as she parted his lips with hers. Their bodies took over, a tangled swirl of limbs and grass and dew and desire. Paul kissed her like his life depended on it. Being with Cerra was like nothing he'd ever experienced. She left him exhausted and exhilarated at the same time. They explored each other until the stars faded from the night sky. As Cerra drifted to sleep, Paul wrapped her tightly in his arms, wanting to make the blissful moment last.

Chapter 20 – Cerra

Cerra opened her eyes to an unexpected view. She lay nestled in Paul's strong arms in a field of tall grass. Dawn washed the sky, and she felt her cheeks flush when she realized she wasn't wearing any clothes. *So last night hadn't been a dream after all?*

She had trouble suppressing her smile. Waking up in Paul's arms felt spectacular. She gazed at his sleeping face. A thin growth of stubble had come in, adding to his already rugged good looks. She couldn't resist rubbing her fingers over it. Paul stirred and murmured incoherently but didn't wake. Cerra slipped out from under his arm and stood up to stretch.

She felt sore, but more from her tryst with Paul than the coven's attack. Memories of Liza's assault came flooding back as Cerra surveyed her injuries. Luckily they'd already healed, but she found herself heartbroken that her own sister had been the one to inflict them. She'd been stupid to trust her. It was always the coven before blood. Liza's actions proved that last night. Her threats for Cerra to never return to the forest still echoed through her mind.

Cerra scooped up Paul's discarded shirt and pulled it on, relishing the smell of him – leather and metal. She'd felt thoroughly worn out from using her powers to help him and his men escape. She hadn't expected to feel so depleted. As she gazed down at Paul, she smiled, knowing she'd do it over again in a heartbeat to have another night with him. She glanced across the bay. The fog she'd induced had dissipated, and with her keen eyesight she could clearly see the ships in the harbor. She searched the shoreline and when her eyes settled on the Old North Church tower a vision pierced her mind so suddenly her knees buckled.

Chapter 21 – Paul

Cerra's screams woke Paul from his slumber. He was instantly on his feet, moving to where she knelt on the ground. Her hands clutched her head, and she rocked back and forth.

"Cerra! Cerra! What is it? What's wrong?"

When he looked into her eyes, he could see the blackness invading them again. She was having another premonition. As much as he hated it, he sat silently by, not wanting to interrupt whatever valuable information she might be uncovering. He couldn't stand to see her in such pain. Finally her rigid body slacked and the woman he knew returned, staring at him with those striking onyx eyes. He enveloped her in his arms, whispering soothing words.

"What did you see?" he asked softly.

"Two if by sea. They're coming. Two if by sea." Cerra gasped with tears in her eyes.

Paul grabbed her face. "You're bleeding."

Cerra swiped at her nose and her hand came away red. Her lips quivered. "Paul, he knows! Gage knows Sam is in Lexington. He's sending the Queen's Rangers after them while the rest of the Redcoats march on Concord. You have to go warn them."

"Come with me," Paul said pulling Cerra to her feet.

"No, you can't be in two places at once. Go to Lexington and raise the alarm. I'll go to Concord."

Paul studied Cerra's face. Blood still trickled from her nose. "Does this work?" he asked. "In your vision… Do we make it in time?"

Cerra nodded. Paul pulled her into an embrace and kissed her passionately. "Then wait for me in Concord. I'll come find you."

"I know you will," she whispered.

Paul grabbed his coat and gun belt, running to the brown mare still tethered to the fence nearby. When he turned back to look at Cerra she was already gone. He heard the caw of a bird and looked up as a single obsidian feather floated down toward him. He caught it and kissed it for luck before tucking it in his hat.

Without sparing another moment, Paul jumped on his horse. He wheeled her around and spurred her into a gallop heading for Lexington. "The British are coming! The British are coming!" he shouted as he raced past the sleepy homes while the sun started to break into the sky.

Chapter 22 – Cerra

Cerra soared higher and higher, beating her wings in desperate measure. She took a longer route to avoid the forest, but her premonition had told her she would have enough time. She glanced behind her repeatedly to make sure she wasn't being followed by the coven. Her keen eyesight caught two tiny glowing lanterns in the Old North Church tower. *Joseph.* It confirmed her vision was true, and the pit in her stomach deepened.

Just like her vision had predicted, Cerra reached Concord as dawn was breaking. She transformed and ran into the farmhouse calling for Will and the men. Once she'd warned them of the troops marching in their direction and urged them to send riders to warn the rest of the colonists, she set off to find Paul and fulfill the rest of her grim vision. There was no time to waste.

Cerra transformed and took to the sky again. She tried to keep her mind from wandering back to the horrifying vision where she watched Paul get ambushed by the small unit of Redcoats waiting in the forest on route to Lexington. She'd seen a way to save him, but she'd also seen the price. She forced the grim thoughts from her mind and pressed on, pushing herself to her limits. When she was in familiar territory, she dove into the forest calling to her sister and the coven. If her plan stood a chance of working, she'd need the coven to help her.

The trees opened up, marking the spot from her vision. She knew she was in the right location. She perched in a low tree branch and waited, praying she'd timed it right. Not a moment later she heard hooves galloping in her direction. Six Redcoats charged toward her, with Paul tied to his horse, beaten and bloodied. She let out a breath. This was it, she still had time to change his fate.

Cerra didn't let herself look at Paul or even think of failure.

She dove from her perch and descended upon the unsuspecting men, talons out – a blur of black feathers. She went for the horses first, startling them. Four of the riders were unseated. She then turned her attention to the two still on horseback. One leveled a musket at her, the other at Paul. She attacked the one who had Paul in his sights, marking him first. Then she attacked the other after his musket fire narrowly missed her. She marked three of the fallen riders, but the fourth was taken out by friendly fire. One of the Redcoats was trigger-happy and didn't take his own men into account when aiming for her.

Cerra transformed for an instant to untied Paul. "Go! Warn them, Paul. You'll make it."

"But you don't!" he cried out. "That's what you didn't tell me, isn't it?"

"Go, Paul!"

"No! There has to be another way."

"There's not. I've known it since the very first vision I ever had of you."

"Then why did you help me if you knew I'd get you killed?"

"Because you're worth it, Paul. What you do today saves thousands. I will never regret that, nor any moment I spent with you."

"Cerra – "

Chapter 23 - Paul

Paul's voice was drowned out by the call of hundreds of crows. The forest around them darkened as the plague of carrion-eaters descended upon them. The Redcoats screamed and fired their muskets wildly. One of the frenzied soldiers steadied his weapon at Paul, even as the crows swarmed him. Cerra saw it happen a split second before the shot rang out and lunged in front of Paul, as she'd seen herself do dozens of times before.

"There is liberty in death," she cried out as she took the bullet meant for him. It pierced her heart and an explosion of obsidian feathers rained down on Paul as he wheeled his horse around and set off for Lexington.

His heart felt like it'd been torn out, but the pain only fueled his drive. He screamed warning to every home he passed – a man possessed, as he blazed a trail to warn his friends. "The British are coming! Defend your liberty! Join or die!"

RISE FROM THE ASHES

By
Kelly Risser

ABOUT

Kelly Risser knew at a young age what she wanted to be when she grew up. Unfortunately, Fairytale Princess was not a lucrative career. Leaving the castle and wand behind, she entered the world of creative business writing where she worked in advertising, marketing, and currently, eLearning instructional design.

When Kelly is not immersed in the middle of someone else's fantasy world, she's busy creating one of her own. *Never Forgotten* is her first complete series, which includes *Never Forgotten, Current Impressions, Always Remembered, and Sea of Memories*, a novella collection. Kelly is one of the authors of award-winning *Fractured Glass* and *7: The Seven Deadly Sins*. She also has a short story in the *Twists in Time* anthology. She will be releasing stories in several anthologies in 2016 and is busy working on her next series. You can visit her at

www.KellyRisser.com.

Chapter 1

Our ancestors concerned themselves with the melting of the Polar Caps. 'Global Warming' they called it, and spent their days measuring the rising water levels and reduction of icebergs. If they'd only known how little that really mattered. It would only take one natural disaster, and thousands had been waiting to happen. Humans thought themselves so fierce, but they were no match for Mother Nature.

When the volcano exploded, spewing ash across most of what was formerly known as the United States of America, a small group of scientists and their families took to secured underground bunkers. Monitoring the underground volcano for years, they noted its increased activity. They'd tried to warn the public, but no one would listen. A handful of brilliant men and women and their families watched as billions of people choked, drowning in thick, gray ash.

Worldwide media covered the event, and other countries witnessed the demise of our own in horrified fascination. Few viewers realized their deaths were imminent too. While their scientists had a little more time to prepare, no one could save a country full of people in the limited confines of an underground bunker. Even the countries with catacombs lacked advantage, for the passages were not airtight and ash easily infiltrated them. In the end, local leaders tried to control mass hysteria, and they probably saved even less citizens than they had originally intended.

The volcanic particles filled the earth's atmosphere, creating an effective block between the sun and us. The surrounding land baked in the immense heat of the volcano. Animals suffocated, plants died. Lush landscapes became dirty dust bowls. The volcano grew dormant, but ash still thickly coated the ozone. The cold crept in, slowly at first, but soon the soft grayness was tipped in frost. And shortly after that, a thick layer of snow and ice glittered like diamonds as far as the eye could see. The earth had become a barren land of ice.

Of course, I didn't experience any of that. The story was passed through my great-great-great grandparents. I was told that storytelling was the way of our ancestors. All I knew was, I could picture the volcanic eruption with precise clarity, and I only had to look at one of our many recorded images to see the truth of those words. The destruction remained over a century and a half later.

Our numbers were small. There were less than two hundred of us in the "Operation Thermal" settlement, known less formally to us fourth-generationals as Thermal. There was no operation anymore, it just *was*.

The original scientists who'd built it had thought of everything. We generated our own power, which allowed us to provide artificial sunlight, both for our health and to grow fresh food. The animals that sustained us had been selected carefully. We kept their numbers under control and were grateful for what they provided — fresh milk when they were young and meat when they grew old and weary.

Couples married and had children, but they were only allowed to have two. The basic rule was you could replace yourself with an offspring, but not add any more than that. To do so was to burden the community, as overpopulation would surely kill us. Numbers had to be controlled.

"Constance Margaret, would you please tell us the answer?"

Cringing in my seat, my eyes darted to the handful of teenagers around me. I hated school, a requirement until the age of eighteen in our community. My gaze was met with sneers and snickers. The only sympathetic face being that of my best friend Jay, and like me, he was probably not paying attention. He was just better about not being noticed. It wasn't the first time I was caught daydreaming, and my classmates would provide no help.

"Could you repeat the question?" I asked meekly.

With an irritated sigh, my teacher called on Jacqueline Marie, who knew everything or at least pretended to.

"World War II ended September 2, 1945 when Japan formally surrendered," she recited, twisting her lips into that conceited grin I hated. "So, we won, of course."

Jay caught my eye and mouthed, "Know it all."

I hid my snicker in a quick cough, although once Jackie's words sunk in, I couldn't resist speaking my mind. "If by winning you mean we stepped in after millions of innocent people had already been tortured and killed. Miss Moran, why do we study history when the world that created it no longer exists?"

Oops. Wrong question. Sometimes I should just learn to keep my mouth shut.

Nancy Moran was a petite woman with faded brown hair and large spectacles that constantly slid down her sharp, thin nose. While no means threatening in stature, she could pierce a student with a gaze that was felt in your very soul. My heart ached while receiving one of those death glares.

"Your obstinacy has got to be dealt with, young lady. Why do we learn? Why not wallow in our own ignorance while we're fifty feet below ground? Really, Constance. Only through knowing the follies of human history can we create a brighter tomorrow for our children."

Brighter. In artificial sunlight and stale, recirculated air.

Arms crossed, I slouched in my desk. Taking my silence as consent, she returned to her lecture and I contemplated my future. *Six more months of this and then what?* Living underground didn't feel like living at all. We studied how plants grew, but no one was alive who remembered what the sun felt like when it caressed your skin or the wind when it lifted strands of your hair. Everything here was sterile, clean, and predictable. I wanted mess. I wanted adventure. I wanted to be like my hero, Amelia Earhart. She was a woman who knew what she wanted and didn't let anyone get in the way of her quest for adventure.

What I desired over anything else was to go to the surface. It was something I dreamt about for years, but my dreams were safely tucked away. Those thoughts would be considered blasphemous. I couldn't risk my family's status. My dad was a respected member of the governing board, and my mom a lead scientist in agriculture. Reputation was everything, and a rebellious daughter was a sure-fire way to lose it. Lose everything.

"Constance, are you going to lunch or are you going to stare into space all day?" This time, Miss Moran's words were lacking their usual bite. She sounded tired. "Honestly, child. You spend your life with your head in the clouds."

I wish. I'd never seen a cloud, probably never would. I read about them, of course, but reading and experiencing were two different things entirely. Before Miss Moran scolded me again, I rose from my desk and hurried out of the room, walking quickly in the opposite direction of the cafeteria.

Rarely did I eat with my classmates. The only one I really liked was Jay, and he spent the lunch hour being tutored. He was dyslexic and struggled with reading. It would only embarrass him if I hung around to keep him company. Instead, I visited my mom in the agriculture sector. I sat under one of the squat trees on a patch of thin, sickly looking grass and pretended I was in a field. Sometimes, I got so lost in my daydreams that I swore I really could feel the wind blowing against me. The image was lost the moment I honed in on the metallic hum of the ventilation system. Somehow, I didn't think the rhythmic pressure of forced air was anything like the unpredictable currents in nature.

"Having a better day today, kiddo?" Mom settled next to me, handing me half of the lunch rations packed in her bag. Shrugging, I ignored the question and concentrated on my sandwich.

"That bad, huh?"

After a brief, but comforting hug, she dug into her own sandwich. We ate in comfortable silence. My parents were older than most when they had me. Mom admitted that they didn't think they'd have kids at all until I came along and surprised them. Being older and established in their careers, they didn't crowd me by trying to be my friend or burden me with their unrealistic expectations like so many of the other kids' parents. They worked hard and left me in peace. For my part, I tried to stay out of trouble and avoid their radar. Avoid everyone's radar. School made that difficult.

"Lunch break's over, kiddo. Time to get back to class." Mom stood and brushed off her tan overalls. All scientists in the Ag sector wore the same jumpsuit uniform. The salt and pepper of her hair was a stark contrast to her smooth, youthful skin. I thought she was one of the most beautiful women in Thermal.

"Are you working late?" Whenever my parents were late, I made dinner. They appreciated it and selfishly, my stomach couldn't wait until they got home. I'd eat and leave the rest in covered dishes to await their return.

"Probably." She rolled her eyes. "You know the drill. It's almost birthing time. That means long hours."

"Okay." I nodded. It didn't matter if it was birthing time for the livestock, sowing or harvest time for the crops, or just some other run-of-the-mill emergency that always seemed to happen. There was an excuse for the late hours, and I understood it as well as I could after a childhood of spending evenings by myself. That didn't mean I liked it. "See you when you get home then."

She leveled her gaze at me and added, "Get your homework done."

"Yeah, yeah."

I hurried back toward class and Jay caught up with me a quarter of the way there.

"How's tutoring?" I asked the same question every day.

"Tolerable. How's your mom?"

I turned and gave him a sly wink. "The same."

"You free tonight or are your parents going to be home?"

"I'm free. Besides, even if they are home, you know I have no problem slipping past them." Jay and I often snuck out at night to explore. He was a mechanical genius. He could pick any lock and disable any alarm. Over the years, we'd discovered some interesting corners of Thermal, and this place went on for miles underground. There were still many areas we'd yet to discover.

I wanted to check out the main observation room, but it was manned twenty-four hours a day. There was no way our leaders and scientists would let a couple of teenagers anywhere near the fancy equipment in there. But I knew about it from my dad. Machines scanned the surface. They monitored the atmosphere, hoping, at some point, it would be safe for us to journey above again. Four generations had waited. Two of those came and went without ever leaving the bunker. I didn't want to be the next generation that was born and died here. My only goal in life was to get to the surface, and as crazy as it sounded, I would do anything to make it happen.

"I'll come by around nine," he whispered as we took our seats. "Dress warm."

Dress warm? I whipped around to stare at him, but Jay's eyes were locked on the teacher. His lips twitched suspiciously and I knew he was holding back a grin. He loved to get a rise out of me. Why would I possibly have to dress warm? The temperature throughout Thermal was regulated to a constant sixty-eight degrees. There was no variance. Ever.

To dress warm, I'd have to wear layers, because although most of my shirts were long-sleeved, I didn't have a jacket. I only knew about jackets from the history we studied.

The rest of the day passed quickly with my mind only partially focused on class. What had Jay discovered?

Chapter 2

As promised, Jay showed up exactly at nine. He was the only completely reliable presence in my life. When I went to answer the door, I found Dad lying on the couch, his soft snores barely heard over the old movie he'd intended to watch before promptly falling asleep. We didn't have anything new to entertain us. There was no time in the day-to-day running of the compound for the creation of arts and entertainment. The books, music, and movies we watched dated to a bygone age centuries ago. It had been a time of self-creation, a renaissance of sorts, when the internet enabled anyone to post a video, publish a book, or create and share music. Then Mother Nature struck. When the atmosphere thoroughly filled with thick ash, the satellite signals were lost and the internet, the connection humankind relied upon, had disappeared.

"You ready?" Jay asked quietly when I opened the door.

"Am I dressed warm enough?"

"How many layers are you wearing?"

"Five."

With a shrug of his shoulders, he said, "You'll be okay."

"Great." I closed the door with a soft click. Mom was not home yet, and she wouldn't check on me until very late. She never did. And if today was an exception to the norm, I'd tell her I was out participating in a study group. That would appease her.

"Where are we going anyway?"

"Have I made you curious?" His innocent expression warred with the devilish glint in his eyes.

"You know you have."

"Well, you're just going to have to wait a little longer. It's easier to show you than explain it."

It wasn't until he turned to walk down the path ahead that I noticed he had his parents' transportation pod. Not every family had one, but those who worked in science and government did, which meant both my family and Jay's. "Your dad let you take the Therm-1?"

"Not exactly." With a shrug, he added, "It's not like they're going anywhere this evening. He won't miss it." He climbed in and patted the seat next to him. The pod had no doors, and barely held four adults. It only went thirty miles per hour at top speed, though, so the danger was minimal. "Besides, where we're going is too far to travel by foot and be home at a reasonable hour."

"Now you've really got me curious."

Instead of responding, he winked and started the engine. It hummed quietly as we zoomed down the dark lane. Most families were home in their apartments, preparing for sleep. Workdays were long and started early. It wasn't uncommon for Jay and I to explore at this hour, although we typically went by foot. Settling back in the seat, I took in our surroundings. We were headed toward the archive area where they kept all of our historical records from the time before, as well as the records of births and deaths since the start of this community. Jay continued past the archives, and the air grew thick with unpleasant smells from the waste and recycle area. I hoped we weren't stopping there. I held my breath, and thankfully, he kept going. The next stop was the long-term storage wing, an area of the commune seldom visited by anyone. It held the larger discarded items that couldn't be recycled.

I could no longer contain my curiosity. "Where are you taking us?"

"Almost there." He patted my leg, not taking his eyes off the path ahead of him. A few minutes later, he pulled over and stopped. "We'll go the rest of the way on foot."

When he cut the engine, the silence descended upon us. During the day, it was rare for anyone to come to the storage area. At night, it was unheard of. Jay hopped down, pulled a flashlight from his back pocket, and motioned for me to follow.

He headed down a narrow row between tall stacks of crates and boxes. Truthfully, this section always gave me the creeps. Boxes upon boxes of things that were no longer wanted, no longer thought about. The air tasted stale and our footsteps echoed. My overall impression was of eternal loneliness. Since I often felt lonely and out of place as it was, the emotion was the epitome of all things I hated. Still, I followed Jay silently, hugging my arms around myself, not so much because I was cold as I was uneasy.

"Where are we going?" I asked again. "You know I hate it here."

"I know." He slowed and took my hand in his. His warmth eased my anxiety and I let out a breath I didn't even realize I was holding. "But I really think you need to see this."

At the end of the row, I noticed a grated vent. Waist-high, it was partially hidden by a stack of boxes. "We're going to have to crawl through here, but I've done it before, so don't worry. Just follow me."

Jay slid his fingers along the top right edge of the vent. After a moment, he pulled. The metal easily swung outward opening like a door so that we could enter. Though thickly coated with dust, I could see the distinct tracks where someone had recently gone through. Jay.

"How did you even find this?" I asked.

"You know I like to explore in here, even though you don't. Last week when you attended the public meeting with your parents, I stumbled across this."

"And you waited until now to show me?"

He squeezed my hand one more time before letting go and dropping to a crouch. Turning off the flashlight, he placed it back in his pocket. "At least I'm showing you. Besides, you don't even know what it is yet."

"True." I wouldn't admit it to him, but I didn't really need to know. If Jay thought it was cool, then I would too. I trusted his judgement more than anyone else's. He knew me. We'd been friends since we started school, the two weird kids who were different from everyone else. It didn't matter; we had each other.

The tunnel was dark and my nose tickled from the dust Jay was kicking up ahead of me. Here and there, the path would branch off to who knows where, but Jay seemed certain of his route. He never hesitated, except to stop every now and then to make sure I was still right behind him. Are you kidding? I was practically on his feet. I didn't want to get lost. Who knew if I'd ever make it out again?

Eventually, the air around us began to cool. It wasn't uncomfortable, but I felt a definite temperature drop. The sounds were different too. While I still heard the soft shuffling as we moved forward, I could also hear what sounded like running water. Were we near the sewage pipes or water treatment area? I could've gotten turned around in the tunnels, but that didn't seem right. We were nowhere near those areas when we entered.

The outline of Jay's body began to glow slightly, and then I realized that it wasn't him, it was ahead of him. The tunnel was widening and emptying into... something. My heartbeat quickened and I swallowed rapidly. What had he found? Were we heading outside the compound?

Jay called back to me. "It's about to slope downward. Don't worry, just let yourself slide. I promise you'll be fine."

"Okay."

It wasn't a gradual slope. I could see the bottom, but I couldn't see what was just beyond that point. Trusting my best friend, I waited until he reached the bottom and then I slid after him, squealing a little at the lightweight sensation. He caught me as I exited, before I landed on my butt.

"Where are we?" I asked.

Spinning me around and pulling my back against his chest, Jay rested his hands on my shoulders. I welcomed the heat his body provided in this cool, dark space. "Look around."

My eyes slowly adjusted, and Jay turned his flashlight back

on, shining it around us. I gasped. We were in a cave. A large natural cavern of rock. And now I knew that much, I realized so much more. The echo of dripping water, the tangy quality to the air. We were free. We were out of the confines of the bunker. We were practically on the surface.

"Holy cow, Jay. Holy cow!" I spun and grabbed his shirt, staring up at him incredulously. "How did you ever find this place?"

His grin lit up our dim surroundings. "I told you, I was exploring the other day when you couldn't come out. I heard the waterfall, and headed toward it. I screamed a lot louder than you the first time I slid down that vent."

"Did you—" my heart was going to burst. "Did you say waterfall?"

"Caught that, did you?" He winked at me and took my hand. "This way."

My eyes didn't know where to land. From the glistening formations on the cave ceiling to the flowing pillars growing up from the floor, it was a majestic sight. The moist walls glistened in a rainbow of colors, but the sound of the waterfall, the promise of fresh flowing water, drove me forward.

We headed toward what looked like a dead end, but once we got closer, I realized there was another area behind the wall. The sound of falling water grew louder, and light reflected in a pattern on the dark wall, but I still couldn't actually see the source. That was, until we walked around a rather large formation and there it was. Not tall, but cascading in several small drops.

"An underground river?" I asked.

"Appears so." Jay crouched down and stuck his hand in the water. "It's cold, but not freezing. Kind of makes you wonder if the surface is still all ice, doesn't it?"

He glanced up and caught my eye. The expression on his face told me he had been wondering that exact question long before he asked it. I sat next to him, removed my socks and shoes, and put my feet in the fresh water. The current flowed around me, tickling my skin with the new sensation. "Where do you think it goes? Do you think the leaders know it's here?"

"I don't know the answer to either question." He shrugged, and then pointed to our left. "But see over there? The river flows through that smaller cavern. Even if we had a boat, we wouldn't be able to use it. The only way to follow the river is to jump in."

Frowning, I said, "I can't swim."

"Well, duh."

"Heaven forbid anyone teach us survival skills."

I rolled my eyes while he gave a soft snort. We both knew it was the truth. In Thermal, we were only taught what the leaders felt was important and vital to our survival. Since there was no need to swim in our settlement, it was not something we learned. We knew people used to swim in oceans, rivers, lakes and pools, but we didn't have those or any kind of standing water, really. Citizens weren't even allowed to take baths, just timed showers. That meant the risk of drowning was slim, and the need to teach swimming, obsolete, at least in the leaders' eyes.

"Someone has to know this is here," I continued. "The founders must've purposefully planned to build the settlement into a cavern."

"Maybe."

"You can't tell me they didn't know this was here." I gestured around. "And I can't believe that this would've formed in the last hundred or so years."

"No, I agree with that." Jay splashed me a little, causing me to squeal in surprise. "Caves take thousands of years to form."

I turned and pinned him with my gaze, capturing his hand in mine so he couldn't back away. "Tell me really. How did you discover this? I don't buy that you got lucky and just happened to find the right vent that led here."

Sighing, Jay pulled his hand free and faced me. "The truth is I found a map."

"Can I see it?"

Without another word, he reached into his pocket and pulled out a folded paper. It was yellowed and cracked with age, so I opened it carefully. "Someone drew this? Do you think it was one of the founders?"

"Probably. It seems really old." Jay leaned closer and together we studied the map. "We're here." His finger hovered over an area of the map, not quite touching its fragile surface. "And it looks like the river maybe drops through that tunnel, doesn't it?"

I followed his trail. "Do you think that's a lake it empties into?"

"Looks like it."

"I wonder how far these caves go."

"According to the map, they go on for miles. But I can't see any way in or out except via water."

The map wasn't extremely detailed, so it was hard to tell if the cave had any other exits. In fact, only one path was fully drawn. My guess was whoever created the drawing wanted it for personal reasons. It wasn't the work of a cartographer or anything. I had seen much more comprehensive maps in our classroom and textbooks. The question was, why draw it in the first place and if the person left, why leave it behind. "Where'd you find this?"

"Remember that grate I moved so we could get into the vent?"

"Yeah."

"I noticed it was missing a screw, hanging at an angle, so I went to check it out." He pointed at my hand. "I found that taped to the back of it."

"Sweet find."

"Right?"

"So now what do we do?"

"Do?"

"Yeah." When he didn't answer, I looked up from the map to find him staring at me incredulously. "What's that look for?"

"You don't seriously think we're going to find a way out."

"Why not?"

"Don't you think if it was safe to go up to the surface, then we would've done it already?"

"I don't know. I guess. I mean, I never really thought about it." I carefully folded the map and handed it back to him. It was virtually useless to me now. We weren't leaving this cave by water. "If you don't want to find a way to the surface, why'd you bring me here?"

I put my socks and shoes back on and stood to walk the perimeter. He took so long to answer my question, I wasn't sure he was going to, but then he said, "I thought it might help. I know you can't stand being cooped up inside that stale environment. At least this gives you a taste of fresh air. Isn't that enough?"

"I don't know. Maybe?" I stopped when he placed his hand on my shoulder and turned to face him. "Thanks, Jay. This is by far the nicest thing anyone has ever done for me."

I reached up and squeezed his hand. His worried expression relaxed a little, but he still asked, "Are you ready to go back?"

"Can we explore a little first?"

"That's up to you. My parents are already asleep. You're the one who's going to need to do some explaining."

"I've got it covered."

The walls were cold and wet under my touch, the ground uneven. It was slow going in the dark as I tried to navigate blindly. Jay had the only flashlight and he was too far behind me for it to do me any good. I tripped over something and almost fell, catching myself against the cave. I turned and slowly lowered myself toward the floor, reaching out for whatever I might have stumbled over. I felt something heavy, thick and damp. I paused. "What's this?"

As my sense of touch grew stronger with my lack of vision, I realized the object was furry. Swearing in disgust, I dropped it, jumped back, and wiped my hands furiously on my pants. *Please tell me that is not a dead animal.* "Jay, get over here!"

He was several yards behind me. Based on where the light was shining, he had been studying one of the taller formations rising from the cavern floor. "What'd you find?"

"Shine the flashlight over here, will you?"

He came over and directed the light near my feet. "You okay?"

Oh, thank goodness. Just a rope. "I'm fine. Tripped over this. For a moment, I was worried it was a dead animal."

Jay laughed. "That would've been gross."

He bent and offered me his hand. I let him pull me up. "Why do you suppose this pile of rope is here? It's pretty thick too."

"Who knows?" He'd already lost interest. Shining the light around us, he added, "This is just another dead end. You ready to get going? It'll take us about a half hour to get back to your house."

"In a minute."

With the benefit of the light, I studied the rope. It appeared to have knots tied at regular intervals and the end on top was frayed as if it broke. "Can I see the flashlight for a minute?"

"Sure."

I shined the light on the cave. There were no indications of anything the rope could've been attached to. The wall appeared unmarred. It seemed to blend into the ceiling. Disappointed, I started to lower the flashlight.

"What's that?"

"Where?"

"Raise the light a little."

I lifted the flashlight and gasped. There was a ring mounted into the rock, close to the ceiling. It looked thick and really heavy. Had the rope been a way out, or in?

Jay tugged at my sleeve. "We need to go, Con."

Reluctantly, I handed him the flashlight and followed him back to the vent. We walked in silence, but my mind was anything but. Who had been in the cave before us? Did the rope rot out and fall or had someone cut it? I couldn't fathom that the original scientists scaled down a rope and crawled through a vent to get into our settlement. No, we knew there were other passages in, even though they had been sealed off from the very beginning. But this rope, this simple way out, had someone used it in the hundred years? Had someone gotten out? Could I use it to escape? And what waited at the top of the wall?

That led to more questions. How could we rethread the rope through the ring? The walls were slick with moisture and mineral deposits. Climbing it would be next to impossible. The ring looked large, but not large enough to throw something up there and loop it through. It seemed hopeless, and my spirits sank. To see a possible way out, so close, and yet have it be out of my grasp.

"You okay back there, Connie?"

"Yeah, I'm fine."

With a soft grunt, Jay kept moving. "Not much farther now."

So you say. To me, it seemed impossibly far.

Chapter 3

School was even harder to get through than usual. My mind was back in the cave, on the puzzle that was the rope and ring. Besides Jay, I wasn't sure there was anyone else I could talk to about it, not even my parents. They both were so close to Thermal operations, and they never seemed to take my desire to go to the surface seriously. So instead, I sat in school, listening only enough that if Miss Moran called on me, I wouldn't look like an idiot again. Throughout the day, Jay kept catching my eye. I knew he was worried I was obsessing on our experience. As my friend, he tried to understand my interest in going to the surface and support me, but he had told me more than once he didn't really understand why I wanted to leave so bad.

"We have everything here, Con," he'd say. "Food, shelter, education, entertainment. There's no disease, no terrorists. Remember what we learned about the world before the volcano erupted. It was filled with violence, disease, and hatred. Our world is nothing like that. It's peaceful."

I didn't agree with him, and we argued about it enough that I had finally agreed to disagree. What he saw as safe and peaceful, I saw as oppressive. What he saw as fair and consistent, I saw as limiting and controlling. I knew what we learned about human history was true, but I also knew that not everything during that time was bad. There was good in the world, too. There would be good in the world again. And everything wasn't perfect in our current situation. Not even close.

When class ended, I bolted from my desk. Jay was at my heels. "What are you going to do now, Connie?"

I stopped and turned to him. "What makes you think I'm going to *do* anything? I could be heading right home."

"I know that look. You're planning something."

We stared at each other, neither budging. Finally, he sighed.

Jay always gave in first. "Can I come along?"

"Sure." I smirked at him before turning back around. "I'm just going to the archives."

The archives were where we kept all of our books, but also all records of Thermal history. I was hoping to find some old maps so I could identify the cave and potentially find a better, more detailed map of it. Before I even tried to problem solve the ring and the rope, I first needed to rule out that there weren't other paths out besides the river.

"Can we get something to eat first?" Jay asked.

"You're always hungry."

"So?"

"No. If you're that hungry, go home. You don't have to come with me."

He made a noise but didn't argue. I figured I'd stay for an hour at most, and then I'd go home and make dinner. It would still give me plenty of time before my parents returned from work. After being gone so late last night, I didn't want them getting suspicious. Jay would be fine. His mom always had a meal waiting for him.

"What are you looking for anyway?" There was a little sulk in his voice, but I ignored it.

"Maps. Specifically, a map of the cave."

"Are you crazy?" He was suddenly right at my side, whispering furiously in my ear, his hot breath tickling my skin. "If your dad finds out, you'll be in big trouble."

Looking over my shoulder, I gave Jay my best stink eye. "Then, we'll just have to make sure he doesn't find out, won't we?"

He muttered something under his breath, but stayed next to me and even held the door open for me once we got to the archives. Few people had any interest in the old books and records outside of our leaders. The building was mostly empty. We placed our bags on two worn leather chairs in a back corner.

The smell of yellowing paper and cracked leather enveloped me in a comforting way. This had always been one of my favorite places to hang out. I preferred the old novels and picture books to movies and television. Jay used to hang out here with me, but the last few years he came less frequently. I was actually surprised he decided to come this time.

From what I remember, the former state of Tennessee had some of the most famous caves, but the underground formations dotted most of the countryside. Thermal could literally be anywhere. Why the founders kept its location a mystery made no sense to me. Were they afraid people would try to leave?

For the next hour, we poured over maps, looking for anything that matched the crude drawing of our cavern, but nothing matched. Disappointed, I put everything back where we found it.

"Now what?" Jay asked as we walked home. Unlike me, he seemed almost cheerful. I had a nagging feeling that he didn't want me to figure it out. What I didn't know was why.

"You seem chipper."

"It's time to eat. Of course I'm chipper."

I stomped next to him, mumbling a goodbye when we got to his house but not stopping until he reached out and grabbed my arm. Reluctantly, I looked up into his dark eyes. "Don't give up, Connie. You'll get there. You're the most resourceful girl I know. If anyone can find a way out, it's you."

He held out his arms and I moved into them, grateful for his words, his confidence. If it weren't for him, I'd crumble. The critical eyes and biting words from our peers and superiors chipped away at me on a daily basis. Jay was the glue that held me together. In moments like this, I felt a rush of immense gratitude for my best friend. I squeezed him back and held off the tears that threatened to fall. I would be strong. Everyone told Amelia she couldn't fly, but she did it. She didn't let naysayers destroy her dream and I wouldn't either.

I was so focused on planning my next steps that I didn't

notice the signs that my parents were home until it was too late. They were both waiting for me in the main room when I arrived, stern looks on their faces. My mom spoke first. She always took the lead while my dad was the quiet enforcer.

"Where were you last night?"

"Out with Jay."

Surprise crossed both their faces, though they were quick to hide it. "What could you possibly be doing so late?"

My dad's face turned slightly red and I squirmed. Ugh. Don't tell me their thoughts were going *there*. Jay was like a brother to me.

"We had a project. For school," I added lamely.

"What kind of project?" Mom asked. They leaned toward me with expectant looks on their faces.

Great, now they take interest.

"A book report. On old world explorers." I was proud of myself for that improvise. If they found out about the maps, it would all tie together. "Hey, speaking of, do you know what caves are near Thermal? I'm curious if we're below the land that, um, Lois and Clarke explored." I threw out the first names I could think of in the spur of the moment. I was fairly certain Lois and Clarke had covered a lot of ground, so as explorers went, they weren't a bad option to land on.

"How do you know that we're near caves?" Dad's eyes narrowed suspiciously.

Shoot! I screwed up. That's another thing that bothered me about our world. No one would talk about where we were. We could be in Texas or Alaska for all I knew. Why was it such a big secret? "They told us in school."

Dad stood up, giving me his, "That's enough nonsense from you," look. "I highly doubt that. Where did you really hear it?"

There was no sense digging myself further into the lie. My parents had crazy alien radar when it came to sniffing out untruths. I collapsed onto the couch and hugged my arms around myself. "I saw it."

"Saw what exactly?" Mom sat next to me and took my hand in hers.

"The cave. I was in it."

"That's impossible!" Dad made angry tracks across the floor. "All entrances to Thermal are sealed. You wouldn't be alive if you were in the cave. The outside air is toxic."

"Dad!" I stood and put my hand out to get him to stop and listen. His pacing drove me crazy. "I'm telling you I did see the cave. I touched the walls. I saw a river, and... and there was a rope, a frayed rope. Near the top of the wall was a ring. I'm guessing someone used it to climb in or out at some point."

While I was talking, Dad slowly backed away from me, his face growing pale. "Y-you need to be quarantined! You could've picked up a disease. Beth, alert the medical team."

"Tim, don't you think you're overreacting?" Mom stepped close behind me. At the moment her hands lighted on my shoulders, Dad winced. "Connie is our daughter. I am not turning her over to be poked and prodded. Can't you see she's fine?"

The stare-down between my parents lasted all of two minutes before Dad cleared his throat. "You're right. Of course, you're right." He pointed at me. "But you will not do that again, young lady. You put us all in jeopardy and I will not have it. I could lose my job if someone found out."

It was always about his job. That was his whole world. What did it matter? He'd get another one. Everyone in Thermal had to pull their weight. If you weren't good at one task, you were continuously reassigned until they found what you were good at.

When my dad settled back into his chair, Mom excused herself to start dinner and asked me to fix the salad. As I chopped the vegetables, we didn't talk about the cave or why I chose to go there. I caught Mom glancing at me curiously once or twice, but she didn't say anything.

I knew my parents tried to understand me, but how could

they? They loved it here. Their jobs. Their friends. This was their world and they were perfectly happy with it. It was safe. It was predictable. They couldn't see things the way I did. In this world, we didn't thrive. Not really. We existed.

"You know," Mom whispered in a conspiring tone, leaning against the counter by me. "If you were looking for the name of the cave, you might check Laney's journals. After all, she was a young girl when she first came here." Mom patted my arm and smiled. "Just a thought."

She didn't say anything more about it over dinner. Dad talked about the updates they were making to the air filtration system, and Mom described the latest feed mixture. "It's so nutritious that the animals require less of it to thrive. We can feed the herd for a small fraction of what it used to take."

If I wasn't running through various escape scenarios in my head, I might've fallen asleep on my plate of meatloaf. "Excuse me," I said as soon as my food was gone. "I have homework to do. I'll be in my room if you need me."

On the way to my room, I passed the bookcase where Mom kept her small collection of books and family heirlooms. There they were—the journals from my great-great-great grandmother, Laney. She was only ten when her family moved to Thermal. I'd never given them a second glance before, but now I stopped and stared. Mom was right. Laney might've written about the time before. She could have information about the cave. Or our exact location.

I took three of them to my room, closing the door behind me. From the opening paragraph, she pulled me in.

July 18, 2020
Dad says we're moving to a top-secret location. I can't tell anyone, not even my best friend Madelyn. He gave me this set of journals and told me to write down everything

I would've told her. Not that I know much. He won't even tell me where we're going. I guess he doesn't trust me. All he said is that I have three days to pack, and I can only bring two suitcases full of stuff. We can't even bring our pets. Ralph, Zilly, and Zazu are going to live with Nana.

Mom and Dad think I'm too young to understand, but I hear them talking after I go to bed. They've been discussing an underground volcano. It might explode. I even heard them say 'end of the world' and that scares me more than anything. I don't want to die. I don't want to move. I don't want to give my dog and kitties away, but I don't want to die.

The last paragraph on the page was too blurry to decipher. I could imagine young Laney's tears falling on the fresh ink. If I had been in her shoes, I would've felt the same way, scared and angry. The next entry was almost three weeks later.

July 31, 2020

We leave tomorrow. I went to the pool with Madelyn yesterday. In front of everyone, including Nick Strauss, I started to cry. It was so embarrassing, and the worst part was, I couldn't even tell them why I was sad. It was the last time I would see them. Dad said we were leaving in the middle of the night. Everyone would assume we went on vacation. Well, that's what he said. Obviously, he doesn't know Madelyn well. If she hasn't heard from me in two days, she'll start texting and calling to see where I am. Unfortunately, she won't be able to reach me now. Dad says we're leaving our phones behind. It feels like we're leaving the whole world behind.

This crazy situation has me scared stupid. I know Dad's a bigwig in the science community, and I know he's been assigned some top-secret project, which is why we're moving, but it feels like we're in the witness protection program. Why the secrecy?

Laney had a point. If that had been my dad, I would've been grilling him nonstop, and I would've told my best friend anyway. There weren't any secrets between Jay and me.

I flipped forward a few pages, scanning to see if she recorded anything about their entrance into Thermal. I was disappointed to read that she was half-asleep when they arrived and only remembered the sterile smell, bright lights, and flurry of activity around them. In the following pages, she talked about settling into their apartment and daily life. It sounded like some people were still coming and going freely.

September 9, 2020

We've been underground for over a month. I miss the sun so much. And the smell of flowers in the air. I even miss the buzzing of insects and I hate bugs. It's unnatural here. Everything's too quiet, sterile.

I asked Dad if I could go outside, just for a few minutes, but he refused. He looked so worried. "Any minute," he said. "Disaster can strike at any minute. It's close now, Laney. So close."

I heard him, but I didn't care. I'd risk

anything just to be free of this cage.

My many-times-great grandmother sounded a lot like me. I wonder if every generation fought with the unnaturalness of being underground, or if, over time, they just grew to accept it. I felt like I was an anomaly. No one understood me. Not really. Not even Jay.

Pages later, I found Laney's account of the eruption.

> *October 26, 2020*
>
> *It's happening. It's really happening. As I write this, we are bunkered together in the most secure area of the compound. And the earth's tremors still wrack out bodies. The monitors give us access to views of the outside world, and what I see takes my breath away. It's an inferno. Death by fire and ash. Nothing will survive it. I think of Madelyn, of Nana, of my beloved pets, and even of Crystal Wilson, the snotty girl a year ahead of me in school. They were all dead. Or dying. Gone. It was the end of the world as we knew it.*
>
> *Dad and the other scientists built this shelter to save us, but I know it will kill me. Just slower and more painfully than the volcano. The ocean cannot survive in a bottle. The stars do not shine in a box. And I, I cannot live in this underground prison. Prison, I tell you, for that's what it is to me. Caging in my very soul.*

I wiped my eyes and took a deep breath. Laney and I would've been friends. We certainly thought alike. I kept going, expecting additional, spirited entries, but after that, her journal focused on daily life, friends, and school. While that told me a lot about the first few years in the settlement, it didn't give me the information I was looking for — a way out.

What had changed? Laney was so passionate at the beginning, but by the end of the initial journal, roughly two years later, her writing was listless. Did Thermal reduce her to despair? Perhaps it was the effect of seeing the outside world die around her. I couldn't imagine it. Watching the green fade to brown. Seeing friends and strangers struggling to breathe the thick air. Were their deaths quick or tortuous?

A knock at my door startled me, and I realized I'd been staring at the wall, at nothing really, while I considered Laney's mood change. Clearing my throat, I called, "Yes?"

"Connie, light's out. It's late."

"'Kay."

I tucked the diaries in the drawer on my nightstand and tried to fall asleep. It was no use. My mind kept drifting. It could've been minutes or hours later, but I was still awake when my door opened. I could tell by the footsteps that it was my mom. She sat on the edge of my bed and reached over to smooth my hair from my forehead. "Can't sleep?"

"Not really."

"Find anything interesting in those journals?"

"Interesting, yes. Helpful, no."

She squeezed my shoulder. "Keep reading."

I leaned up on my elbow. In the almost dark, I could barely make out her face. "Do you know something, Mom?"

She made a noncommittal noise and straightened my blanket. "What are you really looking for, Connie?"

A lump formed in my throat. What did I want? Only one thing came to mind. "Happiness."

"Oh, sweetie." Mom placed her hand against my cheek. "Happiness won't come from out here. It comes from inside you."

Covering her hand with my own, I said, "I know, Mom. But I can't find happiness in complacency and predictability. We've been down here for so long. I can't believe that the surface is still uninhabitable."

"I don't know." Mom dropped her hand, taking mine with it. "If it's safe for us above, why have our leaders kept us here?"

"Because it's even safer here." I sat up fully. "There's no famine, no illness. Crops are predictable. Heck, even population growth. The real world, it's messy. I know that."

"In history, there was so much chaos." Mom's words were soft, meant for her ears more than mine.

"But that's what made it exciting, Mom. I mean, how are we really *living* here? We're sustaining, like your crops, but we're not living as humans are meant to do."

She sighed and stood. "Everyone has their own ideals. Their own version of happiness. While I don't fully understand yours, I'll try to." She kissed my forehead, her lips warm and soft. "Try to get some sleep."

"I will." As she was closing the door, I called out, "Thanks, Mom."

She paused. "For what?"

"For listening."

"I'll always listen to you, Connie. I love you."

"Love you too, Mom."

UTOPiA 2016

Chapter 4

I was halfway through the last journal, and I still hadn't found anything remotely close to telling me how I might escape. I was glad my mom suggested I read them. Learning about Laney's life was interesting. While in the beginning, she wrote frequently, almost daily, over time her entries dwindled to a few per month, and later, a few per year. It explained why only a handful of journals represented her entire life.

At this point, she was in her late forties with a daughter and son, both teenagers. From her descriptions, Nadia and Russ were well adjusted to life in the shelter. Having never lived on the surface, they didn't miss what they didn't know. There were times when Laney's old fire shone through, but mostly, she seemed resigned to this life. She confided in an earlier entry that she knew she would never visit the surface again, but she hoped for the future generations it would be possible.

That's great, Laney, I thought. *But what can you tell me to help me?*

Mom seemed so confident that I would find something in here. Then again, if she knew what I would discover, why didn't she just tell me? At this point, I was afraid to skim the remaining entries. I mean, what if I missed something?

Thirty-five pages later, I was rewarded for my patience.

May 3, 2072
I dream about it often. My life before Thermal. The dreams are so vivid that I wake with the warmth of sunshine in my hair, the smell of flowers in the air, and the taste of the clean ozone on my lips. My heart sinks the moment reality sets in. Just a dream, and I'm faced with another day in this regulated

world.

My first grandchild was born yesterday. Nadia and Paul named her Christine. When I held her in my arms, I felt the strangest pull of emotions. Elated at this innocent beauty before me, immensely saddened at the constraints already placed on her life, and fear for the generations to come. Will we lose that which makes us human? The will to fight, to explore, to thrive? Comfort is no man's friend, and I fear that comfortable is what we as survivors have become.

Our leaders have grown fearful of the unknown. Because of that, they control the knowledge of how to return to the surface. They say they will tell us when the time is right, but I don't believe them. My father, God rest his soul, had intimate knowledge of Thermal's floorplan and operations. When I returned home from the medical wing, I put together everything I knew about Thermal, its systems, and all the former escape routes. They may be sealed currently, but nothing is impenetrable. I've placed this information, more precious than gold, in a sealed box and plan to pass it to my granddaughter as her inheritance with strict instructions to guard the box and hand it down to future generations. There will come a time when someone will want to open it, to own the knowledge contained within. Until that individual exists, I plan to leave strict instructions that the box remain sealed. I do *not want this wisdom placed in the wrong*

*hands, or lost. When the time comes, I have
hope that it will be claimed.*

My heart hammered in my chest and I broke out in
gooseflesh. I had the eeriest feeling Laney was speaking directly
to me, as though, through the pages and years, she knew I would
be a companion spirit and she wanted to help set me free.

Mom! She knew. Did that mean she had the box? Oh, I
prayed that it did. Although it was Saturday, she'd gone into
work to check on some new seedlings. I knew she'd be home in
the next hour, but I could barely wait. Dad was gone all
weekend. It was his turn to oversee the weekend shift in
Thermal's main operations. He had to do that once every twelve
weeks.

In my nervous excitement, I fixed dinner, cleaned the
apartment, and straightened my room. As I did, I started making
a mental checklist of what I should take with me and what would
need to stay behind. There was no doubt in my mind. If Mom
had the key, I would be opening the door.

An hour passed and I had to fight with my self-control. I
badly wanted to tear apart every storage container and closet to
find Laney's treasure. The only thing that held me in check was
the fear Mom would be so angry she wouldn't give me the box.

To pass the time, I tried to read. No luck. My mind kept
wandering.

I considered calling Jay, but what if Mom didn't have it? I
was counting on one entry in a journal as my ticket out. Laney
never mentioned it again. There were only five entries after that
one, and the rest were very bland. It was like, once she figured
out what she wanted to do, she locked that part of herself up in
the box. Plus, knowing Jay, he'd have a million questions. No,
better to wait.

Another hour passed. Where was Mom? I ate dinner by
myself, cleaned up my dishes, and put the rest away in the

refrigerator. Jay called to see if I wanted to come over for a movie, but I wasn't up to it.

"You okay?" he asked.

"Yeah, why?"

"You haven't been the same since I showed you the cave. I thought you'd be happy after that."

"I was. I mean, I'm glad you showed me. But Jay, didn't you think that a taste of freedom might make me want the whole thing even more? Don't you want to know what's on the other side of the wall? What's at the end of the river?"

"We already know that. The map showed us that there's a lake."

I heard the confusion and hurt in his voice. He didn't understand. Jay never questioned things. He loved exploring, but he preferred to do it within the confines of safety. The unknown had always been too scary for him. "Look, I'll see you tomorrow, okay?"

"Do you want to go back to the cave?" he asked.

"Maybe. We'll figure it out in the morning, alright?" If I got the information from my mom, I was sure I could convince Jay to check it out with me.

"Sure. I'll see you then."

"Goodnight, Jay."

"You're not going to see Jay tonight?" Mom asked from right behind me, startling me enough that I dropped the phone.

"I didn't hear you come in."

"I just did. Sorry for scaring you." She smirked and turned toward the kitchen. "And I apologize for being late. Had an emergency fire to put out, you know how that is. Two of the newer scientists mixed the fertilizers and almost killed a whole crop."

"Dinner's in the fridge. I ate already."

I followed her into the kitchen anyway, filled a glass with water and sat across from her. She didn't even bother to heat the leftovers. Guess she was hungry. When she finished in record time, she sat back and gave me a knowing look. "You finished the last journal."

"Yep."

"And you want to see the box."

I rolled my eyes. "Duh."

With a laugh, she pushed back from the table. "Follow me."

"Mom," I started. "Why didn't you just show me the box? Why make me read the journals?"

I saw her slim shoulders shrug. "It was the way Laney wanted it. She was adamant that every female heir read the journals. She said that her kindred soul would recognize herself and seek the wisdom she offered." She looked over her shoulder at me. "Although I knew long before you read the journals you were the one. I just didn't want you to be."

My heart sank. "Why, Mom?"

She turned and welcomed me into her arms. "I know we haven't been the most stellar of parents. We're tied to our jobs, leaving you alone for long hours, but honey, you must know how much we love you. I love you." She sniffed and touched my cheek. "I don't want to lose you."

"You won't lose me, Mom."

With a sad smile, she shook her head. "No, we will. Once you open the proverbial Pandora's Box, you won't be coming home to us. You're going off in the world, Connie, and I couldn't be more proud."

Letting me go, she continued into her bedroom. She reached into the far corner of her closet and pulled out an unassuming black box. "Well, here it is."

Taking it from her, I turned it over in my hands. It wasn't very heavy, but it had a sturdy lock on the front. "How am I supposed it open it?"

"With this." She reached around and unclasped her necklace. On the end was a skeleton key I always assumed was just decorative. Now I knew better.

"Do you want to look with me?"

She shook her head. "This is your journey, Sweetheart."

With a fluttery pulse, I took my newfound treasure and retreated to my room.

Chapter 5

The first thing I found when opening the box was a note, written in Laney's now familiar handwriting.

> *Dear Sister in Spirit,*
>
> *I call you that, for although I don't know your name, I know you're my descendant and a female in search of adventure. How I admire your tenacity, your courage. How I envy that you will see the sky and breathe the fresh air I miss so much.*
>
> *In this box, you'll find a map that shows all five emergency exits as they were designed. The main entrance is also identified, although if you are trying to go in secret, it will be too visible for you to use. You must cross through main operations to get to it.*
>
> *I recommend you utilize the exit closest to the water treatment center. This tunnel ends in a natural cave with a lake. From there, use the other map to navigate the caverns and find your way to the surface. There is no way for me to prepare you for what you might find when you get there, but I wish you Godspeed and good luck. Be brave, my daughter. You've come this far and your true adventure waits!*
>
> *In Faith, Laney*

Jay and I had been so close! We were in a different chamber of the cave, but comparing the maps, I could see Laney was right. The exit she identified was the least obvious and had the best route to the surface. This was it; I'd found my destiny.

*

Together, Mom and I broke the news to Dad. His initial shock faded into a blend of acceptance and admiration. In the week I took to prepare and pack, I tried to convince others to come with me, but no one would, not even Jay.

"You sure you want to do this?" he asked me for what felt like the millionth time.

"I'm absolutely sure."

Tucking strands of stray hair behind my ear, he gave me a lopsided grin. "I admire you. You know that?"

I wrapped my arms around him and squeezed, probably surprising him as much as me. He pulled me closer. "I'll miss you."

"Me too." I wiped my eyes before he noticed. "Sure I can't convince you to come with me?"

Frowning, he shook his head. "I'm not brave like you."

"You are."

"I'm *not*. Maybe someday. Not today."

With a heavy heart, I confessed, "I wanted to make a change in Thermal, and I failed. I couldn't even convince you. A revolution does not start with one person."

His eyebrows drew together in confusion. "What do you mean? Of course it does. Someone has to be the spark, the trigger. Your efforts will not go unnoticed." He nodded toward the far end of the cave, where the path that would eventually lead to the outside was visible. "Go get 'em, Amelia. This is your moment. Don't let me stand in your way."

After another hug, this time the tears flowing from both of us, I ventured across the cavern, feeling Jay's gaze on my back. I didn't turn and look at him again. I didn't want to be tempted by the familiar.

Flashlight in hand, I marveled at the formations that accompanied me on my journey upwards. Untouched for over a century, I was surrounded by the glistening artwork of nature. It kept me calm and focused on my path. My heart wanted to leap into my throat. What would I find on the outside? Was the world still a barren wasteland? Was it a lush oasis? Or more likely, something in between. A land of new beginnings and possibilities.

Instead of cooling, the air warmed as I climbed higher, a good sign. Before I even saw the opening, I tasted the fresh air and felt a draft, my first experience of a natural breeze. Elated, I closed my eyes and simply enjoyed the moment. How could the others not want this? How could they be satisfied in the world below?

With renewed vigor, I broke into a light jog. This was it. This was the moment I'd lived for. Freedom. Real Freedom. Ahead, sunlight filtered against the rocks, and I stopped once again to admire a new sight. How many more wonders would I encounter in my first day above? I touched the rocks and felt the sun's warmth. Pure magic. Then I turned and my breath froze in my lungs. Stunning. There was no other way to describe it. Green fields dotted by bright spots from wildflowers. Young trees reaching their branches toward the blue sky. And then, a screech. I ducked in fear, only to rise a moment later, captivated by the sight before me.

A bird, its wings spread wide, glided on the wind and circled above me with smooth graceful motion. It was a symbol meant for me. Like that bird, I was taking my first flight.

Eat your heart out, Amelia. I'm on my way.

REBELLION

By
Desira Fuqua

ABOUT

Desira Fuqua is a happy human who has travelled six continents, married her high school sweetheart, and kept a menagerie of pets as a child. Although she started her professional life as a software developer, she's also dabbled in business and operations, and today is focused on writing, narration, and dog sitting, because everyone needs more animals to cuddle. She draws from a lifetime spent reading voraciously of every genre and tramping the earth in search of history, adventure, and beauty to write essays that she hopes will inspire others to follow in her footsteps and come see the world, and tread more lightly upon it. This is her first work of fiction.

www.Desirafuqua.com

Chapter 1

A leaf fluttered down from the trees. Thera watched impassively, squinted up at the deepening blue sky, and turned back into the tent. The seasons were turning, and their advantage would come with the winter rains.

Clustered around the roughhewn table inside, the others were still squabbling over the details of their campaign. As she glanced around the table, Thera's expression hovered on the line between exasperation and bemusement. She knew the plan was sound. So did the others, for that matter, but they were still driven to settle every moment. Argus, a fellow veteran, had been sucked into the fight.

"It's best to fall back to the rise, so the archers have some advantage when they come forward."

Except they will have archers of their own and we'll be exposed. We should plan on the trees to the side here"

"And trust they won't have Fire? No, only a little further back to the rocks – "

Thera leaned forward, resting her palm upon the table. "All good ideas, and something to keep in mind for the day of the battle, don't you think, Didymus?" Her eyes swept round the table as her mouth twisted wryly. Yes, they had almost forgotten he was there.

A stirring of robes accompanied the subtle tapping of fingers as Didymus searched for his cane, before the quiet figure who had been bent upon the stool by the side of the tent, stood.

"Thera, you know my heart. We're wasting energy here, but maybe settling a few nerves, too."

Unlike the rest of them, he had been fighting age at the time of the regime change, twenty years ago. The others had been small children. A few had not even been born. They had heard about the era before: of peace and democracy. They could envision it, and they wanted it, but, Didymus knew. Didymus missed it. However, he was not a soldier; he was a scholar, perhaps a seer. A path in life chosen for him when he was blinded at a young age. Now he stepped towards the table, and the others made way.

"What matters," he crooned with a twinkle in his milky white eyes, "lies not with where we go, exactly, but with where *they* go. We will lure them here," he said, pointing uncannily at the region they had marked in red upon the map.

Chapter 2

They had three days left to prepare, and Thera was covered in mud. Her back ached, and she cursed the late rains that had put them at such odds. She knew the attack could not be delayed. It had to come on King's Day. For this fight, pride must be injured to overcome defenses. She was flinging yet another load of dirt and rocks into the gulch when Corin found her.

"Do you have a moment, Thera?"

"No, but if you carry this, you may walk with me," she said, handing Corin the muddy woven basket as she started back up the hill.

"It's about Argus," Corin said.

Thera took a half step in surprise but kept walking. A glance at Corin told her what she already knew and, suppressing her anger, she came to a stop. She turned to Corin and took the basket from her as gently as she could manage. Staring into her eyes she said firmly, "This is war, Corin, not a love song. Very likely, either you or Argus will be dead in a few days, and if I am wrong about that, we can worry about it then." She gestured towards her own filthy clothes, the basket, and Corin's blistered hands. "It does not look to me like either of us have the energy to spare for this sort of thing. If you do," Thera said, placing a firm hand upon Corin's shoulder and offering a friendly smile, "work harder." She saw with relief that Corin was more shocked than hurt. A good fighter, she would find the strength to do what was necessary.

"You're right," Corin said quietly turning away, crossing an arm over her chest to feel the muddy handprint Thera had left upon her shoulder.

Chapter 3

The day had come. The air was brisk, but not freezing. As the silver clouds scudded across the sky, Thera watched lights begin to twinkle on within the city walls. They would attack an hour past full dark, to allow the parade to get underway inside. She watched the others, and they waited, scattered in a rough line through the trees and rocks. Three stolid siege towers and two catapults lay within the vaulted forest. Time passed quickly. She surveyed her lines a final time, and signaled the march forward.

The towers slid forward quickly, each pushed by a team of twelve. The catapults were slower, but the soldiers with both were well protected. A cry came from the walls. They had been spotted more quickly than she had expected. Far to her right, Argus fired a test shot. They had a hundred paces to close the distance for the catapult.

Suddenly, a flaming bolt ripped the sky. It tore into the leftmost siege tower, and set it aflame. Ballista! As the fighters retreated from the burning tower, one of the catapults became mired in the mud. They had tried using boards to keep the wheels moving, but it had failed. The abandoned tower began to list, narrowly missing the other catapult as it crashed down, blocking its path. A second missile was fired, this one into the center tower. It was grazed, and to Thera's dismay, the missile fell upon several fighters as it bounced away. The remaining tower slowed, uncertain.

Chapter 4

From the wall, the King watched. This was his day. He grinned as the tower fell. "Ballista!" As he watched the soldiers begin to abandon the final tower and commence a retreat, he murmured, "Things do not seem to be going as planned for the rebels." As the last of the fleeing would-be upstarts disappeared into the trees, he wheeled on his advisor, Hena.

"I want my cavalry!"

"My liege, I hardly think such a weak attack merits exposing – "

"EXPOSING? That's entirely the point, there's hardly any risk! It's obvious they are not well trained. My soldiers are. If we strike now we can end this quickly. Imagine if they had gotten close enough to launch one of those?" He gestured wildly back at the field and its mired and smoldering siege weapons. "People could have died! No, I won't have it. We will pursue them. They know what day it is; everyone is out of their homes. Such brash violence isn't tolerable."

"Your father," Hena began.

"Yes, well he's been gone quite some time hasn't he, Hena? Eleven, twelve years? Perhaps you should advise *me* as I am still living, rather than hound after his ghost!"

Hena drew a measured breath and raised her gaze just above the King's head. "My liege I *am trying* to advise you, but..." she rushed on before he could object, "I will notify commander Temis to ready the horses. Our hundred best should be sufficient?"

"Hmf," the King mused, "I know who is among them; you will want some archers as well. Twenty or thirty, those that can ride best – and don't let Temis go with them. I want her here. Send the Satyr, it will be a fine opportunity for him to prove himself."

Hena walked to the door, expecting further instruction before she reached it, but there was none. She walked silently down the stone hall, and just as she turned to descend the stairs, she all but ran into Temis.

"He's sent me for you. He wants a hundred cavalrymen, and twenty well-trained mounted archers."

Temis closed her eyes and stood there, relaxing her hands. Without moving she said almost cheerily, "I will speak with him."

"I have tried Temis; we will only delay the inevitable."

Opening her eyes, Temis smiled. "All the same, if we can delay enough, I will argue a morning hunt, rather than a blind night attempt. And then," Temis smiled more deeply and half-closed her eyes again, "then we might still salvage the feast!"

Temis pivoted on her heel and practically danced past her before Hena could formulate an argument. At any rate, she would prefer the King dissuaded. She half-thought to follow, but knew she would rather not be asked to explain letting Temis by, so she merely leaned against the wall and waited. She could barely hear the shouting, and it didn't take nearly as long as she thought for the more stubborn to win out. Temis came prancing back down the hall, all the answer Hena needed was in Temis's feet.

"Hungry?" she said as she passed Thera on the way down the stairs.

Chapter 5

Hena stepped over the bench and made room to sit across from Temis. She laid her plate, heavy with meat, bread, roast vegetables, and beans upon the table and looked at Temis's plate (which was half meat and half cake) with a small shake of the head. She couldn't help but smile.

"So?" she asked.

Temis took a bite and chewed whilst grinning. It was awkward to watch, and Hena became interested in her own plate. Finally, Temis swallowed.

"So," she said, "I'm to have the horses and archers ready at dawn, as well as a small contingent of scouts, to help us make up the time we are spending here – enjoying ourselves." She spread her hands towards the lavish food surrounding them.

"And the Satyr will lead them? Hena enquired.

Temis nearly spat, "Of course not! I'm nearly mad to get outside these walls and have some fun. A good chase is just what I need. Besides, he'll get some experience running things while I'm away. I'm taking only half the cavalry, there's still the infantry to browbeat, and the rest of the archers. Why, he can grease the King's ballista! And who knows, maybe I won't come back," she paused, "then he could run things himself."

"We both know you'll come back. You'll always come back because – "

"Tsk, Hena! Never curse a truth by speaking it! Anyway, he has a name you know!"

"I know," Hena said diffidently. "I just find it strange, and rather difficult to pronounce."

"Well, that is true," replied Temis thoughtfully, as she chewed a mouthful of cake.

Chapter 6

Everyone ate too much, and drank too much to meet the expectation of a dawn departure. Even Hena was late in rising, and she suspected Temis knew this would be so. How can someone so seemingly lighthearted be so calculated in planning? Still, as she entered the stable yards, things were well underway, and Temis soon joined them, looking buoyant. Hena watcher her rush about the yard checking saddles and carrying armloads of supplies to rucksacks, almost as busy as the stable boys themselves. The Satyr, Dzawa, had beaten them both there, and at the moment, was counting heads. She pondered the name. It was spelled simply enough, but when he said it in his own tongue, she knew it was not a sound she could mimic. Frustrated by the difficulty, she simply refused to say it. Her brother did the same. She was lost in these thoughts when suddenly soldiers began to mount and form ranks. Temis rode to the head, and they trotted through the gates. They wound down in a procession through the city streets. Hena did not follow, nor did she watch them from the walls, instead, she climbed back into the fortress in search of a cold breakfast and a hot shower. She knew the King had underestimated the enemy. She felt it unlikely the party would find anyone. They had more probably put in a hard night and would be regrouping. Temis was beyond competent, still, she felt doubt. Something pulled at her mind. She did not know what it was.

Chapter 7

It had been a long night, but a fruitful one. They had made their way back through the forest, taking the time to leave signs, showing the path but concealing their numbers. Finally, they had reached the abandoned cow pastures to the north, and they waited. They posted a watch and slept. Thera was surprised the pursuit was not immediate and wished they had been able to achieve at least one blow to the high and thick western walls. They had allowed for the likelihood of a nighttime battle, but it had not come. She was glad for the respite, and as the day grew near the peak, she knew they were now well rested; an additional advantage. Thera only hoped that soldiers were indeed coming.

Finally, word came. No more than one hundred and fifty. All mounted, and so coming rather quickly now. The final preparations were made, positions were taken. They put fresh bacon on to fry in the encampment, and some even had the stomach to eat it, Corin and Didymus among them. Thera willed the soldiers to come straight on, but the lookouts, perched high in the trees with mirrors, reported that they were flanking on the left. Thera exhaled. When the flank broke the tree line, Thera counted to five before giving the cry. Everyone seemed to scramble, but they all had the sense to fall back through the tents and out the far side. But they did not go far.

Away from the tents, she could clearly see the main body was also upon them, while some mounted arches held to the rear. At Thera's signal, everyone fell back, but not too far. A very calculated risk. Then she gave the signal, and suddenly everything became strange. A loud series of cracks combined with a sudden quagmire appearing before them. The horses in front of them were swallowed. The encampment trembled, collapsing in a confusion of canvas and horseflesh. Quickly, her soldiers spread and formed a front perimeter near the edge of the pits. Archers materialized from the rocks behind her, and the trees behind the enemies. Quickly, the enemy archers who had not fallen, were either killed or had decided to leap into the hole.

She approached the edge, aware they were still armed.

"Lay down your arms and lift your hands," she shouted. She stepped back before the arrow flew, and she winced as her men retaliated. "No harm will come to you, if you lay down your arms!" Surprisingly, this took a few more attempts before they began the process of extraction, and interviews. Thera knew she needed every man, and she was confident many secretly wished to join them. They would be given their chance, and Didymus would question them. She was sure of his abilities.

Chapter 3

After checking on the wounded, Thera ducked into the tent they had set up for questioning. The damage was surprisingly minimal. The cavalry never touched them, but their archers had been quick. The twenty had managed to wound ten, two fatally.

She stood near the entrance of the tent, behind the soldier currently being questioned by Didymus. The questions were short and to the point. First, a brief explanation of their cause. Democracy, elections, no more hoarding of goods in the Keep: by leaders, the police, *or* the army. Second, "Will you die for the King?" This was calculated to bring out those who might support the cause, but more importantly, when delivered correctly, and with the necessary intimidation hovering in the air, it also weeded out the cowards. The cowards, Didymus wanted.

Of course, Thera had balked at that. She had argued they would turn on her own soldiers, but Didymus was very convincing.

"They won't turn. The worst they will do is run so they can claim innocence later. But they will only do that if it seems we might lose. And," he had added archly, "they will make our numbers seem much larger. Successful tactics are as much about intimidation as they are about skill."

Finally, "Is there anything you would die for?"

To find the leaders they would need reliable, good-hearted soldiers to manage the new recruits. It was not that people never lied to Didymus (he did not have the power to hear the truth from everyone) but she knew from experience, he always saw the lie. The man was never fooled.

There was a commotion outside, shouts and cries from both those across the pit, and the soldiers standing guard just outside the tent. A dozen voices mixed in alarm.

"Stop her!"

"--see"

"The horse--"

"There!"

Thera whipped back the flap of the tent and stepped out. Her scanning eyes immediately found the commotion on the far edge of the pit. A captured soldier had somehow scaled the wall and pulled down an unwary rider from his horse. The fallen horseman rocked back, having just hit the muddy earth as the escapee slipped a foot into the stirrup and began to mount with a flourish of movement.

She was not fast enough. Thera saw one of her soldiers with a sword in one hand, and a handful of the escapee's tunic in the other. But before Thera could feel relief, the soldier stumbled back and turned. Somehow, the woman, now fully on the horse and already turning it away towards the forest, had concealed an arrow, which now protruded from her soldier's chest. Thera's eyes moved from the crumpling soldier to the fleeing horse as she ran around the hole. There was no need to shout commands to follow, three mounted men were already giving chase. Her feet crossed the distance to the fallen soldier. The helmet was being removed by others, who had rolled him onto his back. She saw what she already knew.

Argus.

Something came to life within her chest. It wanted out. It beat upon her ribs, and grasped her esophagus. It pressed into her lungs, as she swung her eyes around the camp. It plugged her ears, as she found Corin. Corin, who had been watching with general concern. Corin whose eyes met hers, and in a moment of understanding, widened, whilst all other muscles of her face sagged. She began to move. Thera looked away, moving her vision across the treetops and seeing the evergreen branches sway, and the barrenness of the oaks.

She looked back down to see she was kneeling. Argus was dead. The arrow had not gone far, but it was well aimed, and it had gone far enough, slipping between the ribs and into his heart. She cursed the odds, and her own foolish advice. Corin arrived. Her hands felt at the wound, reached for the shoulders and shook.

"Argus!"

Corin slapped at his face to wake him, leaving a bloody hand print. Thera reached for her shoulders and turned her.

"It's me. It's me you want to hit."

And she did. Corin's fists found her jaw, then her temple. She had always been good fighter. Thera was knocked sideways into the mud, shouting for the soldiers to leave Corin. In that moment, breathing in the mud, the smell of cold earth, she had a million thoughts: of relief to suffer for her mistake of the difference a few weeks for them might have made, of a lie to sacrifice the already dead, to aid the living. She pressed her hands into the earth. Mud seeped between her bare fingers, and clung to her face. Corin had risen to her feet and loomed over her.

Thera rose and met her eyes, then looked down. She spoke softly. "Corin, I am sorry, but…" she felt for breath. "…he wasn't a good man, Corin. He would have hurt you, and I don't mean your feelings."

Corin stared and said, "How could you say that of your brother?"

Thera grit her teeth. "That is how I know." She held Corin's gaze. What she knew was that they couldn't mourn a fallen hero. They couldn't be demoralized, just as the tides turned. Corin lowered her eyes to Argus. Soldiers crowded round. This was no private exchange.

Corin murmured hoarsely, "Still, we will fight for him."

"No!" Thera said with a force that surprised even her. "We do not fight for our dead!" she shouted, turning. "We do not seek retribution for the past! We fight for our future! For our children! For The Castle!" She cast her eyes around her soldiers. Women and men, lean and ready. She looked down into the pit, at the faces remaining there, and saw hope reflected back at her by many there too. Inside, her heart was pressed into her throat. Forgive me, Argus, but I must hold them to the end. Thera would take her own advice and save her energy for the war. As she raised her eyes from the pit, they met those of Didymus, standing just inside his tent. She pushed her heart away. The beast inside her chest gave one last kick at her stomach, and was still.

Chapter 9

It was well past dark when a rider came into the courtyard. Hena had been keeping a vigil for a messenger, taking her dinner near the window instead of the fireplace, despite the cold. But when she recognized just who was dismounting a hard ridden horse, she jumped up and spilled her wine. Thankfully it was white, not red. Two servants were already cleaning the mess before she reached her door. She jogged down the hall, and for the second time in as many days, nearly ran into Temis on the stairs.

"You've returned."

"Yes."

"Alone."

"Indeed."

Whilst Temis steadied her breath, Hena stared at this geminid, whose eyes glinted with fury. She reeked of horse and sweat and leather. Her face and the entire front half of her body was smeared with dried mud.

Finally, the King joined them. "What has become of the others?"

"We were caught. We were played as fools, and acted the part. There was a trap, a pit. It was quite large, actually."

She seemed to need to tell everything at once. When she had finished, Hena needed to fill in the obvious gaps.

"What are they doing with the soldiers?"

"Ha, with those pits, isn't it obvious? None come back out of the tent, or are returned to the pit. I wasn't going to wait my turn to be sure."

"But you didn't see or hear anyone being killed?"

Temis rolled her eyes. Hena was glad to see her humor was returning. "How much sound does a sword make exactly, Hena? Why lure us out there, otherwise?" She seemed to notice the caked earth for the first time, and crumbled some from her hair. "I'm going to bathe. We need to figure out what we are going to do. Better yet, I'd like to figure out what *they* are going to do."

Hena agreed and she looked to the King as Temis went plodding off.

"Don't. Don't. Don't say anything." He sighed heavily. "Even you didn't suspect the failure of the attack on The Castle was intentional. Bring Temis and the Satyr to me in an hour. We will talk – and this time, Hena, I will better consider your advice."

She didn't say a word.

Chapter 10

Thera reached over the fire and dug her fingers into the meat, pulling off a strip that was perfectly cooked, and tender. It felt so good just to sit and eat – and to be warm. It had been a long day. Tomorrow would likely be longer. The soldiers were sorted. From twenty archers, five were dead and six too wounded to fight either way. Five refused to join them, leaving her only four. From the one hundred and ten cavalry, seven were dead, and seventeen were too wounded from the fall into the pits to fight. Fifty-two cavalrymen would join them, but that left a total of sixty-two that would not be coming with them tomorrow. They would leave behind thirty-nine able-bodied enemies, more than she liked. They couldn't risk someone catching up to them and attacking, or interfering with their plans. She, Corin, Didymus, and others had talked about how to make sure this group stayed far enough behind, so that couldn't happen.

For now, the captured enemy forces had been disarmed, the wounded had been seen too, and they were waiting in the pit, which was now reinforced with some fencing. It would hold them for now, but she knew they could quickly escape once her soldiers broke camp in the morning. She had no intention of killing them, so it was a question of how to slow them down. Bezek's suggestion that they, "Part them from their thumbs and great toes," had given everyone a good laugh but wasn't to be taken seriously. Such wounds would prevent the soldiers from rejoining society, and she didn't think they deserved that. Maybe just the one who had escaped, if she ever found out who it was. The soldiers who had given chase had returned empty handed, and mystified by the rider's quick disappearance. She licked her fingers and stood, clapping a hand on the shoulder of the soldier sitting nearest to her, and mustered a smile. "I'll see you and your friends," she cast a glance around the fire, "in the morning,

Olen" They smiled weary smiles and she turned towards the next fire.

Picking her way through the mud, she wondered if taking their shoes would be enough. Her soldiers had the advantage of having nearly enough horses for each man. The mud and the cold would slow the abandoned force's bare feet. If only so many mounts hadn't been injuring falling into the pit they had spent weeks digging. It couldn't be helped, though. She found Amali among the soldiers at the next fire and squeezed in next to her. She was offered some coarse bread they had cooked over the embers, and she took it gladly, eyeing the meat turning on the spit. Yes, it had been a shame to lose so many horses, and grisly to put down the wounded ones, but everyone would eat well tonight, even the soldiers they would leave behind.

Chapter 11

They sat near the fire, chairs brought close to the light of the hearth. Temis was the last to join them, her hair wet, her face clean. They were quiet.

Dzawa was the first to speak. "The question is, what will they do now?"

"There's only a few options." Temis sighed. "They wait for us to come to them, or they come to us."

"They will wait." Hena was confident. "They will rest and sort through the supplies we have given them. They may want to build new siege weapons, but then they will come. We still have a stronger army by the count Temis gave us. We are fortified. They cannot assail us here."

"But they will still be there. And we'll be in here... trapped like rats. Well-fed rats perhaps, but not free." Temis frowned. "I want a small group; I can hurt them. Perhaps turn them away. Let them go start a little village somewhere, and leave us."

"They might expect a second party, knowing you got away to warn us. They might prepare for that rather than come to us, anyway." Dzawa said.

They sat silently, and weighed options. Hena thought how vulnerable they had been and not known it. A small guerilla party, less than half the size of their own army, had caused them so much damage. Yet she couldn't quite puzzle out what it was they wanted. She suspected it was just power - wasn't that what most people craved?

The leaders of the rebels were siblings from Low Town. There had been word from the police that people in that neighborhood had become increasingly aggressive. Shutting doors, refusing to help officers in investigations. Some had been jailed for violence. But it had been mostly petty or so she had thought. The Castle had instituted some new rules for the neighborhood; no large gatherings, evening curfew, that sort of thing. They even banned the baring of doors.

Hena had done a little investigating and learned the names Argus and Thera. But as for their purpose, she could learn nothing reliable. When pressed, even the individuals most well connected to Low Town, merchants and farmers, would only say that the siblings spoke of more food and better resources, which made no sense. It had been a bumper crop year. There was enough food. Things were generally very good at The Castle. For instance, the feast last night, which was open to all, could not have gone better, baring the siege.

Hena paused in thought and glanced up. Was it possible that had been only the day before? And the rebels had certainly attacked that day on purpose. Why lay a siege on a feast day when everyone would already be inside the castle walls? She remembered then that of course it had *not* been a siege, but a ploy to injure the King's pride and elicit a hasty response. They had been baited.

Hena thought again of Low Town, and how a few weeks ago, the police had reported the district suddenly deserted. Hundreds of people had left their homes. It mustn't have happened all at once, such an exodus from The Castle would have been noticed, but the people had simply trickled away – and so it would seem, had formed an army. Although, not all of them; more had left than just fighting age. Entire families were gone. And they must be somewhere.

"We need scouts," she said. "A dozen."

"There's only one army," Temis laughed. "what would you do with so many?"

"We're not looking for the army; we're looking for their families. Perhaps from them, we can find out what this is all about."

"Oh, Hena! I never would have expected such tactics from you!" Temis was nearly beside herself with glee. "When do we leave?"

"Absolutely not, Temis." Hena said. "There will be no 'we'. This is purely diplomatic. There is something we are missing, and I am going to find out what. I won't have you out playing the lion amongst a herd of goats. We need to search all directions as I doubt they are in the same location as the army."

The King spoke at last. "I agree on all counts. We'll send the scouts, without Temis. We'll assume they will lay siege soon. So we'll send a few parties also to gather additional food and supplies from the closest farms. I'll have the Lardner take stock and set a full ration. We've all the food stored here, and it's winter; this won't last long." He stood, hiding a yawn with the back of his hand, "Right, it's late. I will give orders in the morning."

Temis began to protest, but the King cut her short. "I need better results than last time, Temis. You've had your chance to hunt and you returned more than empty handed. Now we need strategy and care."

"Well in that case," Temis drew herself up, "I saw some wine downstairs that looked very lonely."

Looking at the satyr Hena said, "You will select the scouts, you might also consider some of the hunters who came in for the feast."

Dzawa looked up. "Me?"

Hena gave a quick nod as she stood to leave, suddenly uncomfortable.

A smile tugged at the corners of the King's mouth as he saw them all out. He tried to catch Hena's eye, but she wouldn't look at him, or the satyr.

Chapter 12

It had been a long night. Thera had made the rounds to all the various fires, and along the way, had eaten and drunk more than she should. Her mind drifted continually back to Argus, and the grave that had been dug for him and all the others, friend and foe.

She lay in her tent staring at the crossbeam, again thinking over their plans. Two concerns remained. First, the speed of the enemy soldiers who would certainly follow behind them. Secondly, the one who had gotten away. It was possible the King would form another army and come for them. She might meet them tomorrow in the woods. If they brought only horses, at least they might outnumber them now, although Thera knew that such an equal fight, would be bloody and likely unproductive. Between these two groups of enemies, her forces could be pinched.

She rolled onto her side. Things would be so much better if they could wait and arrive at The Castle under darkness tomorrow, but such a delay could cost them. No, Thera would have to settle for a dawn ride and an indirect route. All she could hope was fear of a second trap would stay The Castle's hand for a little while.

Chapter 13

The day passed wearily. The scouts had gone out. Two parties had been sent in opposing directions to gather stores from the largest farms nearby, merely to provide bit more piece of mind. Many watched from the walls. Some were able to find work within the walls, repairs and preparations for what was to come, but many more hands were idle. The streets were quiet, save for the children, who after one day of sitting subdued already, were not to be contained any longer. Their boisterous laughter echoed strangely down the streets, and off ears that strained to hear the sounds of trouble and bloodshed.

Hena watched the half-moon rising. Slowly, scouts began to return. One by one, she spoke with them and what they had seen. Nothing. Uniformly nothing. But by the time the moon had set, two scouts still had not returned. The foraging parties returned, bringing a little grain and fodder, but not as much as Hena would have thought based on what the farmers had told them. She wondered if the rebel families had beaten them to those supplies. An hour later, Hena went to her chamber, and laid on her bed, fully clothed, anticipating action, and hoping that the remaining scouts had found something. She had barely closed her eyes when a knock came at the door.

"Yes?"

The door creaked open and one of her servants, Aleo, peeked in. "There are soldiers at the gates."

She started. "Rebels?"

"No, no, only our own men."

"The men whom the rebels had captured?"

Aleo nodded.

"That's not right." She stood, alarmed. "Have they been allowed in?"

"The King is going to them. They were still outside."

Hena paused to pull on boots, then jogged down the halls, down the stairs, and out the gates of the keep.

Chapter 14

Thera lifted the torch high to see farther into the dark and to avoid the few roots and rocks in her path. She did not suppress the grin that came to her face. The others were a safe distance behind her, and they had been wildly successful tonight. The faint glimmer of an idea that Argus had over a year ago, and that he and Thera had worked to develop into a gleaming gem of a plan, had finally proved fruitful. Spying a faint glow ahead, she fairly skipped on, despite having to lean hard into the rope slung across her shoulder. Drawing the sledge and its heavy burden on, she came out under the light of the setting moon.

"Didymus! We have nearly all of it!" But as she drew closer, she saw Didymus leaned forward uncomfortably on his stool. She was about to reach for him to wake him, but realized the old man was dead.

A blow stuck her across the left ear. Bright light flashed before her eyes and she dropped the torch. She would have fallen but the rope she leaned into helped her keep her feet. She spun, her left hand going to her sword, but her eyes were blinded by the torch light, and before she could blink it away, a foot connected soundly with her abdomen and she flew backwards, sliding on the mat of wet leaves. Her mind slowed and she smelled the leaves and felt the gravel in her left hand where her sword had been. Her eyes tunneled in on the figure of a man that stood over her. High above his head was a simple mace. The moonlight glinted faintly off its facets. The moon was setting. The sky was dark.

Then he began to collapse in slow motion. His knees buckled and his arm swung down through the air. No, she realized slowly, he was striking her. She rolled to her left side, reaching her right hand to the small of her back, and a concealed blade there. There was a strange wet thwack just behind her head. She kept moving, coming onto all fours, then sprinting forward. She was not fast enough, and the ball of hard metal caught her in the soft spot between rib and hip, but she scrambled on, putting a tree between herself and her assailant. They feinted left and right, then stopped. Each breathing hard. Thera wanted to thrash in pain. Her side felt as if it were being devoured by wolves, but she would not touch it. Behind the man, her torch gave a small circle of light, smoldering amongst the leaves where it had fallen. Beyond that, another light approached quickly.

Thera gave a yell and leapt forward slashing at the man's hip, but he only stepped back, laughing a bit. He stopped when an arrowhead materialized, protruding through his forearm. He took a hasty lunge towards Thera, and Corin's second arrow found his back. Thera, shrieking with pain and dissatisfaction, stepped inside of his blow, thrusting her dagger up into his sternum. She collapsed under his weight, crying tears of pain and sadness. "Not Didymus, too," she sobbed, and closed her eyes as the man's blood crept over her, warming her skin.

Chapter 15

Hena could not grasp what was happening. Before her and the King, crowded in the narrow meeting hall of the keep, were dozens of men, cold, footsore, and barefoot. The story they told was unanimous. In the tents they had been searched, loosely interrogated, fed under watch, deprived of their shoes, and much of their outer clothing, and eventually returned to the pit, it having been emptied of soldiers. Several had woken when the rebels had broken camp. They had taken time to scour the site for supplies, had scavenged some additional meat from the fires of the night before, but had found little else but a pile of burned shoes mocking them.

They had returned to The Castle as quickly as they could, but carrying the wounded who had been left, their bare feet, and mostly empty stomachs had slowed them considerably. For the most part, they had followed in the tracks of their opponents, and had expected to find The Castle under siege. But traces of the army had disappeared abruptly not long before they left the trees and came into the open fields surrounding The Castle.

The King ordered the men fed and washed. The wounded were seen to. A few were not likely to make it, having badly broken legs, but most would heal. A headcount was taken, and the rations were adjusted, although, the King said, and Hena agreed, that perhaps, this was no longer necessary. It seemed their rebels had gone elsewhere.

Chapter 16

Thera opened her eyes. It was still dark, and a low fire, mostly embers and blue flame, burned some distance to her left. She wanted to shift her positon, but grunted at the pain and lay still. A figure came towards her from the fire. She recognized Corin's gait in the silhouette. Her face leaned close to see Thera's open eyes in the dim light.

"You slept pretty good. How do you feel?"

Thera gestured to her side where the mace had struck her. "Feels broken."

"Nothing there to break," Corin answered, "but…" she hesitated and looked away.

"But?"

"But," Corin looked at her, "There's the possibility of internal damage."

Thera released a slow breath and resisted the urge to reach for her side, afraid to know too much. "Well," she said confidently," should the worst happen, you know what to do and I'm certain the others will follow you.

Corin, who had been leaning far over to peer at Thera's face, rocked back on her heels. "Never mind that, we've had the medics look at you and they found no immediate sign. Still, we can't be sure, but once Didymus wakes up, he might know more."

"Didymus is alive?" Thera gasped, trying to whisper, wanting to yell.

Corin leaned in again, a toothy smile gleamed on her face. "Yes. He apparently put up quite a fight with that man before being knocked unconscious. Out cold as the dead, but he came around at the smell of food," she laughed. "No permanent damage, but we were afraid to talk to him about you until he's had some rest."

"Well, he's had some now hasn't he? Better bring him to me, if there's anything to be known or done, sooner is probably better."

"I guess that's true enough," Corin conceded.

As she moved to rise, Thera caught her elbow and winced. "Who was that man? A soldier? Alone?"

"He was a scout or spy. We're not quite sure, but they sent word from Home that they caught someone lurking around there as well. They must be from The Castle."

Thera cursed. "Have they moved?" she asked quickly, "They might already have been – "

"I took care of it, they'll be fine for now. Just lie back, I'll get Didymus." She left.

Thera looked up and realized for the first time that she lay in the open. The air was warmer than it had been at midday. She spied the faint lighting in the east, which was the precursor to the glow of dawn, and she corrected herself. It was warmer than midday yesterday. Wind swayed the branches overhead. They had been lucky yesterday. Things could be much worse, and the weather had turned, so at least perhaps they would not be too cold in the coming days.

Chapter 17

Temis had become unbearable. She paced anxiously, constantly. Direct eye contact was best avoided, much less conversation. Hena steeled herself and walked towards the far side of the hall, where rows of windows let unseasonably warm fresh air into the room, and where Temis paced through the pattern of dark and light.

Before Temis could turn and spring, Hena saved herself by shouting, "I have good news!" from halfway across the stone floor.

"Freedom is the only good news I want!" Temis returned.

"Which is why I've come to give it," Hena rejoined.

Temis paused, one foot lifted. "It's not like you to joke, Hena."

Hena came face to face with Temis and smiled into the suddenly still eyes. "It's been five days, and no sign from the scouts. You are not the only one at their wits end."

"So you are opening the gates?"

"For you, and five riders, only. A quick scout to see how things look, a foray to double check their original campsite, and if you return without falling into any holes, we will let people return to their homes."

Temis had brightened the whole while, despite Hena's irresistible jab; now, Temis laughed. "I must admit I haven't understood anything that's happened over the past week. Those people confound me. Why did they attack at all? Where did they go afterwards? Where can they be if our scouts repeatedly find nothing? But," she sighed, "despite being angry about what they've done, I hope we find nothing. I'm ready to be done with this. When do I leave?"

"Now is as good a time as any, pick your men and go." But she already had.

Hena turned and leaned out of the window. The air was too warm, and had been all week. Looking over the field before The Castle, she agreed with Temis. They had sent out scouts daily, both to look for the missing scouts, and an entire missing rebel army. They had sent them in widening circles, in every direction. But they had yet to send anyone more than a few hours ride from The Castle. They'd seen nearly nothing. A few claimed to have heard horses, but they'd never laid eyes on one. It was as if they had been attacked by ghosts.

The King had agreed to Hena's urging, and refused to let Temis join the scouts. Hena was afraid that after her last outing, Temis might actually murder anyone she met, making a peaceful resolution difficult. But, having found nothing, it was time to look farther. And the farther they went, the riskier it would be, and in that case, Temis was an important asset.

Chapter 13

Thera had been surprised by the King's patience, and had taken advantage of the delay to heal, but the others were restless. They had been fortunate in their weather, comfortable enough without fires. Corin thought it was their due after the late rains had forced them to dig harder and faster than any had wanted in the preceding weeks.

Thera knew however that they must be vigilant, and they maintained their watch, high in the trees, following the scouts with their eyes, whilst using mirrors to signal and keep them away from the core army. There had been a few close calls, but they had managed to lure them away each time. All those dusty books on military tactics that Argus had dug up and obsessed about, had actually come in handy.

Now, Thera was one of those on watch duty, for the first time, having recovered enough from her injury to stand the climb, so she saw when the gates opened and a group of riders came out. They did not scatter to scout, and in fact, the normal scouts had already ridden out and returned in the morning. Instead, they rode with purpose across the field, and towards the trees. Thera flashed a light twice to the east and twice to the west, then began to climb down.

Chapter 19

Hena watched Temis go. She stood on the stone wall with the curious and bored, and hoped they would find nothing. But she knew the rebels were out there, because nothing else made sense. If they had wanted to leave, they could have done that easily from the beginning. She could almost feel their eyes. They had feigned an attack, lured a force out to chase them into a trap. Then they had questioned prisoners, and given the nature of the questions, Hena knew the army they faced had grown by the ranks of the King's own soldiers. It was likely large enough now to match their remaining army. Temis, and the soldiers who returned, weren't sure how many had died in the brief battle, or if any had been killed later, but it probably wasn't many...

Refocusing on the puzzle at hand, Hena pondered the fact that the rebels had then broke camp quickly, and made a hasty march right towards the castle, leaving hobbled unarmed enemies behind them. They had then disappeared. The rebels' trail had disappeared in the southwest. No obvious clues there. Initially, she had worried they had somehow infiltrated The Castle, but Low Town was still empty, and it would have been impossible to enter without notice anyway.

Temis had stopped at the edge of the clearing. It was a little far to see any detail, but Hena could not make out, from her perspective, any reason for the group to stop. Minutes passed. Finally, Hena saw with surprise that Temis was turning back, and riding full speed towards The Castle. Hena watched for pursuit. There was none. Hena turned and ran to the courtyard to open the gates of the keep and discover what had deterred the lioness from her hunt.

Chapter 20

Thera's cheeks were flushed and her palms were slick with excitement and anger. She'd recognized that soldier charging towards her, and this time she was glad to watch her riding back towards The Castle.

Chapter 21

Temis dismounted and rolled her angry eyes towards Hena, but she did not speak. Instead, heading through the kitchens connected to the courtyard, she demanded they produce a key to unlock the doors to the larder. As a group, they all rushed down the stairs into the darkness. Temis rushed forward among the stock and began rocking barrels. After trying a few nearest the stairs, she began knocking them over, working her way towards the back wall. They fell to their sides and lids popped off, rolling this way and that. She tested the weight of the crates on the shelves, and began pulling them down, too, by the dozens. Temis screeched and growled; saliva flew from her red face, and she began to sweat in the cool air.

Hena watched silently. Every crate torn down, every barrel toppled, they were all empty. As Temis raged on, the witnesses realized they had almost no food left. The stores were gone.

The Lardner arrived, and panicked immediately. He joined Temis in the search and began to mutter.

"No! No, no, no-no, no, no no! This isn't possible. Just last week I counted; I had cheese here. This was full of those dried fruits from that old farm on the hill, what's it – Nestor's…" He caught site of Hena's eye, and came to her, "I swear it was here! I would never put us at risk, I – "

"I know," Temis interjected. "It was them!" and she began stomping around on the floor, like a mad dancer. Finally, she found a spot which gave a resounding boom in a room of only wood and stone. Temis reached for the lid of a crate and, with both hands, used it to scrape the earthen floor. She revealed boards. The Lardner was there, helping her find the finger hold that would let them lift them, revealing a tunnel beneath, complete with stairs. Hena's ears rung with Temis's scream.

The King came down the stairs at full speed, and stumbled to a stop. Raising his eyes, he took in the destruction and settled on Temis.

"What," he bit out, "is going on in here? I sent you beyond the walls, and you return raving mad?"

Hena moved forward in intercepted Temis as she lunged for the King.

"They're MOLES! Rats!" she screamed. "They've taken our food. They've tunneled in and robbed us blind! We've LOST before it's even begun!"

The King moved past Hena and strove to reassure his sister. "We'll send to the farms, gather more supplies – "

"You won't," Temis growled. Before the King could ask why, Temis offered, "Because they are out there, watching. We have been under siege this past week, and now we are basically out of food. I came here because they told me. Their damn leader TOLD me!"

Chapter 22

Thera watched. It had been three hours since her encounter, and evening was drawing across the sky, when the gates opened and a rider came forth. Thera stood, and soldiers began to gather around her, as word spread through the wood, and the rider came near. The man reigned in his horse, nervously scanning the group of soldiers. Thera stepped forward.

"Parlay, tomorrow, one hour past dawn."

"Terms of your surrender?" Thera asked.

The soldier only nodded quickly, turned his horse, and rode away. Several hands slapped her on the back as he went. She waited until the soldier had disappeared again within The Castle before she turned to address the rebels beside her.

"We are almost done, and it would not do to relax our guard now. Triple the watch tonight! And bring the spy from Home, he will join our negotiation party."

Chapter 23

The night passed without event. At dawn, a party rode from the castle and erected an open sided tent to protect both parties from the weather that had shifted overnight to the bleak grey rain of winter. At the appointed time, two parties set out, one from a wall of stone, the other from a wall of trees. The birds huddled in the forest and did not sing.

Hena rode with the King, as did Temis and Dzawa, with five trusted guards. She could see the others coming. A few women and men of fighting age, an old man. As they drew nearer, Hena recognized among them, one of the missing scouts. Well, this would be interesting. They all moved cautiously under the tent. The King spoke first, as was still his right.

"It seems we are at a disadvantage for I do not know your name."

"I am Thera, and you are?"

The King hesitated, then nodded. "Ollo."

"Thank you, Ollo. We seek your complete surrender of The Castle, and I'm certain you are in no condition to negotiate."

The king nodded slowly. "My only concern is for the people. What is your desire? Power? I assure you The Castle is hard work, power limited to a few thousand souls and some square miles of farm and wood. Nothing is ever settled, every decision comes with endless arguing and negotiation."

Hena watched Thera, and saw that her fists were clenched, her knuckles white, but when she spoke it was coolly.

"Power? No. We're planning on holding a vote for leadership, and setting up a council of elders, elected to create the laws and to rule on disputes. As for caring about your people," a sharp edge crept into her voice, "we are your people. Your 'police' have been robbing us ever since you took power, and," her voice rose and shook, as she gestured to the scout, "this spy was found lurking around a village of children and grandparents. People who we took safely away from the fighting! I can only imagine – "

"No, you obviously can't," Hena interjected. I'm sure how it must have looked to you, but we only wanted to understand your motives."

Thera laughed darkly, but Temis spoke up. "It's true though. Hena might be a famed warrior but she has the heart of a doe. And I know a thing or two about does; I've killed plenty of them. Of course, she wouldn't let me go anywhere near your village, because there would be a few less grandparents if they had tried to catch me."

"I swear by it Thera," the king added, "but," he pulled up a chair and leaned forward, gesturing for the others to do the same, "what do you mean my police have been robbing you? Who? What have they taken?"

"It is easier to tell you what they have not taken. We were left our most meager furniture, our worn clothes. We were left enough grain to live by, and what we could hoard or hide away. We all became accustomed to your tax, but it became hard when our valuables were gone, and then meat and cheese were hard to come by. All the best parts were taken. You can tell yourself you like the rind and the heel and the bone, but we grew thin and it wore our souls thin."

The king turned and looked at Hena, who was as surprised as he was, but Temis smirked.

"I'm not that surprised, I suppose," she said. "Those men were your father's men, and they would have learned from him. Without fear of a strong leader – a cruel leader," she amended, "they took what they knew they could. In your name, I don't doubt."

Thera was staring at Temis. "You don't expect me to believe none of you knew of this? That you're somehow innocent of all we've lost these past years?"

"No, I gather we aren't innocent. We changed policies as the police suggested. I never doubted their honesty, or your, your … lack of it, I suppose. I'm sure our rulings must have looked like retribution for holding back, though from our position, we didn't understand… we didn't try to."

Thera stood. "That's beyond ridiculous! Don't deny you knew, I'm sure you all ate better for it. What a mockery to allow us our own food at your gracious feasts."

"We've clearly failed, but there was no evil in it," Hena said. "What purpose would lies serve now? It won't solve the problem if we don't root out the culprits. You've won; I can't argue that. Without the food you've taken," she ignored a muffled grunt from Temis, "we'd all starve worse than you've done in the past. So I propose you allow us to help you. Between the three of us, we have a lifetime of experience. As advisors to the new leaders and council – "

"Absolutely not. Do you think that after all this, you'll be allowed to just go on with an ordinary life? Much less in a position such as that? I wasn't planning on allowing the lot of you to stay."

"Hena is right," the King interjected. "There are many people in The Castle who are loyal to us. Despite your hardships and good intent, they might find it difficult to follow you. They might refuse to. Remember, not all of our soldiers stayed with you. Many returned to us."

"Without you here to sway them, many of them will come to see. I will make them see the advantages of real freedom."

"Without us here, imagine the nastiest, greediest police officer leading the others in a revolt!" Temis scoffed. "The king is right; if you really want some kind of utopia, it would be a lot less messy with us around."

"You! Don't you try to speak to me of any such thing, a murderer!" Thera was obviously affronted and enraged.

"I did what I had to do, and I don't doubt you would have done the same if you had needed to," Temis replied steadily.

Thera felt a hand on her shoulder. She turned to see Corin standing there, her eyes shining.

"If I remember correctly, you said that this would not be about retribution, but our future, about The Castle. I think they are right. This is the best path forward. It would stop the bloodshed."

"What guarantee would we have that they do not betray us?" Thera whispered.

"No need of that," Didymus muttered. "Not only do I find these soldiers surprisingly earnest in their appeals, but we know where all the food is. And they do not. That should provide us some time to learn to trust one another."

Thera heart pounded, and she stared in disbelief. "So you are both against me?"

"I think you will find that telling lies and making heroic speeches will always come back to get you in the end." Didymus smiled serenely as he leaned upon his cane.

"Lies?"

"He means Argus, you idiot. Of course, I'm not sure it counts as a lie if no one believes you for a second," Corin said softly.

Thera gaped.

"But we saw the point of it, and took it. Now it is your turn."

The king cleared his throat loudly. "We will retire to The Castle, while you deliberate our suggestion. Whatever you decide, we will accept your terms with honor."

Thera remained silent as they mounted their horses. She watched them ride away already knowing what her answer had to be, what her army's answer would be. It had never really been her choice to make anyway.

ALL THE GOOD IN THE WORLD

By
Caroline A. Gill

ABOUT

Caroline A. Gill went to UCLA and to Northern Illinois University for her MFA, in printmaking and metal-smithing. Trained as an artist, she writes her dreams. Vivid images storm out of her head and onto the keyboard: an orphan who talks to houseflies and learns of hidden magic, a vampire hunter destined to fail and fall, or the last warrior left at the end of the world. The kernel of each story is found there, in her imagination. Living in the Pacific Northwest, Caroline enjoys the Redwood forests, the crashing ocean waves and the cloudy skies. She can be bribed with Thin Mints, chocolate, and soft blankets, all of which are put to good use every winter.

www.Authorcarolineagill.com

*

"Quickly now!" Joshua urged, running from the stark terrors of nightfall. Gleaming, the remaining Temple of Time towered ahead.

As the two survivors sprinted those last few steps, hell broke loose. Howling, the undead rose from their final sleep, real magic denied. In the churchyards, skeletal hands broke free of their graves. No priest stood by with holy water, praying to stop the hordes rising. The whole land churned as the dead refused their rest. Hungry for their old lives, greedy for flesh, they poured out of the ground. Murders of crows flocked overhead, their black beaks sharp as daggers.

Evil won. On this day, creation ended. This world could only rot and die in the grip of victorious, screeching demons.

Only when Allie reached the ancient clearing in front of the spires did she stop. Turning towards him, brown hair floating behind her in a halo, she faced the darkness rising all around.

"Joshua," she exhaled his name, her voice full of longing, "I will find a way to return. There's a way. There must be. I won't forget, I swear." Allie pleaded with him to listen. "Hope does not die today. You have to believe that. You have to, Joshua."

To see her there, shivering, her clothes torn, her skin bruised, covered in claw marks, Joshua marveled. *She is a miracle. A miracle.* Watching her eyes, filled with fear and courage, the Timekeeper knew two things: one, he loved her to the marrow of his bones (And that made the second fact perhaps even harder): Allie wouldn't live through the night. *Not here, not on this fallen world.* What he wanted, the life he wanted with her, all of that fell by the wayside.

Allison Beatrice Good must be saved. And there was only one way to do that: the Ascension. Joshua felt the beacon of hope flicker and go out in his heart. He knew better. The future they imagined evaporated from his grasp. He saw the signs. This was the ending foretold. Nothing would help them now. Hope was a weakness he rejected.

"Come on, Allie," he whispered, holding her one last time within the protection of his arms. "You know the way. Only you can do this. It's time."

Her body trembled like a captured sparrow, shaking wildly against him. His fingers touched the soft brown hair that lay across his armored chest. Her tears fell. His did not. Joshua knew this was the way it had always been. The way it must be for worlds without number, back through to the beginning of Time.

"For all of us." He leaned down, kissing her cheeks, her chin, her lips. More than life, Joshua didn't want her to go. Sorrow mirrored back from her beautiful brown eyes. She didn't want to either.

In the distance, behind the last mountains, an ungodly shriek split the heavy fog. It was the final call of chaos. Demon armies revived, nightmares made real.

Cracking into shards, the last corner of the world fell.

Joshua shook, but stood firm. All of his training, his learning of spells and ritual, years spent training as a knight commander, none of it was not enough to stop the destruction that rained down. With every powerful priest of Argent dead, Joshua could only hold back the march of time for so long. The end of this creation came swiftly.

Loving her, this was the last thing he could do -- one last gift. Joshua Trilan knew the magic. He held a few ceremonial keys: Timekeeper, Minute Accounting. Not that they would do any good now. *What good are seconds when the world falls into pieces?* He fumbled to remember even one spell from his training that would help them fight the collapse. What was the point of controlling a few seconds when chaos rode to war? When the ground opened up in heaving chasms, ripping itself into oblivion?

"I wish," he spoke gruffly to Allie, full of regret, "that we could live our lives in between the seconds that remain. I wish…" his voice trailed off. No one had use for wishes.

For untold centuries, the Argent Order, Timekeepers, Yearholders, even the Decaded had tirelessly fought to hold back the hatred of the bodiless, the lies of the Deceiver. So many catastrophes avoided, so many moments rescued, countless victories all in the name of their service. Timekeepers remembered them all: every change to the timeline, no matter how tiny or large a shift. Only those who held the keys remembered the *once was* and the forgotten futures. For millennia, the system worked. Timekeepers won victory after victory against the Deceiver.

None of those successes mattered anymore. This morning, right before the sunrise, all that ended. In a carefully planned attack, the Pillars of the World were brutally assassinated.

Gathered together, undone by trickery, their Daydreamer lights flickered and went out. Piles of powerful Argent priests fell, murdered as the most learned scholars stood at the Pillars' side. Every holder of real magic sank under the crashing wave of snarling demons. The slaughter continued until there was nothing left but blood, bodies, and ash. When it was over, anyone who could have stopped the plans of the Deceiver lay dead on the temple steps.

Every Daydreamer died in the attack, except Allie.

And that had been because of Joshua. *My fault, my blessing…* Last night, the brown-eyed girl had slept deeply, her hands entwined in his crow-black hair, her breath on his shoulder. Lying right next to him, Allie missed the most important meeting of the year. A scandal at any other time, Joshua had felt awful when they woke. But their mistake meant Allie lived. The last of her kind, hunted by every hellion on the planet, she would be cornered, captured, and killed before night fell. With only his weak magic to hold off the inevitable end.

Joshua didn't speak much as they ran. What could he say? Her whole family, slaughtered. Everyone she knew, gone. She was the only one who could change the world, stop the Deceiver. And she didn't know how. Her Daydreaming had just started. Allie's confusion clouded their every step. Gripped by misery and sorrow, they stumbled on all day long, chased by a growing horde of snarling demons. Last night, the world was perfect, filled with joy, completely normal. Now, a day later, the two survivors fled across the rotting land, running for their lives. He didn't mind the quiet between them. She knew how he felt.

Last night, Allie and he said all the words Joshua ever needed -- the important ones, spells that bound them together throughout time and space. Clear as a frozen lake, Joshua watched as the Daydreamer recited the words of Oath and Binding back to him. "You are the last Good. There is nothing I won't do to protect you, now and forever."

Within days, this creation would all be over -- they both knew that. Already, the defiled earth turned to darkness faster than a pack of hell hounds. Shadows fell across the north, cloaking earth and sky. Storm clouds blocked the sun. Horror began its reign.

Screams filled the air, ripping apart peace and drowning life in terror.

Joshua crouched near the stone steps. The prophesied time demanded by his order's vows, those precious minutes ticked on, drawing closer. *Here, at the last Temple of Time, she has a chance. I will give her those moments, come what may.*

Across his back, his battle-dented shield protected them from demon bows. Around their position, stray arrows fell. Darts and stones clattered and spun when they hit the broken marble steps. Unlocking its buckled grip from behind his back, the Timekeeper braced the shield's cover over his left arm, securing his defense.

He had no weapon to fight with, no way to stop the murderous tide that surged toward them.

"Where's my damned sword?" Frustration. He knew where it was, in the head of a giant demon, shattered into pieces, lost in a skirmish two towns ago. Now when he needed it most, Joshua had no weapon. Surrounding the temple, a wave of demons crept closer. Joshua clenched his empty hand. It was useless against hell-forged blades. *Is there something, anything I can use?*

A glimmer of metal nearby caught his eye, deep in the shadows cast by the temple altar. Scrambling over to the side of the main block, Joshua pulled out an ornate decorative hammer. Hefting it, he tested the weight. *It'll do.* One dented shield and a weapon more jewelry than tool -- that was Joshua's whole defense. Forged by ancient smiths, the hammer's grip molded to his palm. It felt right. Only meant for ceremonial display, it was barely a weapon. That was all he had to protect her.

Joshua set his stance, ready. It was a Timekeeper's calling, what he was born to do: to defend the Daydreamers with his life, with his blood, to the very end of Time.

His forces, the Battalion of the First Argent lay dead and dying, lost in the billowing, dense fog. All of his old friends and the rest of humanity — gone, consumed by the demons, remade into distortions. Betrayed, broken, dust to dust, they existed only as memories now.

Joshua was lost, too. He just hadn't died yet.

There were still his vows. They held him straight and tall. This was the last thing he was called to do. Come hell or high-water, Joshua would see the Ascension finished.

Nodding to Allie, though they both knew the truth, he swung the hammer from Time's temple. And like his heart, the weapon moved steady and strong, clearing the surrounding area.

To the left, ancient trees broke in half, their giant trunks splitting. Each fell to the ground, shaking the foundations of reason. Thunder echoed across the forest as fallen hordes and their hounds surrounded the valley.

Heart in hand, her fingertips hovered over his eyelids, cheekbones, and jaw.

Closing her eyes, Allie gathered her courage, a phoenix emerging from her stone egg, wings on fire.

Joshua guarded the steps of the temple, giving her time, his last gift. All around her, he could see the gathering flame. The air around the Daydreamer crackled with energy. With the lightest touch, the girl he loved stepped to the imposing, polished stone altar.

With her steady gaze on Joshua, Allie grasped the base of the ornate candelabra. Neither of them knew what to expect next.

The second she touched the metal, her fingers burst into flames. Allie looked at him, shocked. Her hands burned with a bonfire's light. She didn't cry out. Instead, her eyes mirrored an eternal fire across the deep lake of their sorrow.

Guarding her, Joshua watched the ground around the temple begin to crumble and fissure into bits, exactly like the future they had promised each other.

Floating on a lake of brimstone, Allie glowed with life and power beyond imagining. Then, with a whoosh, the force of gravity lost its claim on her burning form. Shining with immortal flames, the Daydreamer rose, her body lifted over the altar. A feather in the wind, Allie drifted above him, the waning sun pulling her home. Weightless, pulled ever higher, soon she soared over the treeline.

Looking down at him, Allie smiled through her tears. Relentless, the magic took her, lifting the Daydreamer to freedom. She ascended to a future they would never share.

Joshua's heart pounded ever louder, watching the miracle. *Save the Daydreamer. Protect the Daydream.* That vow held him steady even as he lost the woman he loved to the elemental fire.

Joshua shielded his eyes from the heat that dripped from her body like rain. Sparks crackled and fell all around him. He did not move. Stubborn and loyal, he waited, hammer in hand, protecting the last sands of time. Tilted, the hourglass inside the last intact temple emptied onto the ground. Soon, less than ten handfuls remained. Those, he guarded with his life.

Joshua looked up, stealing a glance at the wonder. Above him, Allie flew into the darkening sky along the ladder of angels. The Daydreamer, hope of all nations, burned brighter than the North Star. She traveled home. Safety lay somewhere beyond this realm. The farther she flew, the smaller her glowing body became until she was one star among millions across the wide night sky. There was a splash of blue light that bloomed in a circle from the farthest point of her ascension. Through the portal, the last Daydreamer stepped. And then, she was gone.

Gone.

Imps and demons, ghosts, and horrors all charged the last shining beacon of Time. Hefting the weapon in his hands, Joshua's eyes reflected their rage. "You have not won. You have not," he swore to the gleeful monsters. "I will fight you until my last breath."

Above the gathering, out of the ragged, blood-red sky, a tiny star glimmered. The distant light descended, its gleam parting the smoky gloom as it fell. Growing larger as it sped through the sky, the bit of brightness floated down to land near Joshua's planted feet. Out of the corner of his eye, he saw it: a single shoe. Her shoe. One delicate, shining bit of the Daydreamer glowed with the purest white to ever bless the earth. Not even the mud dimmed its illumination.

Snarling, Joshua swung his hammer as the demons attacked.

By the light of Allie's lost slipper, Joshua fought. Fury and spit filled his mouth.

With a stroke of the old hammer, he swept the ground near his feet clear. Every contact erased a demon. Not sure how it worked, Joshua was grateful all the same to the ancient smiths. Pop after pop, the leering, savage faces of lust and greed vanished. Joshua grinned, counting each death for what it was: a small victory. There was no winning. He knew that. Defeat rode straight at him, on the backs of hellions. *But for now, I will stand. With this breath, I fight.*

Faster and faster, the demons just kept coming. Ten replaced every single imp he obliterated. Swing after swing, the army that surrounded him grew. Dark, heavy clouds filled the sky from horizon to horizon. The air turned bitter cold. Still, Joshua swung his hammer. For a while, the polished white stones of the fallen temple of time still shone, but even that light faded. Darkness squelched any opposition.

Finally, there was only the steady, constant glow from the dropped slipper. *Allie.*

Joshua groaned. Terror built up in his lungs, fear he could ill afford. "Doubt not. Fear nothing." That's what the wise, wrinkled priest in his demolished village used to say. Doubt nothing at the end of the world. Fear nothing as life died. Fear didn't help. It just made him tire quicker. Wasted emotion, weakness he could not afford. Squelching the rotten corpse of despair that scratched and clawed inside his mind, the lone man struggled on.

Relentless.

Hordes attacked, howling their glee and Joshua answered each screech with the smooth swing of his weapon. Sweat built on his forehead. He did not wipe it away. There wasn't time for such gestures. *No time.*

There could be, though.

By the sole light of the Daydreamer's dropped shoe, Joshua thought as he fought. The wave of demons kept coming, insatiable. Their dull black eyes absorbed light. That was what the last man standing searched for: the pits of flat despair. His shoulders ached. And he knew. Joshua knew he would fail soon.

I will fall. Everything will end. As it was foretold. *As it has always been.*

"But not as it should be!" he swore.

Clouds formed with each of his exhales as night's reach smothered the dying heat. Soon, there would be no way to survive, not as a lone man stranded on an ice planet. Now scarcely seemed the time for prayers. But Joshua knew: vows fueled by need, sealed with blood could never be broken. And Joshua did not intend to break. Ever.

From under the far mountains, a cackle boomed, rippling across the valley. It was full of victory and gloating. That sound echoed through Joshua's bones, shaking the earth and his slowing body. No one lived to tell him what made that sound. No one needed to. Joshua could feel the impending collapse of reality as the fragile world shook. The Deceiver. That thing -- it was rising. The second of its final victory approached.

He placed one bloody, sweating hand on the unmarred altar's polished surface. "Never. Never will I let this happen." Words fell from his lips, sealed in his heart, marked by the crimson handprint on the cool, white stone. Wasn't much of a prayer, but it was all he had left. But the hammer kept swinging, his determination flowing to tired muscles. *Again. Again. Strike. Smash. Pivot.*

Suddenly, from right behind his position, came the sound of glass breaking, crushed underfoot. Footsteps: a sound he had never thought to hear again. From the sides of the jagged, crumbling walls, a single man stepped forward. And then another. Two more raced past them, swords drawn. All four, no, five, plunged into the fray, surrounding Joshua's swinging hammer.

"We told you that you would never fight alone, brother," Alaric the Bold shouted. Next to him, Stephan the White punched out a demon while stabbing two undead through their miserable, shrunken hearts. Loric the Quiet said nothing. He didn't need to. As always, his sword spoke far more eloquently than a poet. Joshua's shock was muted by exhaustion. But still, he grinned. Impossible things happen.

Protecting Joshua from every side, the twins Jans and Relm stepped into the line, facing the fallen together. Wiping his beard with one hand, Jans guffawed loudly. And he kept laughing as countless demons popped.

"You are always late," Joshua mumbled, the smile in his eyes speaking volumes of gratitude. "Always late."

"But we never lose!" finished Alaric, kicking a demon in the head while decapitating another. The wall of demons poured down, teeth and weapons, claws and evil splattered to the icy mud. The six warriors answered the challenge, refusing to give ground.

In front of the last Temple of Time, they stood firm. Every warrior in the line took terrible wounds, but they did not fall. They did not fail.

"Can you hold the line?" Joshua whispered to Stephan and Loric, his words an echo of his old commands. Without pause, Stephan and Loric stepped into Joshua's position, sharing the burden. Their swords did not pause. The last line of mankind held, if only for a few glorious moments.

Joshua wasted no time. Sprinting over to the broken hourglass, he carefully scooped up handfuls of sand, pouring each into his leather waterskin. The sack had been dry for hours, but now it bulged with fragments of exposed time. *I am the last Timekeeper. No second should be squandered.*

Then, spinning to his left, Joshua grabbed the gleaming slipper from the ground. Her shoe. Up close, he could see the mud and grass marks from their frantic sprint a few hours before. Its surface marred by travel, scuffed and dirty -- still, it was perfection. Holding that tiny shoe brought a rush of emotion and memory to Joshua's worn and defiant heart. Love filled his weariness, more powerful than water or food.

Holding it in his hand, the light from the Daydreamer's slipper lit the whole valley, blazing with the beacon of her final hope.

Stepping forward into the knights' defensive line, Joshua brought the impossibly bright shoe with him, tied to his belt. Swinging the ancient hammer, Joshua continued to resist. He would, right up to the end.

Something had changed.

The gathered horde blanched. Caution slowed the demons. Weakness that the overwhelming enemy had never considered possible. Instantly, Joshua knew. The last Timekeeper saw doubt settle into their hate-filled faces. For the first time since the earth-shattering betrayal this morning, the demons paused in their rejoicing. Allie's shoe -- its light made the imps hesitate. Just that little trace of a Daydreamer stunned the vile horde. That was all the six survivors needed. Fully committed, the knights pushed back.

Relm did not stop fighting, nor Alaric, nor Loric or Jans. And Stephan wouldn't pause until someone put a beer in his hand. This was a moment to be seized: the split-second that the battle turned.

Howling their anger, screeching their frustration and gluttony, the demons attempted to break through one last time. The towering wave of anger and hatred fell with the weight of a mountain onto the shoulders of the six remaining knights of the First Argent. Crushing despair and soul-ripping rage: emotions capable of tearing apart worlds smothered the last warriors. And not one man paused. Not one broke the line. Not one failed.

Together, they stood, fierce and loyal, strong and determined. Together.

The vast pits of hell emptied onto their heads. Horrors attacked in numbers never before witnessed. Nightmares slashed and bled across the field. And still, the men stood firm. Their circle lit only by the glow of Allie's dropped slipper, the knights fought the looming hatred of darkness.

The enemy was too great; they knew that. Resistance was only a gesture. Soon, one would fall. Then they all would die. But for now, for right now, the brotherhood of six withstood the harrowing demonic army. Their faces shone with the light of the Daydreamer. Their swords fell, parried, and swung again. Life danced in the face of death. Life refused to give way.

Joshua saw the next wave ripple across the valley. He saw ghosts on dead horses armed with lances. In a line, they charged the temple grounds. Lances had reach. Lances trumped even the mightiest of swordsmen.

"Retreat!" he commanded.

And in the space of three breaths, all six men rushed inside the heavy temple doors, slamming the iron-bound oak behind them. As a trained group, they moved instinctively. Relm and Jans lifted one end of the tremendous beam while Loric grabbed the other. With a heave, the three men blocked the massive doors.

"Iron helps. We've gained a few moments," Stephan warned. "But that is all."

Alaric's grumble echoed through the main hall, "Whatever you have to do, brother, do it now." The oak doors began to bend under massive assault. The main hall would be breached and soon.

Joshua understood. He was already in motion. In fact, he had not stopped running from the moment he called the retreat. Behind him, the five knights prepared to defend the temple door in pitch darkness against a demon horde that had already broken through the top of the stout door with their axes.

"No time. No time," Joshua mumbled, sprinting down the second hallway, leaving behind the five remaining Knights of the First Argent, side by side in the entry room. Their voices faded as Hell's army swarmed the main hall.

Some gave all. He could do no less.

Lunging up the stairs, Joshua ran to the clerestory, to the nave of the third floor, to the end of the tunnel of Time, located on the very edge of the ornate building. Even on this, the darkest of days, the Timekeeper's feet did not fail him. Far ahead, down the length of each hallway, Allie's shoe shone. Its tremendous light guided his search. Joshua raced against the final collapse.

Above him, towering walls shivered. The sounds of invasion, tunneling and burrowing demons made every bit of the building sway and creak. There were only minutes, perhaps even less than that, left. Grinding noises came from under the foundation stones. The floor trembled. Joshua sped for the sanctity of the last holy room. The entire wall flexed, bending as he ran inside, slamming the plain wooden door.

Joshua knew what that meant. This building was coming down, its structure failing under the pressure of thousands of destructive hands. Every Temple of Time had been built the same. Every single one. They fell, one after another, in the same exact pattern.

Joshua and Allie had seen two destroyed before they could reach those polished white walls. Defiled altars were useless for Ascensions.

Reaching far out into the surrounding valley, flying buttresses held each of the enormous walls open. Crushing weight shifted off of the interior temple stones to anchor points outside of the main building. Obviously, each of those locations were now engulfed by spawns of hell. They surrounded, pounded, demolished every cornerstone. Fortifications rocked.

Within moments, the last temple would fall.

Inside the nave, Joshua clung to the banister along the wall. When the shaking lessened for a moment, Joshua regained his footing and grabbed what he needed. In one hand, he clutched a quatrefoil-marked dish. In his other, a stick of chalk. Opening the madness-filled Book of the Dead, he began one careful word at a time. Soon, a continuous chalk line inscribed symbol after symbol, intertwined. Sweat drops marked the ground but did not mar the incantation. Furiously, the Timekeeper worked to save any bit of creation he could with the only magic left on earth. The one power he still held: Minute Accounting.

Slowly, carefully, he listed off the seconds, naming each one. Dropping sand, one grain at a time into the central dish, Joshua spoke names of tremendous power. The air vibrated like a metronome. Tick, tock. Tick. Tick. Tick. Reality swung back and forth to the spell the Timekeeper cast.

Ancient and rippling, the true name of time's tiny portions fell off his tongue. Emerging in great oily drops, each name sealed the seconds within the spell he cast. Furious wind pulled at his hair. Somewhere nearby, demons cried out in victory. Every part of the nave shook. Roaring with the thunder of a waterfall, the farthest corner of the temple dissolved. A section of wall broke away, tumbling outside, ripping away most of an elaborate glass window. Shards of delicate artistry crashed to the grounds, littering the hallway floor and most of the nave.

Like a spinning top, Time lurched and shuddered. His words slowed its weary march. Time screeched and sputtered.

Then, time stopped.

Throughout the temple grounds, stones froze in place. Mortar cracked and crushing gravity demanded they fall. They did not. Each of the gigantic, disintegrating polished stones trembled and paused. Fifteen seconds demanded power, denying forces that split the last building into a pile of rubble. Like icicles, the stones rested impossibly, held in place by eternal spells. Ancient phrases gathered in the crystallized air around him. Even then, Joshua did not stop. As his words sunk through the inscribed pattern and rippled out, spreading across the floor, the symbols flooded the room. Magic filled the floor and walls, rising up the shelves of decaying books.

Each layer of his vow spun a shield and a seal, one after another, delicate and unbreakable. It wouldn't hold forever in its shimmering grasp, but the Timekeeper didn't need that long.

Unfortunately, the Timekeeper's own body still existed within the span of days of the world-that-once-was. Now, he alone moved through the hours, feeling the drain of every heartbeat on his physical body. Joshua stood at the brink of extinction and took stock.

Searching his pockets, the weary man found only a mouthful of bread from the last sunrise meal he shared with Allie. No water. *At best, I have three days, not much more.* It wasn't enough. He knew that. But he squared his bruised shoulders, defiant.

Standing on the precipice of the end of everything, the time he stole held Joshua's only chance. *First, I have to finish the bindings. Then...* he looked at the old texts, glowing with the Halting spell's shimmer.

Maybe there is something in here. Maybe there is a stone unseen, a healing undiscovered? A way, something simple, something overlooked. I will find it. All of this can stop. How many worlds had ended just like this one? Planets beyond numbering. This was the pattern. Joshua knew that simple fact. And like every other sane man, Joshua admitted the truth: *I--don't--want--to die.*

But it was more than that. Allie was gone. Without her, life drooped and wilted. Hope decayed into the dullness of lead. *She is safe. Safe and far from this.* Still, her dropped shoe lit his world, holding the shadows from falling, binding him to her. His vow to her still rang true. More honest words were rarely spoken. "You are the last Good. There is nothing I would not do to protect you, now and forever."

Holding her shoe, Joshua poured over the decaying papers, scrambling to find some path, any way, even the tiniest of spells that might save him.

Two days passed without any success.

Bleary eyed, Joshua rubbed his forehead, vainly trying to push away a terrible, numbing headache.

His hands shook, grasping at old writings, sifting through fragments of wisdom -- coming up empty with each attempt. Joshua held a game piece in his cheek, trying to keep moisture in his mouth while he feverishly searched. It didn't work well. Thirst clawed at him like an insistent housecat, relentless, unanswered. *Need. Water.* He even tried licking the outer wall for moisture, but only ended up with a mouth full of dust and cobwebs.

Focus. Joshua was running out of time. Out of power, out of options, his body failed him. He needed food. He prayed to find a rat, a bug -- anything. At this moment, frozen in time, Joshua would eat whatever he could find. Book bindings were no good. And there were no animals anywhere in the dust-filled room. He'd checked twice.

Determined, he turned again to the library, searching for answers to the impossible.

But the books were full of strange drawings, charts of unknown stars, and nonsensically bad poetry. He turned another page that tore with the bending. *There is nothing. Nothing. No answer. No end to the apocalypse. No salvation for me. No return for this poor land. We are only dust waiting to float away.*

A crushing sadness smothered the room, casting thick clouds of frustration in every corner.

Death would not be fooled. The last sleep was coming for him. *What will I say with my last breath? What regret do I have?* He knew as soon as he asked. Allie. *Allie.* That was the only answer he had. The key to his loss and his sorrow.

Closing his eyes against the fatigue, Joshua saw her again, running through the fields of grain, turning back, her yellow sundress laughing soundlessly over her shoulder as he chased her. Every bit the girl he knew as a child, every part of her a woman grown. He missed every lock of her soft, brown hair.

Swimming in front of his gaze, the page before him blurred, full of archaic words which were hard to read. "Seven is the structure. Seven is the Portal. Seven Worlds, Lit by Seven Stars. Seven Dreamers hold each one. This planet, the first to rise, will be the last to Fall. When the Deceiver comes, all Dreamers die. Protect the Flames or Chaos fills the empty sky."

Seven is the structure. That made no sense. But dreamers? Joshua knew who they were: Allie's family. They had lived among humanity for so many centuries, the Daydreamers even looked like people. *She had become one of us. She...*

Again, he saw her hair flying about her face as Allie turned to him, running from the destruction that rippled across their land. Again, the Timekeeper saw the sorrow and the defiance in her eyes. *She loves me. She loves me, I know it. And she is safe. She made it through the portal.*

The Deceiver is still bound to this world. That was all that mattered. *I did my duty.*

Allie ascended above all the horrors, taking the light of the world with her, taking Joshua's heart. Safety lay somewhere else. That was all he knew. Where did the Daydreamers go when they rose? No answers were found in the holiest of libraries. But he didn't need to know, not really. Love transcended distance and Time. It was as simple as breathing: he loved her. *Wherever she is, she loves me still.*

Closing the book, he stood, body aching from his frantic studies. Hungry, thirsty, alone, Joshua prepared himself for time to begin again, for the last few moments that lay frozen beyond the doorstep, held back by magic, paused mid-destruction, to break free of his spell bindings. Running his hands through his hair, he hefted the ancient hammer; the weight of it almost dropped him to his knees. Most of his strength was gone, along with most of his hope.

Steady, man. Head up. Taking a breath or two, the Timekeeper strode to the plain wooden doorway and pulled on the handle.

Intricate spells shimmered and snapped. Instantly, everything sped up. As time rebounded, the seconds rushed past, blurring together. Both of the back walls of the nave burst apart and fell away into the blackened earth below. Inky darkness swelled from the hallway, surging in like spilled paint across the polished stones.

"There's nowhere left to go, old friend," a deep voice murmured. It came from Alaric's empty face, hatred seeping through the dull blackness that filled his eyes. "This world has ended. It is ours now. And there is someone waiting for you."

Stephan and Loric, Jans and Relm stood woodenly in the doorway, no trace of emotion, no sign of the things that made them human. The last of humanity blocked his passage. Risen demons rode the bodies of his loyal friends. And Joshua could do nothing. Perversion spoke through Loric's lips – language he had never spoken in life. The sounds now were a travesty and a lie.

"There is a use for you," the demon snarled. "There is a place for you in our kingdoms."

Joshua didn't listen to his dead friends. Lifting his other hand, the magician held up the glowing shoe of the last Daydreamer. Its light blinded Joshua. Rays of captured sunshine burned through the doorway and down the collapsing hall. Stunned, the demon-ridden dead fled back into the shadows. Around the shaking wall, Joshua heard them draw their swords.

Softly, he began to count down. "Fifteen." He spoke the number with a caress in his tone. The way he said it felt like a longing for the beauty of sunlight and love, a memoriam for the dead. With a wrenching sound, furious, howling imps tore off the ceiling of the nave. Ancient papers and brittle books were thrown into the air, their delicate bindings ripped apart, shredded with glee by demons and the wind. Joshua didn't hear the howls of destruction. Bits of paper and ash fell like snow on his upturned face.

"Fourteen. Thirteen..."

With a thunderous roar, the last Temple of Time collapsed, knocking Joshua to his knees. Tilting, the floor became a slide, vaulting him out of the clerestory as stones as big as ten men rained down around him. Smashed imps mewled piteously on every side.

Sharp pain made him wince as he bit his tongue. Blood filled his mouth.

"Twelve..." He spat onto the ground. In his shaking hands, Joshua held up the glowing shoe. His back muscles tensed lifting the suddenly heavy hammer. Its ponderous weight dragged him off-balance. Only the light Allie left him formed a beacon to the eternities. He readied himself, preparing for the onslaught of overwhelming hatred.

But the howling demonic army didn't charge.

Most of the creatures scattered to avoid the falling temple walls and the choking dust. The immediate area around Joshua cleared of imps and demons. The light of her shoe made the whole ground, upturned grass and jagged stones alike, feel like a magical sorcerer's garden. Bits of ash floated everywhere, filling the scene with otherworldly grace. Nothing moved. Joshua's stomach cramped and his fingers twitched as he stared up at the overcast sky. It was peaceful, serene even.

"Eleven." His voice trembled a little as the seconds slipped away. Still as death. The Timekeeper blinked. Shadows moved in the corners of his vision. By the light of the shoe, danger crept closer. There was nowhere to run. *I will not hide...*

Five deadly beings picked up their fallen bodies and walked with supernatural grace toward the holder of the shining slipper. Each face blanked, each hand clenched on sword and shield, the emptied remains of the knights of the First Argent advanced. Surrounding Joshua one at a time, they stood far enough away that he couldn't strike at any. Not yet.

Even then, he didn't look at them much, giving the mighty

fallen not more than the briefest of glances. Joshua's eyes returned to the ash-filled sky, so polluted with smoke and destruction that not one single star shone through the grit. Still, the sky was where Allie had gone. So that was where the last Timekeeper looked in the moments before he died.

When it came, the pain inflicted by the sharpened blades mixed with a strange numbness. Pushed back by the force of Jans' weapon through his shoulder at the same moment as Relm's blade cut through his other arm, together they skewered the last man alive. Alaric and Loric moved like serpents in the grass. Joshua looked down to see each of their honed blades stab clean through his legs. The four demons held the weapons there, pinning Joshua to a wretched, eclipsing pain.

"Ten," Joshua mumbled as shock set in.

Stephan stood in front of him. A harsh sting pinched Joshua's skin and muscle, above his rib cage. The point of his old friend's finely-sharpened sword cut Joshua's chest where it rested. Crimson red bloomed through the ripped cloth.

Dizzy, Joshua's head fell forward. Dull blackness used Stephan's eyes to watch the tortured man, drinking in the damage, blood, and sweat that covered his pain-wracked body. Leaning in, the demon lifted Joshua's fallen head, forcing the captured human to stare into the eyes of chaos. Rough fingers moved the skin of his face and neck, a farmer inspecting an animal at auction.

Whispers floated in the space between them. Joshua understood some of the words, but they felt distant, removed. "You have a purpose. You are preserved for a reason, mortal. There is one more needed. One more to break free."

"Nine." That was all he said. Numbness climbed up the Timekeeper's fingers. His hand betrayed his will. Even though he concentrated, it wasn't enough. Joshua dropped the slipper.

Shouts of victory sounded across the valley, spilling over the far mountains with hell's jubilation.

"It's over. It always ends this way. We win. We always win." Stephan's face loomed close to Joshua, his gloating all that the tortured man could see. The grin of his dead friend filled his vision, a nightmare of loyalty and bravery twisted into trash. Ponderously, Joshua tried to speak, tried to blink. But three days without water had left him near voiceless. The thing that animated Stephan's corpse leaned in, listening to the slight sound carried on his breath.

"Eight."

With one terrible strike, Not-Stephan moved, slashing across the delirious man's exposed throat.

Hot blood rushed out. Evil would not be thwarted. They always won. The time of man ended with a whimper. Ripping the four blades out of his failing body, the once-Knights guffawed at his collapse.

Joshua blinked so slowly. Opening his eyelids again took tremendous effort. Warm liquid covered his chest and arms. He bled out like a pig. To the hellspawn, that's all he was good for: carrion to be consumed.

Then with a rumble, the ground stirred beside Joshua's cheek. A hole appeared, mounds of dirt pushed away from something hidden in the earth. His eyes barely stayed open, but the Timekeeper still saw the Deceiver break free, rising to claim its throne of destruction. Snout first, a serpent slithered out of the underbelly of ripped grass, black as tar. Prophesied moment, worth the witnessing. That didn't matter to Joshua. He didn't watch its silken movements.

Instead, Joshua searched the clumps of disturbed ground, hungry for one last glimpse of the wondrous slipper. One last connection to the girl he defended to the end of the world.

No sound came out of his mouth as the dying man's lips recited, "S-seven. Six. F-five…"

The thing of nightmares sprawled next to Joshua's bleeding body, licking at the thick, red blood running down his shoulders.

Opening its scaled mouth wider than any creature could, the voice that crooned out of its mouth made grown men weep with fear. Slick words twisted every emotion.

"There is no death. There is no lie. There is only me. No deceit, no truth, just the end of all. My beginning, my rule. And to you," its dull black eyes studied the ashen skin of the dying man, "I grant eternal life."

Nonsense, the Timekeeper thought, his vision narrowing, every breath a battle. *Four.*

Triumphant, the thing slithered closer. "You have lived to see the end. Your body is my new chariot. See your defeat. Despair. Now watch my reign begin." Clamping down on Joshua's exposed neck wound, the creature's venom poured into the weakened human.

Joshua closed his eyes for the last time as the emptiness of hell spread to his brain, numbing every nerve, severing every atom. His hand shook twice, fingers contracting as he reached one more time for the last light on earth.

Allie. Alli--

The glow of the shoe filled his failing vision just as the love he felt for the Daydreamer, for the simple act of living, filled the man's faltering heart. Like the sensation of sunlight on a summer day, the impossible slipper warmed him – held and comforted him. Its glow refused the venom of the Deceiver, denied creation's ruin. *Three.* The shoe's luminous shine did not fail.

A terrible, wrenching pain seized Joshua's heart and mind as the poison took control. But Joshua was already far away. His last gaze filled with the truest of lights.

First, his heart died. Then, flooded with the dull black thickness of Deceit, every cell in his brain stopped firing, the switch flickered and turned off. Something dark, blank, and hideously distorted moved into the empty spaces left behind. The last of his blood pumped out of his veins, soaking the upturned earth.

It was a good death, a heroic end. Not that it mattered to Joshua. The rest of eternity spent in Hell lay before him, full of mourning and loss. It was always going to be this way. Every prophecy in every ancient text stated the law clearly: All men must die. He was the last to walk through that final door.

Floating there, the Timekeeper's ghost repeated one name: *Allie*. Allie! His destroyed body had no voice. Still, his mouth moved with finality. *Two...* There was a power in names.

Allie.

Abruptly, the discarded slipper shook.

More of a shudder at first, then violently, the shoe's light splintered. Fire shot in every direction, a hail of a thousand darts.

Every demon struck by the explosion crumpled, instantly undone, melting into a puddle of red hot lava.

Hell looked confused. Elementally chaotic, every imp and demon nearby paused as the light expanded from one tiny, insignificant shoe into a ring of purest fire. Mowed down by each flaming point, the confusion that froze on their melting faces spread across the assembled horde, scorching the land. Riding the violence of an eruption, the gathered rays of light expanded ever outward, catching rows and rows of demons before they could flee.

As the confusion spread so did the brilliant Daydreamer light. More glorious than a fallen star, the slipper's combustion seared through the hatred of hell. Stabbing greed, jealousy, burning pride and gloating, one tiny shoe torched the desecrated ground and every bit of hell it contacted.

Nearby, the five knights stood back to back, shields up, spared from the brunt of the blast. Only a few sparks of light hit their animated bodies. But that was enough. *Darkness cannot abide where any Light shines.* Dull dark evaporated from their eyes. Clarity returned to their faces. Awareness of what they had done showed on each one. The same friends whom Joshua had led into countless battles, now reacted in horror and despair.

Horrified, Jans ran to the dead body of his friend. Alaric's face twisted, appalled.

Stephan shook, a wall of grief flooding his fragile grip on the fragmented world around him. Every single one of them knew what had happened. What their bodies had done. What uses Hell had for their world. Returned from the filth of possession, the Argent knights understood impossible things, well beyond the grasp of any mortal man.

Loric walked to Joshua's bloody remains. With one slash of his blade, the quiet knight cut the head off of the monstrous, burning snake that thrashed nearby.

All five men stumbled together, forming a circle surrounding the body of the last Timekeeper.

One by one, they laid bare hands on the man they had murdered, touching the corpse of their friend.

All together, they uttered the same words. "Daydreamer," they shouted. "Daydreamer!" the knights bellowed to the pitch black sky.

Pausing, they waited.

One at a time, the warriors planted their sword blades into the land around Joshua's corpse. And then, the five men touched the wounds their hands had inflicted, the wrong done with their own flesh. Looking skyward, the knights demanded justice. Their pleas echoed across the valley, the sound amplified into far more than two words. With each syllable, their fierce loyalty shone. From their fingertips, a glow kindled. The same kind, exactly the same light as the wondrous shoe.

Every few minutes, the five knights called again, refusing the silence of the clouded sky. Every time, the same words. Every voice held the same plea. No answer came, but they did not stop. Hand in hand, the men of war refused defeat. And make no mistake, this was a battle. The greatest battle ever fought. One impossible thing – that was all they demanded. And they were stubborn.

Especially Stephan, who wore his grief like a heavy cloak.

Again and again, they searched the empty, opaque sky. Their hands glowed with an otherworldly light that spread up their arms bit by bit. Each cry, each earnest plea burned their flesh a little brighter. No one stopped to speak to the other. They concentrated everything they had on the work, on the words.

Jans held the tortured body, pushing aside the bangs that strayed out of place, denying death's deterioration. Each man held the wounds caused by his part, from the damage of his sword. Sorrow was a heavy burden to bear. Together, they lifted the terrible weight, steadfast.

There was no sign of the sun. No stars, no true reckoning of time to guide their way. But the fallen warriors did not need to see. Their voices sped through the thickest air. They did not need the heat of the sun's orb to believe that they could change what was.

The lost demanded justice.

Without ceasing, those five men called to the vanished girl, to the Daydreamer who loved Joshua, to the Timekeeper's beloved. Soon every bit of their bodies glowed with light. No answer came. Heaven was gone, burned away in hell's rising.

But they would not, did not stop.

In a circle, the five men held their fallen friend, wrapping his corpse in hands of fire. Soon their faces shone brighter than either of the moons. Each warrior focused entirely on that one, singular task: calling for help.

Joshua wanted to answer.

His ghost flickered in and out of awareness, but he heard their cries. He wanted to live. The ravaged body left by the Deceiver was useless. Still he tried, moved by the pleas of his friends, by the devastation in their voices, by the toll of their regret. Joshua stretched back down to the tether that held him there, that tied his spirit to the destroyed world. Reaching inside the ruined form, he felt only the coldness of clay, the immovable mountain of flesh that lay blue and bloodied under their shining hands. There was nothing there. Venom and decay had done their work. Already the stomach, his stomach, started to swell.

Joshua could not do it. *I am not strong enough.* Curling around the ancient hammer, his ghost fingers slipped right through.

Allie.

Hands lit. Voices combined. United in purpose, they did not stop. The cries of the knights did not fade away. Instead with each demand, an invisible bell echoed through the argent portals, even from across the universe.

Somewhere, a door flew open.

Above the pleading men, a single dim star lit the night sky. The first celestial sign sparked and faded. Then, it shone again. Brighter. The first star since hell broke loose shone in waves, weak and small.

"Daydreamer," Stephan called, glowing with the force of his loyalty, the cost of belief.

"Daydreamer," Jans sighed, his hands resting on Joshua's pale face.

"Daydreamer," Alaric intoned, daring the sky to defy him.

"Daydreamer," Stephan whispered, his plea holding every bit of pain and regret.

"Come back," Loric the Quiet spoke to the quivering star. "Daydreamer, come home."

A cry shook the heavens, fierce and piercing, defiant. Distant light stabilized, growing stronger, speeding toward the destroyed world. Screaming through the outer layers of clouds, the star arced across the horizon and spun closer and closer, burning ever brighter. As it collided with the densest clouds of ash and dust, the strength of the light sliced right through the gloom.

A star fell and burned the sky with its passing.

Screaming her despair and pain, the brilliant star shone. Her wings were on fire, so terribly bright that none of the warriors could look at her without squinting. Born of flame, the creature of fire lit the fallen, dreary world. Dark and grey dissipated; misery burned away at her gaze.

She fell to earth, until she hovered in the air, just above them. Feathers of scarlet, purple and orange danced around her human form. Two truths in one body.

"Daydreamer," the men cried one last time, bowing their heads.

Dream-like, she drifted lower. Her shining form flew closer to the rubble of the ancient temple, closer to the broken body that once held Joshua. Her wings beat in great movements, holding her just above his remains. Fire and flame, flight and fury, she was all those things, a being of surpassing beauty and grace. Scanning the damage, searching the bowed figures who had called across galaxies, the wild creature saw everything.

And then she looked right at Joshua. Seeing the physical wreck and ruin. Examining the pale ghost lingering there, her fiery gaze cut through his misery. He was uncertain of his path. Filled with sorrow, his entranced spirit drifted in a void. Her piercing golden eyes saw the tears he never shed, the pain he endured, the weight of soul-crushing loss, the scorching of hell's venom. There was a question in her unbending stare. Only the shade of Joshua saw her true form. Only she saw his broken heart.

Reaching out, the ghost of a man lifted his eyes to meet hers. The immediate connection was exquisite. Light could not separate the ghost and the creature of fire. Not when Time fell. Not even across the wide and unending universe, there was no distance between their hearts.

Joy lit his eyes first. And then his smile beamed from a transformed face.

The five knights still bowed, still repeated her name, asking for redemption she could not give.

Leaning so close to the upturned rubble that she touched his cold cheek with her lips, time froze again for a heartbeat. Then, a single tear dropped off of her lashes, falling to the shattered corpse.

The very second it touched his pale skin, the one drop exploded into many. Fire roared. Burning with a white-blue flicker, flames spread across his bloodied face and hair.

Heat cleansed.

Fire claimed. His face shimmered under the intensity. Within a second, his eyebrows and eyelashes burned away. Spilling like oil along the ruined form, it took only moments before the dead man's remains were consumed.

Startled, the five undead warriors stood back confused.

"Why, Daydreamer?" Stephan asked.

"No!" Jans and Relm cried out, the glow increasing around their bodies. Then, quickly they were also consumed.

"Stop! Please stop," someone cried. But she did not. One by one, all the knights of the First Argent burst into flames. Along with the corpse, in the courtyard littered with broken walls a bonfire raged. Combined heat melted the ground around the destroyed temple into glass.

The flames flared higher and higher. Brighter than the sun, six pyres burned. Then, the bonfires receded. Charred remains smoked. A swift wind blew through the demolished building, scraping the ground. Blackened piles broke apart, their bits floating away in every direction.

Shattered temple stones glowed with the heat of the cremation. And in the middle of all of it, stood one girl, cloaked in a fabric of scarlet and red. Her brown hair burned with starlight. Golden eyes scanned the ravaged landscape, defiled beyond repair.

Six piles of ash surrounded the fire creature. And then she

spoke to the empty air, the shattered land, the ruined planet.

"This is not my home. And it is not yours, either."

Swirling sparks shot up, colliding, building, growing ever taller, wider. Taking on the general shapes of men, each of the six piles of ash flexed and solidified. Bright as cherry coals seconds later, six statues formed in perfect detail.

One of them blinked. Another shuddered and stretched obsidian arms wide. A fine coating of charcoal flew off of their skin. Their shining, perfect, glowing skin.

Smiling, the burning, smoking firebird spoke, "Seven Portals. Seven. And Seven Daydreamers to hold them."

Joshua looked up, his skin shining, body perfect and whole. Wings of brilliant purple and scarlet spread out behind him, shadows on his shoulder. Love shone from his glowing face even brighter than the fire.

His heart spoke. One word. The only word Joshua had ever needed: "Allie."

THE LAST THUNDERBIRD

By
Tricia Zoeller

ABOUT

Tricia lives in Marietta, Georgia with her husband, Lou, her little yappy dog, Lola Belle, and her big orange mutant cat, George. Her two stepsons, Joseph and Robert, make stopovers as well, making sure to keep life an adventure.

Writing has always been a part of her life—like breathing and chocolate. She tells stories full of mystery, magic, and mayhem. Urban fantasy *First Born* grips the reader from the first page, bringing him/her on a harrowing adventure, chock full of Chinese mythology.

The Darkling Chronicles, comprised of five novellas, features a portal story for the Young Adult/New Adult audience. Step through the portal to a world full of shadowcasters, dragon lords, nymphs, sprites, and satyrs.

www.triciazoeller.com
Facebook: Tricia Zoeller, Author
Twitter: @tzoellerwriter
Instagram: Triciazoeller

Chapter 1

I moved the damp cloth from Grandmother's forehead. The Owl Spirit had called outside our cabin all afternoon. I heard it. Hal heard it. The Medicine Woman, Gail, had told us to prepare.

"Two went up the mountain. Only one returned." Grandmother's eyes opened, reminding me of the great owl with their flashes of amber. "Did you hear me, *Little Bird*?"

She'd used my tribal name. We weren't encouraged to use those anymore.

"Yes, Grandmother. Hal goes up the mountain tonight. But don't worry, he's strong." I swallowed and steadied my trembling hands.

My brother was fourteen. Tonight, he would become a man. The ritual required he go up Thunder Mountain, be blindfolded, and remain there all night by himself. If he returned, he had passed the great test and would be honored to work in the mines with the other men. The women of Menolark didn't know what happened on the mountain, other than sometimes it *took* very good men.

Her hand gripped my arm like a talon. "You must follow *Walks with Lightning*."

"But—"

"Take my quiver."

Her quiver hadn't been used for *so many moons*. Grandmother's people had been belomancers. They'd shot arrows in pursuit of *answers* not animals.

Only the Mayor still conjured spirits for guidance through the use of divining crystals. Grandmother thought he'd brought the eternal thunder into our world by following solely the traditions that suited him.

"I saw the snake," she said, her breath rattling. Seeing the snake was a death omen, indicating the interference of witchcraft. Her grip softened, and her body stilled. The screech owl trilled one last time.

"Grandmother?" I heard my own blood rushing in my ears. *She's gone.*

"No." I shook her frail shoulder. "*Awenasa, Awenasa, Awenasa.*" As I wailed her true name, my vision blurred. The rest of our people called her Winnie, but she was *My Home*, and I would call her as I saw fit.

The door creaked open. "Anna?" Hal's voice sounded as fragile as I felt. He stepped into the room and studied Grandmother's state, his chin quivering. By the time he reached my side, he'd cloaked his emotions behind a hard mask. With steady hands, he shut *My Home's* eyes. He patted my shoulder, then left.

Time slipped by. I was vaguely aware of the village priest removing her body and Hal leaving for his initiation ceremony.

The only thing anchoring me was Grandmother's traditions, so, I broke furniture and shredded linens, then fed them to the fire. I lit Father's old pipe and blew smoke in every corner. Finally, I put a buzzard feather over the door to ward off witches. I wondered what she'd felt when she saw the snake on her deathbed and realized someone had wronged her.

After purifying the cabin, I walked to the river and submerged myself. The freezing water took my breath away, but I didn't care. I wanted to be numb. My clothes rose to the surface, and I allowed the river to carry them away. Without shame, I clambered up the bank, now cleansed. Gail wrapped me in a blanket.

"I'll take care of her," she whispered in my ear. "You take care of yourself."

I retreated past gaping bystanders to our cabin, which churned black smoke into the wintry sky. Just inside the cabin's entry, a fierce bear's head startled me; it was just my reflection in the mirror. Gail had draped me in a *bear* fur—usually only given to males.

Grandmother's wishes drove me to the trunk positioned at the foot of her bed. Leaning over, I watched droplets of river water run off the rounded lid from my hair and create mini tributaries in the dust. When I lifted the lid, the strong scent of cedar hit me. I stared at the cane basket quiver, well over a hundred years old. I didn't find any arrows, so I added six from my own set and placed it by the front door with my bow.

Next, I retrieved her ceremonial paint. Drumbeats sounded in my head as I drew black and red stripes across my face and one red stripe from my forehead, down my nose, to my chest. The person in the mirror was still me, but different—a past version come to life.

I heard a commotion outside. Hal opened the door. He wore a pair of sweatpants, no shoes. His eyes bounced over me, noticing the paint, the bear, and my still-wet hair.

"I wanted to check on you before I go." A horn blared in the driveway. "I'm coming," he called over his shoulder.

He'd left in the middle of a ceremony? I couldn't believe he'd defied the Mayor. I took a red warrior's feather I'd found in the chest and tucked it under his damp, jet-black hair.

"Gail told me you walked out of the river naked as a jaybird," he said.

I shrugged.

"You're scaring me more than the mountain does." His voice broke, as it often did these days, not knowing whether to be light as a child's or heavy like a man's.

Shouts came from the truck.

"I have to go."

"You're strong," I managed.

After he left, I crossed to the window and watched the red tail lights zoom away. The Mayor and the Manager would take him up Thunder Mountain.

Wolves howled in the woods; sleet scratched at the windows.

Follow him.

Raw panic animated me. I changed into all black clothing, slung the quiver's buckskin loop over my shoulder, and strapped the bow to the quiver at my hip.

Outside the cabin, I headed east toward the mountain. Night had descended, but I could make out the faint light of flashlights blinking up the pass. By the time I reached the mountain's base, I'd lost any trace of them. A force dominated the ground and sky all around the mountain. Lightning slashed through the fog, illuminating my surroundings in short, concussive blasts. As quickly as it came, the light died, and I was once again blind, feeling over the mountain's terrain as if it were braille.

Thunder rumbled over and through me, sounding like a pride of angry lions, roaring in contest. The cold sleet felt gentle in comparison. I slipped on the rocky terrain too many times to count. Every time I fell to my hands and knees, I thought of my brother's bare feet and pushed forward harder and faster than before.

I followed a twisting path up the mountain, asking the spirits to guide me. The noise grew so violent and disorienting, I focused inward, attempting to hear my own breaths.

In a short pulse of lightning, I caught the unmistakable silhouettes of the Mayor and Manager, one tall and lean, the other a short barrel. I slid to the side, feeling the terrain with my feet and hands. The gnarled arms of mountain laurel embraced me, and I prayed, hid me.

In town, the nightly storms never felt so intense. Here, it took hold of me and shook. I couldn't hear if they spoke because my heartbeat pounded in my ears. I held my breath in the cold and waited until their beams of light diminished from view.

Venturing onto the path, my legs quivered, and terror swelled inside my chest. I swallowed a sob. If something had happened to my brother, I would be lost, anchorless. In the chaos of moaning wind, rumbling thunder, and stinging sleet, I found an ounce of clarity. This mountain was angry, and so was I.

I'd heard it was bald at its peak due to constant lightning strikes. Landslides happened often, sending rock and debris hurtling into parts of town. And so, I thought I knew what to expect.

The air changed as I crossed through a layer of clouds. The storm moved below me. Moonlight hit my face and bathed the ridge in silver. As the grumbles of the storm died away, I listened for some sign of my brother.

Frantic, I climbed over the peak and dropped through space.

Chapter 2

My stomach rose into my throat, and I flailed my arms to grip something. Finally, I hit rock. My breath left me for a good fifteen seconds. A stream of swear words hissed through my clenched teeth. A quick assessment told me I wasn't broken. I'd fallen, perhaps seven feet, and landed hard on my hands and knees.

As I pushed to stand, pain stabbed my kneecaps. Shaking my head didn't completely clear my vison. As my eyes adjusted, starlight illuminated a crater.

Something in the night made me reluctant to give Hal's name, so instead, I gave the cry of the whip-poor-will, a signal my brother and I'd used in the woods. My ears strained, and I waited for what felt like forever. I caught something on the wind. When I heard it again, I rushed to the spot.

Hal sat on a rock, shivering so hard his teeth chattered. He was not only blindfolded, but bound at his wrists and ankles.

"An-Anna?" he asked, his voice hoarse.

"Yes!" I touched his shoulder. It felt like ice. When my hand nudged the knot of the blindfold, he jerked his head away.

"D-don't."

I yanked the dirty cloth over his head, despite his protest.

"Why'd you do that? You're n-not supposed to be here." His eyes flashed dark and dangerous.

"Grandmother told me to come."

"She's dead. Put the blindfold back on."

"This isn't a fair trial of manhood. They're gonna kill you." His body shook so violently, it pained me to watch.

"I'm n-not a quitter."

Grandmother had said to follow him, not free him. The cold and stress had taken its toll on me. I couldn't think. "I wouldn't ever cheat you of honor, but this is wrong. You could die of hyperthermia or get attacked by a wild animal. You can't protect yourself."

"Th-that's the point."

Chewing my lip, I looked around. Fog danced around us. The conditions had shifted to a cold drizzle.

"Well?" he asked.

"Since I stepped foot on this mountain, I've felt like *something's* here."

He scanned the area. "I thought it was just my imagination."

The blindfold, stiff from the cold, hung from my finger. I figured Hal's hands and feet were bloody messes from his journey. Anger burned inside me, causing me to burp up pipe tobacco. It was difficult to see in the dark, but I squatted down and drew my hunting knife from my ankle sheath.

"Anna. Stop."

Tears burned my cheeks as I looked up at him.

"This isn't up to you," he said.

"You're all I've got. I don't care if you hate me the rest of our lives, I would never forgive myself if I left you here."

The ground quaked beneath us, and lightning shot from the middle of the basin straight into the night sky. Burnt ozone stung my nostrils.

"What was that?" Hal didn't wait for an answer but shook his hands in front of me, fear causing a change of heart. I worked the blade through the wet rope on his wrists, and then took care of the ankle bindings.

Once free, he rubbed the raw areas and rocked on his perch, wiggling and shaking circulation back into his extremities. When he chanced a step on his raw feet, he winced.

The ground shook beneath us.

"Eeeeeeeeeeeeeeeeeeeeeeeeeeee."

We dropped to a crouch behind the rock. The screech echoed off the walls of the crater. It came again, accompanied by a light show from the center of the basin. Knife in hand, I glanced at

Hal. He reached toward my quiver, the bow attached.

"Where are the arrows?" he asked, brow furrowed.

Fumbling in the quiver, I came up empty-handed. My stomach soured. I wore my own quiver positioned at my back. Grandmother's side model needed to be at the correct angle or the arrows could drop out.

"They were there before." I spun around, attempting to search the ground.

"Never mind." He shook his head. "Give me the knife."

I did as he said. I owed him that. When the shriek came again, I realized I'd never heard anything so loud or tortured.

"It's gotta be an owl, or an eagle," he gasped.

"One the size of an elephant," I added.

Watching him with the knife, I saw my father's strength. Hope filled me to where I let the fear slip away. Using the rock as a shield, I peered around the side to investigate. An open beak breached the center of the basin. Lightning shot skyward. I ducked back down and tried to remember how to breathe. I seemed to be only exhaling.

"What?" Hal asked, eyes wide in terror.

"B-b-big bird."

The lines on his face smoothed; his demeanor changed to a calm determination. He sailed over the rock before I could catch his ankle. Everything slowed. The creature's full head emerged, revealing the shimmery blue-black feathers of a crow with the strong, hooked beak of an eagle.

Lightning blasted from empty eye sockets straight at Hal. He convulsed once, froze, and then collapsed.

"Hal!" I bashed my knee on the rock as I cleared it. Instinct sent my hand into the quiver, only to be disappointed again at my stupidity.

The bird's head dipped back into the hole, followed by a flutter of wings. Peals of thunder rolled around the rocky bowl, and I realized it came from the bird's desperate movement. It was trapped in the mountain.

I dropped to my knees and pressed my fingers to Hal's neck, searching for a pulse. My mouth covered his, and I began giving breaths. The rhythm of breaths to chest compressions became all I knew.

"Don't you dare do this to me," I cried, pumping on his chest. I resumed the rhythm. Finally, he coughed and retched.

"Hal?"

He looked at me with sharp eyes, *recognition*, but he didn't answer.

Instead, the creature did. "Eeeeeeeee!"

Something snapped inside me. I detached my bow and left it by Hal. The quiver jounced at my hip as I strode to the hole. My fingers struggled with the deerskin loop, but I pried it over my head.

"What did you do to him?" I launched the quiver into the black hole. My body shook with stress. "You evil creature."

All grew quiet. A curtain of clouds drew back from the moon, which gilded everything in its light. I couldn't move. Hal's loud moans behind me snapped me to attention.

"We have to get out of here," I yelled. I dashed over to him, hooked my hands under his arms, and dragged him. We made it to the edge of the crater.

"I can't lift you in the air."

Roots of scrub brush jetted out like knuckles on the wall. I could get a foot and hand-hold, but I wouldn't be able to fireman-carry Hal. I settled him on the ground. Pacing under the lip, I tried to think. I could shove the bow over his head, pull his arms through, and use it as a pulley or sling.

Pain exploded in the back of my skull as my head jerked forward. My fingers found the sore spot as I turned to see what had hit me. Grandmother's quiver lay at my feet. My mouth ran dry, but I mustered the courage to look up. The beast wasn't there.

How had it launched the quiver at me? I'd been right on the cusp of hysteria. The monster returning my family heirloom pushed me right over. I hooked the strap over my shoulder.

"Get up," I screeched. I yanked Hal to his feet. He swayed. "Climb." From behind, I helped attach his hand to the first root notch. Then, I boosted him by driving my shoulder under his backside and pushing with all my might. Ever so slowly, he managed to progress.

Hal leaned against me as we walked in the dark and fog. The eastern pass lay eerily calm. We didn't talk. When we emerged in the woods that skirted the mountain, thunder and lightning resumed. It was the middle of the night, but I didn't want to chance running into anyone, so I took the back way home.

Once inside our cabin, I barred the door. Hal collapsed on the couch. I retrieved a dry pair of sweatpants for him. He changed while I worked to restore the fire. Once in dry clothes myself, I piled blankets on him. He didn't shiver or moan. He simply closed his eyes and slept.

I regretted having fed spare furniture to the fire during my purification of the cabin earlier because I had nowhere to perch and monitor Hal. Defeated, I dropped into a blanket on the floor and curled up. I fell into a familiar dream about flying.

In the morning, Hal was gone.

Chapter 3

The washcloth felt like sandpaper as I removed the paint from my wind-burned face. I poured rubbing alcohol into the cuts on my hands and yelped from the pain. Every muscle in my body screamed from overuse, reminding me of last night's trauma.

I was on my third cup of coffee and wearing a groove in the wooden floor with my pacing when, I heard the neighbors cheer. After grabbing a few things, I dashed from the house, slipping on the icy front steps.

Hal staggered into town, pale, bruised, and shivering. Bloody gashes crisscrossed his arms and chest. He truly did look like a successful candidate who'd spent the night blindfolded on the mountain.

I rushed to him with a bottle of water and my father's old beaver-fur boots shoved under my arm. He chugged the water but ignored the boots. He set off toward the river, drawing a curious audience with him.

The sinewy muscles of his back tensed before he jumped into the freezing waters and cleansed himself. A single, red feather bobbed to the surface and floated away. On the bank, Gail wrapped her husband's coat around his shoulders. I placed Father's boots in front of him. Hal showed no outward sign of discomfort when he slid his raw feet inside them. As I looked at my brother, I could almost perceive the two men's spirits present for this triumph.

All mining applicants went through the ritual, no matter their age at the time of initiation. The mountain had claimed Gail's husband; the mines had claimed my father.

Looking at my brother's dimpled chin, I saw Father. Had he taken off his blindfold during the ritual, seen the bird? How had he and Hal survived the lightning when others hadn't? There had never been bodies to bury. Had the bird eaten them?

I shivered as the creature's empty eye sockets flashed in my mind and its tortured cry echoed in my ears. My neighbors' jostling brought me back to the present. We walked the narrow road to the Mayor's home, keeping several paces behind Hal while showing our support. Feeling guilty for my dark thoughts, I thanked the Great Spirit for my brother's return.

The Manager opened the door. His official badge glinted in the sun. As the town's law officer, he served on the Council. He spent most of his time as the Mayor's shadow. When the rough pine door closed behind Hal, I felt helpless.

Now, another test begins. Would my brother tell the story that needed to be told?

I felt a soft flutter at my shoulder. Gail's dark eyes watched me. Our breath clouded the air as we walked unspeaking to the little graveyard. The recently disturbed soil brought back the sadness. There was no headstone for *Awenasa*, just a circle of stones.

Kneeling in front of it, I said a quick prayer. Gail stayed at my side, her walnut forehead lined with concern. I was grateful she'd seen to Grandmother's body yesterday so I could see to Hal.

Explosions shook the tranquil day. They came from the mines of Cypress Mountain, which loomed in the west.

"She saw the snake," I said, getting to my feet.

Gail's mouth dropped open. She didn't speak, just shook her head.

The horror of everything hit me. *I need to get away.* As I whirled away from the cold circle of stones, hot tears filled my eyes, causing the landscape to melt around me. I ran without a glance back at Gail.

An hour later, I knitted on the couch, waiting for my brother's return. I kept dropping stitches, but refused to put down the pathetic scarf, afraid to still my hands.

A soft knock at the door brought goosebumps to my arms.

When I peered out, I saw Russell Stillwater, his blue-black hair glistening with drops of melted snow.

"*Little Bird*," he whispered.

Certain people merely have to give me a look or say my name, and I turn into a human rain cloud.

"May I come in?"

"Of course," I said, swiping at my tears.

He stomped the snow off his boots on the mat before stepping inside. The fire had dwindled, but his presence always made me warm.

"Brownies," he said, holding out a covered plate.

"Thank you." I crossed the room and placed them on the counter. When I turned, he was there, just a big wall of a guy with his arms ready. I dove into the hug, my face brushing the rough wool of his coat, feeling his long, silky hair on my cheek, and smelling Russell—lightning struck cedar, sweet grass, walnut—all the scents of the musical instruments he handcrafted.

"Shhhh," he said.

I closed my eyes and let go of everything, just leaned on him, releasing my hurt, fear, and heartbreak. Russell was never the first to break a hug. He stroked my hair as I trembled.

"He's okay, Anna."

"I know." I broke away and wiped my eyes on my shirtsleeve. "So, how are you?"

"Worried about you."

"Well, I'm fine now that I used you as a human tissue." I hugged myself and swayed.

"I've had worse done to me."

"Let me take your coat." My eyes traveled with his fingers as they undid each button. When he slid it off his shoulders, I grabbed it and turned from him, hiding the warm flush I felt in my cheeks.

We sat on the couch, and he found my hand.

"What are you going to do when Hal leaves for the mines?"

"Work, knit, domesticate raccoons." We sat for a moment in a safe quiet.

He took his hand back. "I don't like you here by yourself."

"Well, I think we both know the solution to that."

He jerked his head to me, eyes wide.

"Should probably get a dog," I said.

His cheek twitched with suppressed amusement. But then he grew serious, and I figured he had a lecture inside him. He rubbed his hands on the knees of his jeans.

"I loved your Grandmother, but she had some peculiar beliefs, and so does Auntie." He meant Gail who was his great-aunt.

"Someone cursed Grandmother," I blurted out.

"She had pneumonia."

"She *saw* a snake."

He sighed. "Running around in a bear blanket and sticking feathers over your door isn't going to bring her back, Anna."

I watched him closely and dug my nails into the side of my leg, hoping to hold my tongue. "I'll take that into consideration."

"People do peculiar things when they're grieving." His older brother had gone up the mountain and not come back. "Reckless, sometimes." Russell rubbed the half-moon scar on his chin. It was from a bar fight. He hadn't taken the loss of his brother well.

Footsteps sounded on the front stoop. *Hal.*

We stood as the door swung open. Hal stepped inside, wearing too-big jeans and a flannel shirt. He held a miner's uniform folded in his hands.

They cut his hair.

Russell moved first. "Congratulations, man." He went to knuckle-bump him, saw the bandages, and gave him a guy hug instead—quick lean in, two hearty pats to the shoulder, over in two seconds.

"Thanks." Hal's face was devoid of emotion, but dark shadows had formed under his eyes.

"You two need some time," Russell said. He edged past Hal

and grabbed his coat. "See you later."

I waved even though he had already slipped out the door. My attention zeroed in on Hal.

"There's stew on the stove," I said.

"Thanks, but I already ate." He dumped the blue jumpsuit onto the ladder back chair by the door.

We both plopped down on the couch. He studied his bandaged hands.

"You okay?"

"I made it, didn't I?" He tried a smile, but the pain turned it into a grimace. The tiny gap between his two front teeth made him seem even younger.

"They cut your hair."

"Hair grows. I'll live." His hand kneaded the middle of his chest, as if he had the worst indigestion. "I suppose Initiation Night is really tough for Russell."

"It stinks for all of us—victims and survivors."

Hal's Adam's apple bobbed in his throat.

"Did you see anything when you—"

"Died? Got struck by a lightning bolt from a creature of the mountain," he said.

We both laughed. Nerves had us giggling for a good minute.

"I don't recall anything useful. Came-to flat on my back with your ugly mug over me. Heard the *bird*."

"It's trapped."

"Some would say it's contained," he suggested.

We stared at each other. The fire popped.

"I leave for the camps tomorrow." He rubbed his chest with his bandaged hand, again.

The idea of separating from him triggered a panic inside me equal to the one I'd felt on the mountain.

"You can't go up the mountain, Anna. That thing will kill you. Promise you won't."

I didn't blink.

"Of course you're going up there."

We both laughed again.

"For crying out loud, don't lose all your arrows this time." His eyelids drooped. "I'm so tired, I can barely stay upright."

"Rest. We'll talk more later."

In no time, soft snores came from his room. My mind raced. Every night, when the sun set over the mines, it thundered over Menolark. Knowing what made it, I didn't think I'd ever sleep again.

He woke from his nap in the late afternoon and stumbled into the kitchen. His newly cut hair stuck out from a fitful sleep as he devoured the beef stew I'd heated for him.

"Go get Grandmother's quiver," he said.

All the hair rose on the back of my neck. I hadn't told him about throwing the quiver into the bird's hole and it returning to me. While he rummaged through his bedroom, I sorted through the blankets I'd heaped on my bed in haste. I unearthed the quiver. Touching it seemed dangerous, so I froze.

"What's the matter with you?" Hal asked, now at my side.

"Maybe I shouldn't use it," I whispered.

"Did she give it to you?"

"Yes."

"Then you should use it. *Awenasa* knows best." Hal's eyes glistened. He turned from me to hide his emotion. He bent over and grabbed the bottom of the quiver, tipping it on end. Three black feathers fluttered to the floor. They were longer than any eagle's feather.

"I didn't take those," I insisted.

He placed the quiver on the bed and bent to retrieve the feathers.

"It…it gave them to me." I squirmed in place like a child. "I was upset it hurt you, so I threw the quiver at it."

His eyes grew huge.

"When I was helping you up the rock wall, it launched it at

my head."

Mouth wide, he didn't blink as he laid the feathers on my quilt. "How does a bird throw something?" he asked.

"Do I look like I have answers to anything right now?"

He dismissed the mystery with a shrug before pulling arrows from his deerskin quiver. His eyes went to the feathers on the bed. "Let's use them for fletching."

Under Father's old magnifying light, Hal and I worked at the kitchen table using a single-edged razor to adjust the feather size. Once the glue had dried, we studied the arrows and the blue-black feathers.

"I wish it wasn't dark or we could go test them," he said. "You know, just on a target in the woods."

I didn't meet his gaze.

"Are you going to kill it?"

"I don't think it's good luck to kill a Thunderbird, do you?" I asked.

"Thunderbird." He tried the word on for size. "Thought they were make-believe." He traced the barbs of the one unused feather.

"That creature was very real," I scoffed.

"Oh, I know." He chewed the inside of his cheek.

"What happened at the Mayor's house?"

"You know I can't tell you," he whispered.

"He's sending people to their deaths. Something or someone blinded that bird."

"Maybe they had a good reason."

Chapter 4

A white van pulled into the driveway with its music blasting. In the blue miner's uniform, Hal waited by the door with a duffle bag. The driver honked. Hal glanced back at me, mouth set in a frown.

"I'll call as much as I can."

"I know," I said.

"I'll send half my paycheck home."

"You don't need to do that."

"By your age, I'll be able to afford a big house and land."

The unspoken part of that statement was *if I live to be your age.* Working in the mines was dirty and dangerous, but profitable. He shifted on his feet, appearing to weigh something else. The driver honked two more times.

"Don't worry," I said.

With a nod, he acknowledged my promise—no one would know I followed him up the mountain.

The van pulled away, taking a big chunk of my life's purpose with it. My father had pulled away from that same driveway four years ago, never to return. I'd been Hal's age at the time of the mining accident. Our mother had died giving birth to Hal. Father and Grandmother had been our center.

After drinking the dregs of cold coffee, I slipped into my coat and set out to work. I'd never felt so disconnected from reality or ill-equipped for life. My usual route took me past the town square. Today, the sun's first rays lit the square's main feature, a statue of Mayor John's ancestor holding something precious in his hands. *Gems? Gold?* Mining had changed the whole valley.

I walked to the side to view it from another angle. His head was bald except for a topknot or scalp lock. The water had frozen in a twisted snake-like pattern around the figure's hands. I shivered. *It's a statue, Anna.* Still, I noted the tremendous feather attached to its head. I'd thought it was a huge eagle feather, but now, I realized it wasn't.

"You knew about the bird," I whispered.

As the winter sky turned pink, orange, and yellow, I stepped closer to look at the two round stones in the figure's hands—*divining crystals?*

A car honked, pulling me out of my trance. I waved to Gail, knowing she was on the way to her shift at the hospital. Her form of healing was rare these days—mixing modern medicine with knowledge of the old ways.

A quick five-minute walk, and I was in front of the school, dark and institutional-looking. Menolark had a population of 3,000—a decent size for the towns on this side of Thunder Mountain. I worked in the high school library, which was a bit awkward at times since I'd just graduated last spring and was the same age as several of the students.

I floated in and out of awareness as I did the mundane tasks of flicking on lights, starting computers, and straightening stray books on the shelves. The morning was quiet, so I researched the Thunderbird.

I had my head down when I felt rather than heard a presence. "Oh! Afternoon Mayor." I drew a notepad over the book page.

"Anna." His gray eyes studied me.

"What brings you to our little library?"

"My condolences about your Grandmother." He looked down as if in reverence.

"Thank you. She's with the Great Spirit now."

He nodded before casting his gaze to the four students at a round table by the window. They'd been goofing off but ducked their heads over their books at his attention.

"I'd like to talk to you about your brother."

When he leaned his elbows on the reception counter, I glimpsed a deerskin pouch around his neck. *Divining crystals.* A cold tingle traveled the length of my spine.

"Did something happen?" I pushed to stand, my stomach dropping as if I were falling.

He shifted away and tucked the pouch under his shirt. My hand found the desk, and I steadied myself.

"Sit down, Anna. I didn't mean to alarm you. As far as I know, your brother's fine."

As I sat down, I scrutinized him—work jeans, flannel shirt, cowboy boots—laid back, easygoing, some would say. There was little sign of tribe left in him, other than the roundness of his face and the shape of his eyes. *And the fact he uses divining crystals.*

"I was curious about his night on the mountain."

"Aren't we all?" I laughed, trying to make light of things.

"Did he say anything to you?"

"No. My brother would never talk about something he shouldn't."

"And what about you? Would you talk?" He flashed his teeth, stained yellow from tobacco. It wasn't a smile.

"What you mean?"

"Just trying to figure things out. Your grandmother's sudden illness concerns me."

"What does that have to do with my brother?"

"Well, he's had quite a bit of loss for one so young. I was just worried." His weathered, brown hands grasped the counter. The lines around his eyes were slight. I guessed him to be in his late sixties.

"Life's lessons can be painful," I said. "Doesn't mean they aren't necessary. Like the ritual of sending men up Thunder Mountain, possibly to their deaths." My pulse beat at my temple, and my mouth ran dry.

His eyes narrowed.

"Some would question if sacrificing young men in their prime is worth upholding a tradition. But is there really any better way to test a man?" I flashed my broadest smile.

He nodded.

"Of course, I do wonder why no women are tested on the mountain."

"Women talk too much." His voice turned gruff, as did his whole demeanor. He stood taller. "Don't you agree, *Little Bird?*"

I shrugged.

"I'll be seeing you around," he said.

Out the window, I watched his truck pull away.

Why had I antagonized him?

Chapter 5

On my day off, I rose at dawn. With my quiver and bow, I set course for the woods. The birds sang as the sun popped its head up. Nature presented a pretty picture with the trees dressed in their lacy gowns of snow and the light setting it to glow. The birds' chatter made me think of Grandmother. I tasted the salty tears as they hit the corners of my mouth.

She'd told me the birds had many jobs. The first was to wake everybody up. Grandmother had said to greet the day with a thankful heart. And so, I sent a thank you to the Great Spirit for this day, even though I felt so miserable and lonely in the moment. She told me the hummingbird was a tiny messenger who always brought good news of spring and flowers.

"And see, Little Bird. You're a messenger of happiness." Grandmother's voice sounded so clear, I caught myself turning to look over my shoulder.

She claimed the bigger birds, such as the eagle, flew closest to the creator and carried people's messages to Him upon their wings.

"So where does that leave the Thunderbird?" My voice echoed in the field I'd entered just past a stand of fir trees.

Some believed Thunderbirds were a bad omen. Myths even told of them making off with children. The missing males of our town could be considered evidence of such behavior. Except, it hadn't hunted them; the Mayor had *fed* it. I'd never heard a story of a great bird sweeping over Menolark.

If my Grandmother's dying wishes were to be fulfilled, then I needed to shoot the arrows, and I needed to use them to divine something. I'd attached different notes to three arrows: *go up the mountain, do nothing, get Hal and leave town.*

I shed my jacket and arranged my quiver so I could draw easily. Each piece of paper was exactly the same size and shape so I wouldn't be tempted to cheat in my divining exercise.

I nocked each arrow and released, pleased with the great distance they traveled. As I ran to the farthest arrow, my boots christened the undisturbed snow.

"Just tear the Band-Aid off, Anna." I grabbed the shaft and ripped the note off. *Go up the mountain.*

"Ah, nuts. I knew it." I stomped in a circle, feeling satisfied from the loud crunch as my boots broke the hard crust.

Curiosity steered me to the second farthest arrow. Before temptation got the best of me, I grabbed the shaft and shoved it into the quiver without looking. I did the same with the final arrow.

As the birds' song grew louder, I made my way home. After leaving my boots by the door, I brewed more coffee. I had a choice between a stack of mail and the plate of brownies. I chose chocolate.

Drifting into Grandmother's doorway, the scent of rosewater hit me. The cabin felt wrong, a scene frozen in time. Grandmother's pink slippers peeked out from under the bed skirt. On her vanity mirror, she had placed an old saying, *The frog does not drink up the pond in which he lives.*

I pushed myself through menial cleaning tasks so I wouldn't keep straying back to those little, pink slippers. As I washed laundry and scrubbed toilets, I contemplated the Thunderbird's job. What would it do if freed?

There was a reason the Mayor kept it alive. Maybe I just didn't know all the facts, and if I did, I'd understand why things were this way.

Trust is slippery. The only person who may have answers was Gail, but she'd discouraged me from talking that day in the cemetery. I couldn't blame her. The mountain had taken her husband; a witch's curse had taken her best friend.

Deep down, I felt the fear wallowing inside me with the emptiness. But fear can be good, push a person to act. Before I changed my mind, I snatched my coat from the hook and slid my feet into my boots.

Gail owned one of the large ranch houses on the other side of the square. I pushed open her side gate and followed a path to the back, knowing she'd be in the greenhouse babying her herbs and plants. The icy path required all my concentration so I almost walked into full view of the Mayor and Gail.

Through the steamed glass, I could see her, face contorted, finger pointing at him. Try as I might, I couldn't read her lips. He grabbed her arm. I stepped farther into the open space, preparing to yell if he hurt her. When he dropped her arm, I retreated behind one of the evergreens and peered through the branches. His hand cupped the deerskin pouch. She looked away, hands clenched, lips pressed tightly.

Was he threatening her with horrible predictions?

His head swung around to look out the window. I held my breath and froze, hoping the green fringe adequately camouflaged me. When I peeked again, they were gone. Turning from the tree, I started back the way I'd come.

"Anna?"

I slipped on an ice patch. My arms wind-milled, but I didn't fall. "Hi, Russell."

"What are you doing?" His hand rested on the tailgate of his red pickup.

"Looking for Auntie. Was gonna check out back, but almost fell on my butt, so figured I'd better use the front—"

The front door banged open.

Coming here was a bad idea.

Trust is slippery. I ran the rest of the way to Russell and threw my arms around his neck.

"I didn't thank you properly for the brownies." In my peripheral vision, I saw the Mayor's tall, lean figure moving toward the street.

Russell looked down into my eyes. I waited, a soft plea in my look. He cocked an eyebrow. Then he kissed me. Hard. Unrelenting. Warm lips sucked my bottom lip, teased them apart, until his tongue found mine. His hand cupped the back of my head, and the other came around my waist. After a while, I loosened my hold, intending to break the kiss. He stopped but didn't let go of me.

I heard Gail's voice.

"Is this the kind of distraction you needed?" he whispered, a smile on his lips.

I couldn't believe he'd done that in front of his Auntie and the Mayor. Heat swept up my throat and face.

"That...was...g-good."

"Well, I know it was *good*. I just wondered if it's what you needed." He released me.

It took a minute before my brain was able to tell my body what to do. Finally, I removed my hands from his chest. We both ignored the Mayor as he started his truck and drove away.

"Russell?" Gail called.

"Coming." He turned his attention to me. "I need to bring this firewood round back for her."

"Fire," I repeated.

"You on fire, *Little Bird*?" He chuckled. "I see some red in those cheeks."

I scowled, which made him laugh more.

"You want to come in?"

"No. No. Just, do me a favor. Don't mention—"

"That you were snooping in the side yard," he said.

I wanted to yank his long ponytail.

Chapter 6

At mid-morning, I was doing a half-hearted clean-up of branches and debris from the storm last night. Winds had raced through the valley, pulled shingles off roofs, and ripped wires free from poles. The power had been out but buzzed back on in the wee hours.

"I appreciate your help," I said to Russell.

"No problem. I wanted to talk to you about something, anyway."

Russell didn't get nervous often, but when he did, he had a habit of chewing his bottom lip. He'd been worrying it for the last half hour.

"I'm thinking of joining the Council."

Disappointment feels like a punch to the kidneys. I'd elevated Russell so high in my opinion, he walked with the spirits.

"I think that's the worst look anyone's ever given me," he said.

"Sorry. I just don't trust the Mayor. Why would you want to work with him?"

"Because complaining about things and not taking action is the coward's way. And, doing something in direct opposition to the elders is disrespectful."

Ouch. "He visited me at work."

Russell raised his eyebrows.

"Wanted to let me know women talk too much. Also, prodded me about my brother's visit to the mountain and Grandmother's death."

Russell froze with an enormous tree branch balanced across his shoulders. "Auntie's on the Council. She's the one encouraging me to join."

I shrugged, feeling distant from him but scared for him at the same time.

When he left an hour later, I walked back to the porch, noticing the buzzard feather was missing from above the door. A reasonable person would say the storm took it. Maybe I wasn't being rational. Russell's words were bothering me.

My Grandmother didn't raise a disrespectful girl; she didn't raise a quiet one, either.

I took the one unused Thunderbird feather and fixed it over my door with tiny tacks and a bit of wire—a bold statement. Goosebumps prickled along my arm.

Fear will light you up, send a current through you like lightning. I was charged and ready.

In the afternoon, a horn blared in the driveway. I opened the door to see my brother in ripped jeans and a hoodie, hauling two big duffel bags. I wanted to tackle-hug him, but I controlled myself so I wouldn't embarrass him in front of the guys.

"What's up?"

"Back here for more explosive training at the center."

In just a week, he already looked taller to me. By the time he reached the porch, the van was gone, so I threw myself at him and blubbered.

"Can't...breathe."

"Sorry. I'm so excited to see you."

After dumping the bags in his bedroom, he stopped at the threshold of Grandmother's room.

"It doesn't seem real." The muscles in his jaw twitched. "Everything feels *wrong* without her here."

He actually initiated a hug, and for once, I was the first to let go.

Hunger eclipsed grief, thanks to puberty. Soon, he was foraging for food in the fridge. Between the two of us, we put away five peanut butter and jelly sandwiches, a row of Oreos, and two bananas.

Cheeks full of food, I reached for another cookie.

"You been on a hunger strike or something?" he asked.

"I haven't had much of an appetite."

He finished chewing, then gulped down the rest of the milk straight from the jug. I was so happy he was home, I didn't even fuss at him.

"They're taking Sam Rivers up the mountain in a few nights." He stared at me, waiting.

"It's gotta stop," I hissed. "Why are they doing this?"

"Money. One of the old timers drank too much at the fire one night and told stories. Seems there used to be big birds on the mountain we mine."

"There were more?" This saddened and sickened me. "What happened to them?"

"I don't know, but one wound up trapped in Thunder Mountain."

"Driven from its home," I added. "And now, our town profits while the bird suffers."

"What do you want to do about it?"

"I *should* confront the Mayor." I picked the Oreo crumbs off my sweater.

"If anyone talks to the Mayor, it should be me." He shook his head, quite like my father used to do. "I was on the mountain; I went through the ritual."

"I don't trust him, Hal. I've considered approaching the Council members individually. They can't all be bad."

"Is that what you *want* to do?"

"No. I want to free the bird," I whispered.

"I was hoping you'd say that. I have a bunch of dynamite in my bag."

We both jumped when the phone rang.

Hal got to it first. His whole body tensed.

"Today? I thought we started tomorrow? Fine. Okay. I'll be there." He kicked a stray throw pillow that had tumbled to the floor. "We start training in an hour."

"That's ridiculous. What's the rush?"

He plopped himself in the middle of the ugly, flowered couch and ran his hands through his hair. Bouncing his knee, he looked up at me. "We're at the management's mercy."

"We'll talk more when you get back."

He rested his head on the couch and closed his eyes. I let him have a few moments of peace.

*

After he left for training, I settled at the kitchen table with my arrows, a box of single-edged razors, and super glue. We'd used a cheap glue earlier, and one of the feathers had shifted.

The wind picked up outside, sending the wind chimes dancing and tinkling in a frenzied song.

My fingers traced the barbs on the arrows' fletching before I put them back in the quiver.

A knock at the door caused me to start. The wind had muffled the approaching footsteps. As I pushed away from the table, I swept up a razor blade and slipped it into my pocket.

"Who is it?"

"Sam."

The drums I'd heard after Grandmother's death played in my head. I cracked the door and peered out.

At eighteen, he stood broad and proud, wearing only a t-shirt and jeans. He narrowed his eyes at me. The Manager and Mayor were behind him. The Manager's coat was open, providing me a view of his holster and gun, which he gently nudged as a warning to me.

"I'm taking you up on your offer to be the first woman tested by the mountain," the Mayor said. He twirled the Thunderbird feather in his hand.

With my quiver on the table and my bow leaning by the coat hooks, I took a moment to consider my options. My stomach rebelled, and I thought I might hurl.

"Anna?"

Looking at Sam, I knew I couldn't refuse.

"Yes, Sir. I'm coming. Will I need to bring anything with me?"

"No. Just yourself."

"I would like to tell my brother—"

"Not necessary. Our people will let him know the next break he has from training."

Crap. Despite snow flurries, I left my coat. They wouldn't let me wear it anyway. Sam walked in front. I followed with the Mayor holding my right arm as if he were some gentleman escorting me on a date.

They hustled us into his truck. The inside smelled of cigarettes, sweat, and aftershave. I looked at Sam, but he ignored me. If he was nervous or scared, I saw no signs. His heavy-hooded eyes stayed fixed on the back of the Manager's broad head, which featured an obnoxious white cowboy hat.

My thoughts raced. How could I get a message to my brother? I looked at the automatic window switch. When I looked up, I saw we were passing Gail's house. Russell's broad back was to the road, a mere twenty feet from me.

Turn around, Russell. Please, turn around.

He leaned in to ring Gail's doorbell. As the truck turned the corner, he glanced over his left shoulder. I put my hand on the window, but I doubted he could see anything through the tinted glass.

Chapter 7

Keep it together, Anna. I swallowed around a boulder-sized lump in my throat. This was where I was supposed to be. The only chance Sam had of getting through the night was having me by his side. I knew what to expect, kind of.

The Mayor's home looked warm and inviting, but we didn't go inside. Instead, they took us through a side gate to a courtyard. A domed building, constructed of animal hide and stones, stood at the center—*a sweat house*. Before I could ask, I was pushed toward a side entrance of the Mayor's home, which wound up being a restroom.

Inside, I found Gail.

My heart warmed until I saw her face clearly. A black mask of paint had dried into the deep lines around her eyes. This wasn't the person I'd known growing up.

"Undress."

Feigning modesty, I turned my back to her. While fiddling with the zipper of my pants, I dipped my hand into the pocket and slid the wrapped blade into my palm. After shedding my clothes, I glanced over my shoulder. She thrust a simple, white garment at me. In the process of putting my head through the neck of the threadbare gown, I shoved the blade into my mouth and used my tongue to push it into my cheek. I struggled for a moment since it didn't fit lengthwise but managed to maneuver it vertically.

When I turned around, Gail dipped her thumb in a clay mortar and applied a sage rub to my forehead, neck, and down my arms. I stared at her, hoping to see some answers in her eyes, but she never returned my gaze.

"She was your best friend." My voice shook, and my eyes grew wet as I thought of my Grandmother and the betrayal.

Ignoring my outburst, she stooped and removed my ankle

sheath and hunting knife—it had been worth a shot leaving them on. When I attempted to slide my feet into the boots, she kicked them away.

"No shoes."

I swallowed again, tasting the bitter metal of the razor blade and the pulpiness of the wrapper. She led me out into the early evening. The cold slammed into me, causing me to tremble like mad.

Flames shot up from a fire pit in front of the east-facing entrance of the dome. Between the fire and the entrance towered a Thunderbird skull larger than me. My breath hitched and my head swam. I saw Hal's still body, felt his cold lips and my terror, as I'd breathed life back into him.

Bile burned up my throat. I wondered what Sam thought of it. Did he think the skull was fake? Attached to a post, it served as a barrier wall to make sure we wouldn't stumble into the fire when we emerged from the sweat house.

Gail pushed me inside the dome. The pitch-black disoriented me, but strong, rough hands steered me onto a bench smelling of cedar. Gail sat with me. As my eyes adjusted, I detected the faint outline of Sam seated just opposite us.

The Manager had lost his cowboy hat and replaced it with one single eagle feather tied to his braid. With tongs, he carried a hot stone from the outside fire to the pit in the center of the sweat house. He did this seven times. I realized he would be fire keeper for whatever warped ceremony followed.

Mayor John stepped through the door in full headdress. He wore a buckskin shirt with his jeans and created a silhouette that to me was an abominable interpretation of our ancestors. The feathers glowed like the ones on my arrows. He closed the door behind him, and again, I was thrown into darkness, except for the luminescent headdress.

A hiss caught my attention. The Manager had poured water on the glowing, red stones. Steam filled the room, invading my nose and eyes until I felt smothered. *Don't panic, Anna.*

The Mayor sat on a small bench next to the heated stones and removed the leather wrap from his neck. He straddled the bench so both sides could see as he held the crystals in his hand. He chanted in an unfamiliar tongue. The crystals rolled in his palm, moving on their own. When they faced me, I stared directly into the eyes of the Thunderbird. My stomach dipped as if I'd dropped straight off a cliff.

We soared over the valley, a magnificent family of Thunderbirds bringing blessings on the people's crops. The brown faces turned skyward and welcomed the rain we drove from the clouds, the lightning we blinked from our eyes, and the thunder we created with the beat of our wings. We sang to the setting sun and welcomed the emerging moon as we climbed to gather the clouds. In the morning, as the sun returned as a fine line of light, we retreated to our nesting ground deep in the mountain.

Curled together, we slept, still as stone in our hibernation. We'd rest until it was time to greet the moon the next night and soar high above the villages, bringing forth our strength as the people called to us. For centuries, we brought our power and received praise in return.

One night, I awoke to smoke and the shrieks of my brothers and sisters.

"We can't fly! We can't fly! He stole our feathers."

Their wild thunder of panic filled my head, but I couldn't see. Smoke filled my senses as the mountain burned. Flapping my wings, I crashed into rock, my talons scraped the wall, but I was dizzy and in pain for I had no vision. I screeched to them to follow me, but their cries were gone. By the grace of the Great Spirit, I cleared the peak of the mountain and found the open sky.

I tracked the Chief's voice, remembering his whisper in the dark before he'd stolen my eyes and crippled my family.

The drums called me. In a rage, I followed the music to the eastern mountain. Below, my friend, the Priest, called for help. Blood filled my senses. I dove, hoping to help him. The loudest thunder I'd ever heard, rumbled above me. Rocks exploded all around me, burying me alive. I woke many moons later, in pain and trapped with the corpse of their high priest.

A slap sent my head sideways. My connection with the bird severed. Spots pulsed in my vision. The Thunderbirds' shrieks echoed in my head, as did the explosion set by the Chief so many moons ago.

Light from the eyeballs extinguished, throwing up the suppressive curtain of darkness again. Sweat poured into my eyes, bringing with it the sage rub, which caused my eyes to burn. How much had they seen? Did they know the bird spoke to me?

I felt the sharp sting as nails dug into my arm. The Manager jerked me to my feet. I stumbled out of the sweat house, only able to maneuver because he led me. The ointment blurred my vision. My toes met frigid waters as he dragged me down stone steps into a small pool and dunked me seven times.

I grit my teeth and only opened my mouth partially to gasp for air, fearful I'd lose the razor blade. Out again into the freezing air and back into the sweat house. We made four trips. Afraid I'd pass out, I allowed some of the pool water into my mouth. If I didn't, I knew I'd dehydrate.

Rage kept me conscious. Truth fueled me. Thunderbirds never ate humans; they helped them. Which meant the Mayor had been murdering initiates to perpetuate his ancestor's lie.

After the near drowning, they threw huge blankets over us and ushered us into the back of the truck. I heard the *thunk* of the locks and saw Gail's pale robe as we drove away from her. Water from my wet hair dripped down my neck and back. Next to me, Sam shivered.

If Hal and I'd been able to talk, perhaps I would have a good plan. Instead, my cooked brain couldn't quite keep me upright, let alone summon a solution. If I spat out my blade and sliced one of their necks, would I be able to break free, go for help? Would I be able to reach the right people in time?

As we bounced over the bumpy road to the foot of the mountain, I concentrated on the storm. Based on its strength, I'd say the Thunderbird was pissed. The Manager hauled Sam out of the truck. The Mayor took care of me. His grip on my arm was iron-tight. In his other hand, he carried a flashlight. My frozen feet stung from the jagged rocks and sharp sticks. It took every bit of willpower not to scream or cry.

I directed myself to the task at hand. When would they blindfold and bind me? With the Mayor's grip on my arm, how could I raise my hand to cough out the razorblade? Panic took up residence in my chest, and the smothering sensation I'd experienced in the sweat house returned.

"Stop here," he instructed the Manager. "I'll take her up first. Blindfold him."

That panic exploded as a pitiful sob. I didn't endure all this hell for them to separate me from Sam. As my head whipped back and forth, searching the trees in the glow of the flashlights, the thunder subsided. The air felt and smelled charged, but no rain fell. I heard the softest sound—the song of the whip-poor-will. *It can't be.*

The Mayor pushed me. "Time to meet our friend."

My feet hurt so terribly, I didn't want to stay upright, but I wouldn't plead with him.

"What I can't understand is why you thought you would get away with it," he said.

I was so astounded by him, not a single reply came to my lips. He truly believed I had done wrong in helping my brother, in questioning his methods.

Halfway up the mountain, I stumbled, then fell to my knees, sputtering. The paper had all but disintegrated in my mouth, so I was able to cough out the blade into my palm and maneuver it between the knuckles of my index and middle finger. Delirious, shivering, and nauseated, I tried to think. He hauled me to my feet.

After the third time I fell and was slow to rise, he grabbed me, pulling my one arm around his neck and securing his arm around my waist. He half-carried me up the mountain. My right hand dangled inches from his carotid artery. With my arm at such an awkward angle, I couldn't put much power behind my movements with the razor blade, so I focused on the cord around his neck. Straining, I caught the call of the whip-poor-will again.

By the time we reached the enormous bowl, the bird had created a spectacular thunder and lightning show. The Mayor turned me to face him, and held me by my dominant arm.

"You're strong, *Little Bird*. I'll give you that. But I have the strength of the Thunderbird. There's no way you could win."

He pushed, and my heels hit the edge of the lip. In one last ditch effort, I jerked my right arm free and swung for his throat with the razor blade. He grunted and shoved me away. I clawed the air, latched onto the cord, and fell through space. I attempted to twist in the air but didn't fully rotate. My hip hit the sharp rocky floor first, and then my temple struck. Black spots flashed in my vison.

The flashlight landed next to me, flickered out, then buzzed back on. Breathing didn't come for several seconds. Pain announced itself in every joint of my body. I doubted I'd cut the Mayor. Shouts from above, spurred me to move. He was coming after me. The razor blade had cut my right hand, but I'd lost it.

The Thunderbird's head breached the hole. Light flashed from its eyes sockets, illuminating the basin. A tremendous *boom* shook the whole mountain, driving me back to my knees. Rock and debris rained over me. I tucked my head and prayed.

Dazed, I lifted my head to see the sharp beak disappear through the small space and re-emerge in the new cavity created by an explosion.

Hal.

The Thunderbird thrashed and fought, working its way free of the prison.

"Yes!" I yelled. "You did it!" I wasn't sure if I meant the bird or Hal, but it didn't matter. As I struggled to my feet, my ears rang from the blast.

The bird flew straight up, banked to the east, then returned. It repeated this pattern. I stood, dumbfounded. *What the heck is it doing?* The soft deer hide sack warmed my left palm; the severed cord fluttered in the wind.

"The eyes." *It can't see.*

When I opened the sack, the eyeballs looked at me. Cupping my hands, I raised the crystal orbs to the bird, hoping she would sense the organs and where I was. Turning in a circle, I attempted to orient her to the terrain of land and sky. My ears popped and my hearing returned.

"Eeeeeeeeeeeee." The bird's cry rent the valley.

I continued to turn but stopped. The Mayor stood fifteen feet from me.

"Give them back," he demanded. He rushed toward me.

I backed away, not caring if I fell into the mountain, just wanting to get out of his range. I let the eyes look upon him. The bird dove, directing its deadly beam at the Mayor. His head flew back, his back arched, and his limbs splayed wide before he dropped to the ground, smoking and smelling of ozone and sulfur. I just stared, witnessing fate's blow.

Finally, I looked away. The stars painted the ridgeline silver. Thunder rolled through the valley. Lightning danced in the highest clouds. *She's taking her victory lap.*

"Anna!" Hal and Russell dropped into the basin. As they ran toward me, I saw soot smearing their faces and pride lighting them from within.

I laughed and cried while I held the eyes above my head, aiding her return. When she hovered above me, I admired her magnificent wings, spanning fifteen feet. She landed and walked to me, smelling of earth and ozone, fire and air, beast and *triumph*. My body quaked from strain and emotion, fear and joy.

Dried blood mottled her disheveled coat of feathers. Her battle over the years could be seen in the horrible gouges in her beak and the raw, bare patches on her body. Her head came down and her beak nudged my cheek. At the touch, my head thrummed with her happiness to be free.

Through our contact, she showed me my dreams—flying on her back over the valley. *Free. We're all free.*

With her eyes returned, she could control the storms, finesse the thunder and lightning. We would bring honor and the blessings of the storm back to my people. Separate, we were both too broken. Together, we would perform the job of the Thunderbird.

SHATTERING GLASS

By
Nooce Miller

ABOUT

After long, boring years as a medical writer and editor, Nooce Miller finally shrugged her shoulders, said "why not?" to no one in particular, and ditched her office and desk for a cushy armchair to engage in her true passion, fantasy fiction writing. The career change made perfect sense since she visited Middle Earth, Earthsea, Hogwarts, and countless other far flung locales a lot more frequently than she did her own relatives.

Thus far Nooce has written eleventy-two highly regarded books. *The Rooftop Inventor* and *The Voodoo Queen*—the first titles in the fantasy steampunk series known as The Adventures of Theodocia Hews—have actually found their way into print. Theo, the seventeen-year-old heroine, is brave, brutally truthful, and mostly untutored in the ways of polite society having grown up under the lax attention of her kind but absent-minded inventor father. Nooce anticipates several more books in this series because Theo is proving to be quite a handful.

Nooce lives in Indianapolis, Indiana with her handsome husband and her faithful Labrador retriever, Stinky.

www.noocemiller.com

1

I stand peering out across the snow. The forest isn't nearly as dense as I remember from when I was a little girl. Unlike that long ago December day, when evergreens grew thick and tall, and bright sunlight picked out sparkling diamonds from the blanket of white at my feet. Here in the year 2043 there is no blue sky only the perpetual covering of low gray clouds.

The relentless wind makes me squint, so I snuggle my shoulders into the thick polar bear fur I'm wearing. As I watch, an impossibly tall mounded shape emerges from the forest, followed by several others. The hunt is on.

I jog the last few steps to my assigned position beside a cluster of shrubs. I kneel down and slip my compound bow free from my back, nocking a steel-tipped arrow. Elbow up in perfect Olympic form, I draw the string back against my cheek and hold, watching.

The beasts move slowly, cautiously. There are seven, no — eight of them.

The man named Warren, was right. The herd is heading toward stunted willows down by the frozen creek.

My eyes widen. The bull in the lead is a shaggy monster with corkscrew tusks stretching ten feet in front of him. Getting past his guard to bring down a smaller cow won't be easy. Reaching the two babies in the protective midst of their elders, even harder.

"Hey Greer." A male voice puffs steam and my name into my ear, making me jump. "Uh, Warren sent me over just in case the big guy causes trouble." He takes a knee right next to me, but not behind the shrubs. The long spear with the wicked steel tip in his right hand wobbles back and forth as he tries to plant himself in the snow.

I turn my head ever so slightly, keeping my eyes and aim on the animals. "Shhh. Be still."

But it's too late. The big woolly mammoth has already swung

his head in our direction. He picks up his pace, trotting straight toward us.

"Shit," the man says, no longer whispering. "We gotta move."

Seeking a likely target with my eyes, I don't answer.

"Come on!" he says urgently.

"Wait." I concentrate and hold my breath, almost ready to let fly.

"They're faster than you think." He tugs my arm, disrupting my aim.

The bull gallops, so I let the man pull me up and we run toward the creek bottom. He grabs my arm again and drags me down the bank. With the insane trumpet of the mammoth ringing out, we squeeze through a crack in the tall rocks. I can hear the beast snorting and crashing through the willow stumps. The man is pressed up against me.

I scowl. "Dammit, I had a shot. Now we won't eat."

"Don't be ridiculous. Warren will get one—now that we've moved the bull out of the way."

"You ran on purpose?"

He grins and shrugs. "That bull is smart. He won't follow just one person. It takes two to lure him away."

"Why didn't you tell me the plan?"

"Because most people who wander through here don't wanna be bait."

I glower at him, but he smiles and winks. 'The bull can only run ten miles an hour in the snow. I knew you'd be faster than that."

The bull moves back toward his herd.

I snort. "Bait! What did you say your name was?"

"Nash McIntyre."

"Well, Nash McIntyre, the danger's past so you can take your hand off my ass."

Red faced, he squeezes past me to climb back out.

"He's gone," Nash says, holding out a hand to me.

I ignore him and climb out on my own. I return the precious arrow to my quiver and sling my bow onto my back. "You people are idiots. Why put me out there if you didn't want me to shoot?"

His chin drops down. He makes a big show of adjusting his mittens. "Sorry. Let's get back to camp. The meat will be incredible, I promise."

Two days ago I ate my last packet of stale crackers. So I swallow my anger and follow.

2

Inside the tent, the man named Warren bites a chunk of roasted meat and grease drips into his beard before he continues with what he's saying. "So you see, we could really use your help."

I stretch my legs out to the fire. With a loud pop, sparks fly. My eyes follow them way up through the open hole in the lodge roof. My knife cuts another bite, though I'm already full. Freshly roasted meat is infrequent enough so it's best to gorge myself when I get the chance. My body needs protein. Plus it's as delicious as Nash promised.

"I'm going to Glass City, but I'm not doing any negotiating for you," I say.

These people have no idea who I am — or why my expensive bow has stars and stripes on it. Nor did they know they didn't have to put themselves in harm's way, going in close to spear the young female, when I could have easily brought her down from a safe distance.

Warren, group leader, continues to try and persuade me. "All we want is to combine forces with them. They grow the crops. We'll provide the meat. But they only let women in. King won't even talk to us. He doesn't know what we're offering."

"Not my problem," I lick juice off my fingers. "You know, it's funny, just thirteen years ago, my family visited Mammoth Park. At ten, I never dreamed I'd eat one."

"No one thought we'd have a new ice age either," Nash said.

In spite of several broad hints from me, Nash sticks by my side the entire evening. Speaking softly, solicitously offering me the best pieces of meat and the best spot by the fire, it is plain what he wants. He is roughly my age and handsome, even if he is sort of short. But I'm not interested. I've looked for Boone, the love of my life, for the past seven years, ever since the blue plague separated us. I know he is alive — I saw proof at his abandoned apartment in Chicago — a note in his handwriting and a map pinned on the wall that pointed me this way. He'd said he'd head to New York. I'm determined to keep looking, even if it takes me another seven years. I'm stubborn that way.

My eyes travel over the lodge tent again, picking up more detail. This portable structure is a cut above the usual camping tents of other transients I have come across on my travels. It seems unusually well designed, with a smoke hole that actually works and arched pole pockets that spread the roof wide I've never seen an insulated floor before. All the men have good quality matching white parkas and snow pants.

"What exactly did you guys say you did before the ice came?"

They shift uncomfortably. No one looks at me — except for Warren. He meets my eyes, though I can tell it is costing him. "We were the senior design team at Mammoth Park. Except for Nash there; his father was with us."

I know better than to ask what happened to the father. These days, if someone mentions family or friend using past tense, they're dead. Blue death, murder by roving mob, starvation, or freezing, the means doesn't really matter.

I mull over his answer. "You mean you're the guys who brought the mammoths back from extinction?"

Warren nods.

"Fantastic. And now you're killing and eating them so you can survive."

"Ironic, isn't it?" Nash pipes up, grinning.

Warren clears his throat. "I am — that is, I was — the lead scientist. Our cloning and breeding program succeeded far better than expected. We brought back the white-grass from the seeds we found inside the old ice age mammoths so they'd have something to eat, and we manipulated it genetically," He pauses for a moment, swallowing down his guilt. "Unfortunately, it out-competed native grasses."

The man stares at me a moment, trying to gauge my reaction. "We made some changes in the mammoths too," he mumbles.

"I'm sorry, I didn't hear that last part?"

"The mammoths and the grass are GMO," says Nash. "Most survivors we come across don't like to hear that part. You know," he waves the bite speared on his fork, "engineered meat."

I look at my plate of scraps thinking back to the all-organic, free range diet I'd eaten while at the U.S. Olympic Training Center. "Beggars can't be choosers. I appreciate the meal." I stretch and yawn, hoping my hosts will take the hint and let me sleep. I have long miles to travel tomorrow.

Warren won't shut up. "My working theory is that the vast plains of white grass reflected the sun's warmth back off the planet. When it combined with the successful effect the Speck Project had lowering global temperatures, it triggered the new Ice Age."

"Are you saying *grass* is the reason all this craziness happened?"

"No, not exactly — the blue plague was an unfortunate coincidence. Bad timing. If three quarters of the population hadn't died those first two weeks, some scientist might have stopped the Speck Particulate Generators from filling the atmosphere with reflective dust before we reached the tipping point." Warren trails off, hanging his head.

"Yeah, well I don't hold you personally responsible or anything." I stood up from the furs. "Would you excuse me? Got to get some air." I lift the flap and slip outside.

Before I can take two steps, my little shadow is beside me again.

"It was nice of you to say that to Warren. He always feels like he has to tell people what happened. It haunts him every day. Mind if I walk with you?"

His smile is so wide his teeth gleam in the darkness.

"Okay, um, Nash McIn—"

"Call me Nash."

"Whatever. I get it. Really. End of the world, not many girls our age left. Survival urge and all that," I shake my head, "but I'm not interested."

That wipes the grin right off his face.

"It's not like that," he lies. "I mean, not that I wouldn't—" He wisely abandons that line of thought. "Just thought you might want to join us?"

There it was. Every single time. They all wanted me to stay. Keep me like a specimen under a bell jar. "Yeah, sorry, no. I'm looking for someone. Has Boone Delaney been through here?" I usually ask the question first thing, but hunting mammoths threw me off.

"No. But we've been on the move. We covered a lot of territory before the gas ran out and we had to ditch our snowcats and snowmobiles. Came down into New York following a herd."

"Fine. Well you guys can kiss up to Mr. King by yourselves. I'm going in there, looking for Boone, then leaving. I'm sure you understand."

We crunch over the snow silently. Then, damn him, he pipes up again.

"So what happened to your family? To your parents?" he asks.

"I don't want to talk about my parents." He doesn't know it, but I'll never talk about my parents. What happened was too terrible.

"Oh. Sorry."

My feet carry me back toward the lodge tent.

3

The next morning I finish bundling my gear then sling my pack onto my back. My bow is on top, where I can reach it quickly if I need to.

Most of them are still sleeping off their feast. I push my way out of the flap and begin walking.

I swear I don't know where he comes from, since he wasn't in the lodge a moment before, but Nash appears at my side. He takes a big step in front of me and swings around to face me. "Hey, it's dangerous to be alone. Why don't you look around Glass City like you said, then if you don't find what you're looking for, travel with us for a while."

I pull the two hidden handguns from slits in my jacket front and hold them up. "I can take care of myself."

"I'm sure you can. But the coldest part of the winter is coming."

I laugh. "Like that makes any difference."

He tilts his head, reminding me of a golden retriever we once had. "Sometimes it's good not to be alone."

"Look, Nash. You don't know me. Honestly, I'm not that nice."

I stick out my gloved hand to shake his.

"Good luck," he says.

I begin my long walk south.

4

Trudging through abandoned upstate New York, I think about everything I've heard about Glass City. In what used to be Manhattan, a group of engineers fortified some office towers and installed glass — lots of glass — on the upper floors to plant crops inside. Some people say the tops of the towers peek out of the clouds sometimes. I must admit, I'm hoping to get a glimpse of the sun. It's been a long time.

I hadn't heard the part about them only allowing women inside before. That sounds a little odd. But I'm not afraid. I'll play nice and get inside. If Boone isn't there, I'll just leave, simple as that.

As far as Warren's people wanting me to parley a trade deal, well, that's not my problem. Maybe they'll figure out how to talk their way in. Maybe another woman will happen along to help. Whatever.

I follow the snow covered highways south. It is three days since I left the mammoth hunters, evening is coming on. I manage another mile, keeping my eyes open for a structure to spend the night in. I avoid houses or businesses. They draw other wanderers. I want a barn or a shed.

Just before dark, near a small town, I spot a small steel-walled utility shack alongside an old electrical substation. It'll be cold as hell, but at least no one will be looking for food there. I circle around the field behind it so the wide blurred trails of my snowshoes won't lead directly to the front door. I crawl through a hole in the chain link fence.

Most people who've survived this long have hunkered down somewhere against the cold. Not many are on the road like me anymore. A final look around and the lock rattles in my hands as I pick it open. Just then, something moves at the edge of my vision.

I freeze. There's a farmhouse across the road, but I see nothing. I wait a while longer to be sure. Then some distance away I hear the call of a great horned owl. I relax. No reason to be so jumpy.

I go in, unroll my bedding, and wiggle inside. I place one loaded pistol on the blanket beside me and sink into sleep.

5

I know I'm getting close.

The ghostly remains of New York City surround me, and if my map is correct, I'll cross the George Washington Bridge soon. I wanted to take the Lincoln Tunnel, but it's submerged and likely full of ice.

Crossing, I see no recent signs of people at all. I know New York was hit especially hard with blue plague because of the dense population. Word has it that Glass City took in survivors from a three state area, so I don't really expect to see anyone. I slog through the snow-covered, debris-strewn streets. And then, rising up through the canyon of empty buildings, I catch my first sight of Glass Tower City. It's true, they've taken a cluster of the tallest buildings and made them into vertical greenhouses. Steam spurts from vents up on the sides of the buildings. It's unusual to see evidence of so many living people. My heart leaps – of course Boone would want to come here.

I jog the last couple blocks and skid to a stop. The bases of the buildings are reinforced with slabs of stone and brick, secure against any potential invaders. Here and there, metal plates cover old doors and windows up to a height of at least seven stories. Above that, glass covers everything. The streets here have been cleared of everything except the ever present snow and occasional concrete barrier. It has the look of a bizarre third-world military operation.

How on earth will I get in? Is anyone keeping watch?

Almost in answer to my thoughts, four people emerge. One waves. Their weapons are slung on their backs instead of in their hands, so I march right up to them. It's two women and two men, wearing mended black clothing, knitted caps, and coats that do not match.

A grim faced woman steps forward. "State your business."

I keep my hands loose by my sides. "I'm looking for someone."

"Kind of cold for that, isn't it?"

"Sure is. Could we go inside to talk?"

They stand there looking at me for a good while. Perhaps they mean to intimidate me. I'm not a patient person, so I speak up before they've finished their stare-down.

"Look, if the answer's no, I'll be on my way."

Ms. Friendly holds out her hands, palms up. "I'll need all your weapons."

I'm reluctant. Pistols are hard to come by. And my bow is like a part of me. "Will I get them back?"

"When you leave."

It's my turn to eyeball her. "How about I keep the bow, and give you the arrows?"

"I think I can stick my neck out that far for you," she says without warmth.

I hand everything over. She has trouble holding it all, but finally manages to bundle the arrows under one armpit. "Follow us."

They lead me on and I realize while we were messing with weapons, a doorway has opened in the side of a building. Inside I am enveloped in moist heat. They lead me up twelve flights of stairs, and I'm soon sweating. I haven't been this warm in years.

"Hey, do you mind if I take off my fur?"

"Okay," the lead woman says.

I shrug myself loose and the second woman says she'll carry it. Kind of catches me off guard, since before this, she hasn't said a word. Because of coat-check girl, I get this weird feeling I'm going to a party. Makes no sense. Maybe her action has woken up some memory of better days.

Crossing the empty floor, we approach a bank of elevators. Coat-check girl pushes the up button and it lights, adding to the freakiness. The bell goes ding, the doors open up, and we step into the dark car and ride upwards in silence. Finally, the car heaves to a stop, and the doors open up.

Sunlight hits me square in the face, blinding me. I almost start crying it's so damn beautiful.

I rub my eyes until they can handle it, then I notice the guards have gone. A slender woman waits patiently in front of me. She has on a long tank top over slim ankle length pants, and her feet are enveloped in stylish high heeled sandals. Not typical Ice Age clothes.

It's way too hot. I peel off my parka. Several other women walk through the sunny atrium, talking animatedly amongst themselves, carrying paperwork. I can't help but stare.

"I'm Layla," the woman says. "Amazing, isn't it? When you're ready, the king would like to meet you."

The king? What the heck kind of place is this? I try to be casual. Maybe this king can tell me if Boone's here. "Yeah, whatever. I'm ready now.".

Horror crosses Layla's face. "Oh, no. Not yet, you have to freshen up. Please follow me."

I reluctantly leave the sunlit reception area to follow her down a side hall. Several more women emerge from a door, paying no attention to me. I realize coat-check girl and Ms. Friendly have disappeared with my things, but the thought slides away again when I realize this clean, warm hallway is furnished with decorative sconces at intervals, and *they're bright*. "This place is lit with electric light."

"Yes," she glances back over her shoulder. "All of Glass City is lit and heated by electricity. There is a large seam of coal running directly underneath us. The men who live in the north-most tower rigged up the power plant. They mine the coal from a shaft directly under their building. They give us electricity in exchange for fresh food. A mutually beneficial arrangement."

The men. So far I've only seen women. Maybe the mammoth men were right.

When I think the hallway can't possibly stretch any further, we reach a doorway. I read the letters on the wall: MF&C, Attorneys at Law.

Layla pushes open the set of mahogany double doors. I gasp as we enter a large chamber with a soaring ceiling of blue-green glass. We must be on the north side of the building, because the sun isn't shining in. Outside the tops of clouds are lit up in shades of white, cream and palest blue as far as I can see.

Across the room, a tiny dark haired woman is seated behind the large carved mahogany reception counter. She greets us, just as though the attorneys were still here. There are two tasteful lamps on either side, both of them turned on in spite of the plentiful daylight in the room. The normalcy of the scene completely disorients me.

"She needs spa treatments," Layla says, evaluating my current appearance with her eyes. "And ring up the hair stylist."

"You're not cutting my hair," I growl.

"Of course not," soothes Layla. "Let me know when she's finished. No hurry."

The spa lady has come out from behind the desk to stand next to me. "What's your name?"

"Greer Mason."

"Greer. What a lovely name. I'm Amy." She gestures gracefully with one hand. "Follow me, please."

I can't believe it, but the entire place is set up just like a luxury spa. Relaxing music plays from hidden speakers, and clusters of potted palms and bamboo are arranged just so. We enter a locker room and Amy helps me off with my things, handing me a white robe. I stow my belongings in two ample lockers and I'm about to lock them up with the keys jutting from the keyholes when she stops me with one hand. "Would you like your clothing and boots to be cleaned while you're enjoying your treatments?"

I look at my things with new eyes, and I find I'm ashamed at how dirty and bedraggled everything looks. "Uh, sure. If it isn't too much trouble."

She dazzles me with her white teeth. "It's no trouble at all. Little Amy here will take care of you today."

From that moment on, Amy leads me from a tingling warm shower to a fragrant soaking tub, from a massage table to the hair salon. I lose all sense of time in the sybaritic pleasure of unobtrusive women tending to my body.

"I feel like I'm taking advantage of you guys," I say.

The woman rinsing a beautifully fragrant conditioning treatment out of my hair laughs. "You're not. Hardly anyone new arrives any more. We're not at all busy these days."

After a bonus hand and foot massage, Amy gives me a manicure and pedicure, complete with pink nail polish. From time to time it occurs to me I should be asking if anyone's seen Boone, but I push it off until later. I've slipped into some sort of pleasure dream world. I don't want to wake up.

Regretfully, it finally does end, and I'm ushered into a long room lined with racks and racks of clothes and gold framed mirrors.

"This is my favorite part," giggles Amy. "Time to go shopping! You just help yourself."

I eye the racks of colorful lightweight garments. "Oh, I can't possibly. I don't have any money."

She giggles again. "I only say shopping because there isn't

any other word for it. You don't have to pay — everything's free."

I run my hand over the beautiful fabrics. I can hardly wear my usual thick layers of sweaters inside this hothouse tower. I might as well indulge myself. I choose a flowing purple silk dress, sleeveless and with a gold braided neck. It might be floor length on another woman, but on me, it comes down just below my knees. I look at the shoes and sandals on display, but in the end I decide to just go barefoot. I haven't felt soft carpeting under the soles of my feet in years.

"Don't you look nice?" says Amy. "You must be getting hungry. The king would like to offer you dinner."

I can't help myself, I crack a smile. "Who is this king of yours? It may be an ice age, but we've hardly gone back to medieval times."

She laughs, but doesn't answer. Amy leads me toward that bank of elevators. The doors open and we are whisked upward. When we finally stop, the sun once again shines directly on my face as I step out. The doors close on her and I cross the room alone, stopping at the window where I close my eyes to better enjoy the warm glow of sunlight.

"Hard to imagine all this exists when you're down there, isn't it?"

I whirl around. A very tall man stands some distance away. He's dressed in immaculately pressed linen pants and a soft blue shirt. His tanned hand rests casually upon the back of a wingback chair.

"You're Greer Mason the Olympian, I'm told. Pleased to meet you. I'm Paul," he says.

"Are you the king?" I blurt out.

He laughs. "A little joke played on me by the people who live in this city. My name is Paul King."

He waves me to join him at a round table covered with a white cloth.

Unlike the converted law office downstairs, this space was obviously a residence before the blue plague and the ice age came. A very large and fancy penthouse suite.

"You mean the women who live in this city," I say. He holds the chair for me as I sit down.

"I'll admit, the women do outnumber the men, but that wasn't my doing. Blame Amanda Pellot, our city planner."

"Mr. King, do you personally greet all the travelers who come here?"

"Please call me Paul. No. Not all. But we seem to have run out of interesting visitors lately." His lips curve gently upward. His eyes are the palest blue I've ever seen. He pours two glasses of wine and passes one over to me. I take an exploratory sip. It's very good. He catches me trying to see the label on the bottle.

"It's Californian, 2029 vintage. Pre-ice age. We're making good progress, but we're not bottling yet. Soon though." He takes a long swallow.

The view outside captures my attention again. Here and there, other glass towers pierce the clouds, but none are as tall as this one. The sun is sinking in a glorious blush of pink. Paul calmly lights the candles. I can't shake the odd feeling. Yesterday I was tromping along through the snow like usual, and today — it's surreal.

Two waiters glide in bearing covered trays in their white-gloved hands like we're in some five-star restaurant. Paul steeples his fingertips with polite anticipation. "Ah. Trent and David. What do you have for us today?"

One of them, David I think, rummages inside a nearby credenza and extracts polished silverware and gold rimmed plates to set the table. The other man begins placing hot and cold dishes in front of us. It's obvious these guys were professional servers before the end of civilization. The smell makes my stomach growl so loudly I'm afraid Paul will hear. It's all I can do to keep myself from tearing into the bowls and platters, for the meal is made entirely of fresh fruits and vegetables, something I haven't seen in over six years.

Trent uses silver tongs to serve mixed greens onto a small plate. "Balsamic vinaigrette, Miss?"

"Yes, please."

He drizzles it on and deftly applies a few grinds of black pepper. I pick up my fork and have at it. The greens are fresh, clean, and perfectly chilled, and they crunch in my teeth in a way no stale packaged food or mammoth meat ever can.

"More wine?" murmurs David. I nod.

"How is it?" asks Paul.

"Delicious." I'm cramming the fresh food greedily into my mouth, one forkful after another, and I don't care.

Trent and David are the perfect servers, doling out creamed broccoli rapini with goat cheese, sweet potato ravioli with walnuts, chilled watermelon soup, eggplant caviar. The bread is crusty and hot, and I tear off hunks of the steamy yeasty stuff. The waiters stand nearby, unobtrusively whisking empty platters away only to replace them with more new delights. The meal ends with a fruit tart. The sweet glaze on top nearly undoes me. I haven't tasted fruit or sugar forever.

Finally, I have to push back from the table. Paul laughs. "I was wondering how much you could put away. Very impressive."

"You're making fun of me."

"Only a little. You can't imagine how pleasurable it is to feed someone who has done without for so long. To bring her back to civilization."

I dab my lips with my napkin, fold it, and lay it on the table. I've had my fun. Time to get down to business.

"I'm here because I'm looking for someone. Can you help me?"

"Perhaps. Who?"

"Boone Delaney. Dark blonde hair, brown eyes, about six

foot five. I believe he was headed this way."

Paul pulls a small pad of paper out of his pocket and writes on it with a silver pen. "Trent, please take this to Ms. Pellot. Have her search the registry."

I rub my nose with my hand. I am just a bit intoxicated. Well, maybe a lot intoxicated. It doesn't take much these days, and the bottle on the table is empty, as was the one before it.

"Where have you been looking?"

"I was out in Colorado and I didn't get to Chicago until 2039. I had to wait until it was safe, and then it took a while to get out of — the plains."

"That was probably wise. Fewer people by then."

Somnolent from all the food, I stare out the window and try to collect myself. My feet are curled up under me in the chair. I can hardly keep my head up.

Paul notices and he's instantly by my side, gently urging me up. "Why don't you come sit over here? You'll be more comfortable." He helps me over to a long, low white sofa. I sit down and rest my head and without meaning to, drift off into sleep.

6

When I wake, I find myself stretched out full length on the sofa, a thick down comforter spread over me. I'm too hot, and my head is throbbing. It must be morning, because a bright dawn now fills the wide glass window, delicate colors painted across the sky.

I sit up, knocking the covers to the floor. Paul and the others are nowhere in sight. I stand up cautiously and I've only just started tiptoeing across the carpeted floor when a side door opens and a young woman in the spa uniform comes into the expansive living room.

"Good morning Miss Mason. The king didn't want to disturb you last night, you seemed so tired. I'm here to show you to the guest bath."

"Uh, thanks?" I follow her, at a loss for anything else to do.

She leads me into a gleaming marble bathroom and shows me where toiletries and towels are stored. There are crystal sconces and a chandelier, and a sunken tub in the middle of the floor. "I've taken the liberty of bringing you fresh clothes. They're hanging in the dressing room through there. I hope you like what I picked out."

"I'm sure they'll be fine."

She leaves. I lock the door and slip off the rumpled purple dress, examining my body. I can't remember anything happening after the meal, but everything seems intact. Relieved, I put up my hair and run a hot bath complete with bubbles and climb down into the water to soak.

When my fingertips begin to wrinkle, I pull the plug and take a cold shower. It wakes me up to the point where I almost feel human again. I find the clothes the woman left for me — a white shirt trimmed in blue that matches my eyes and white shorts — and once I've put on the white sneakers, I leave the refuge of the bath looking like I'm about to play a game of tennis.

Paul is waiting for me out in the living area. It's another bright sunshiny day, and this time he's sitting with his legs elegantly crossed on a white leather chair. He takes off a pair of glasses and puts down what he's reading so he can rise and walk over to me.

I speak first. "I'm so sorry I fell asleep last night. I meant to talk longer — I had some questions."

He waves one tanned hand back and forth. "No, if anything, I should apologize to you. It's probably been a while since you had any wine. My sources tell me alcohol is getting pretty scarce out there. Here, I have just the thing." He opens a nearby cabinet to reveal a wet bar. I'm about to say I can't possibly handle another drink, when he drops two tablets into a glass of plain water and they begin to fizz. He hands over the glass, and I take a sip.

We head over to a pair of chairs arranged to take advantage of the view.

He smiles. "Sometimes it's hard to believe all we've accomplished in just seven years. Six, really, if you consider the chaos of that first year. But I had a jump on things. You see, I'm an agricultural scientist—was an agricultural scientist. I'd been working on some of the largest greenhouse growing operations before the ice came. When the temperature plunged, it occurred to me I could easily do the same thing vertically if I could just find enough manpower. That was hard in the early days, survivors were so scattered. Everyone was wandering."

"You've obviously done well for yourself."

"The first thing we did was fortify the bases of the buildings. No sense in building all this if someone could come in and take it from us. We've been very selective about who we accept. There's a whole application process."

Trent comes in, pushing a rolling cart. "Coffee?"

"That sounds nice," I say.

He sets up the silver coffee service on the low table in front of us, catching and holding my eyes oddly with his own. Yet for some reason, he doesn't say anything. He places a plateful of fresh baked pastries beside the sugar and cream, and then leaves.

Paul pours two steaming cups of the fragrant black liquid. "I got lucky when old Ed Easton came to me with a crew of retired engineers. They'd all worked in the last of the coal fired power plants before the switch to solar. It's a miracle so many of them survived. They solved the problem of power, and before the year was out, the first glass tower was producing food. We've added one a year since then, except for last year, when we brought two on line."

"Impressive. Look, I don't want to be an ungrateful guest, but I need to know what your registry turned up."

"Of course. Forgive me." He pushes a button on the edge of the table.

A moment later, an older woman with a short hairstyle and glasses walks into the penthouse, her sensible heels clicking on the slate tiles of the entry. I wonder if she's been kept waiting just outside.

"Greer Mason, meet Amanda Pellot, Glass City Planner."

She comes forward and shakes my hand brusquely, staring aggressively into my eyes.

Paul doesn't seem to notice her rude manners. "Greer asked about a young man yesterday." He turns to me. "What was his name?"

"Boone Delaney."

Paul looks at Ms. Pellot expectantly.

She shakes her head. "Not on the registry. I took the time to look back through all six years of data, which was a big job—let me tell you, since we don't have computer systems, only paper." Her mouth pulls down at the corners.

My heart flops over and sinks into the region of my stomach. Somehow I'd believed Boone must be safe and living here, maybe just the next tower over.

"Anything else?" she snaps.

"No, that's all," Paul says, and shows her to the door.

When he comes back, I've collapsed onto my chair and drawn my legs up into my chest.

He places a gentle hand on my shoulder. "I'm so sorry."

I don't know this guy at all, but I don't shrug his hand off. Honestly, he's been nothing but nice. But in spite of the posh apartment and all of the luxuries, a bleak, empty feeling envelops me.

"I'll give you some time alone." Paul backs out of the room, leaving me with the coffee and the view.

My brain churns uselessly in circles. New York had been my only goal. Where could Boone have gone if he hadn't ended up here? My eyes sting.

7

A couple of hours pass before anyone comes in to disturb me. It's Trent, clearing up. I don't want to raise my tear stained face, but I can feel him standing there looking at me.

"It's Greer, isn't it? I need to talk to you," he whispers.

"About what?"

"This place. It's — it's not what it seems."

I blink up at him uncomprehendingly. Yeah, I do happen to know I'm in a bizarre glass tower and the world has gone to shit outside. What in the hell is this guy talking about?

A loud click sounds behind us and when I turn, Paul is rapidly walking our way. "What'd I miss?" he says with a smile.

"Just asking Miss Mason if I can bring her anything else," Trent says.

"Do you want anything?" Paul asks me.

"No, thank you."

"That'll be all, Trent." Paul's eyes follow the man all the way out the door. "A true professional. Incredibly loyal. Would do anything for me." Paul turns his charming smile full blast on me. I don't answer.

"So tell me," he tries again. "How are you enjoying your little vacation from — out there?"

"It's been nice."

"Only nice? Well, I'm going to have to try harder," he laughs, and he puts his hand on my knee.

I casually cross my legs, dislodging his hand.

Undeterred, he leans forward in his chair, turning his body toward mine. "You know, even if your friend isn't here, you're still welcome to stay."

I stare out at the other towers. "I don't think—"

"Not in those, I mean here, with me. Today."

"Isn't there an application process I'd have to go through?"

"I'd get Ms. Pellot to waive it for you."

I laugh, a single, short bark of sound. He'd been amazingly patient, displaying all his luxuries for me first. Spa treatments, food, and warmth, and a lavish lifestyle up in the sunlight. Still— there it is again. It's the same thing they always want.

"You've been very nice, but I'm going to keep looking."

His face loses its friendliness. "Your *friend* is most likely dead. What are you going to do? Wander the east coast for the next few years looking for a ghost? Or go back to those mammoth men?" He spits out the words like they're something foul in his mouth.

Seeing my stunned look, he smirks at me. "Yes, I know where you were before you came here. Don't be an imbecile. You need to stay with me."

I sit up straight and stiff in my chair. If there's one thing I hate, it's someone telling me I *have* to do something — or calling me an imbecile. Trent's right, Paul's not at all what he seems.

"What I need, is my stuff. Thank you for your hospitality. I'll be moving on." I get up and start walking.

"Bad decision."

I don't so much as look back at him. He can stick his opinions right up his ass.

"There's nothing out there for you." The volume of his voice rises a little higher. "You'll be back here inside of a month."

I reach the door, wondering if there will be a guard out there to stop me from leaving. What had I been thinking, agreeing to come up here? All of a sudden, this sunny glass tower has the same feel as the basement in Kansas where those unspeakably horrible people locked me up for nearly three years. I have to get out.

No one stops me. All alone, I ride the elevator down and get out on the floor where the spa is. Amy looks up from behind the desk, obviously surprised to see me.

"Keys," I snap.

She hands them over to me, eyes wide. "Aren't you going to stay?"

"I have some things to do," I mumble, and head for the room with the lockers.

To my surprise, my stuff is still inside — except for my pistols, ammo, and arrows. But I'll find more. It's enough to just have my bow back. I strip the kept-woman clothes from my body and dress in my own things. It feels good.

"Where are you going?"

I ignore Amy and ride the elevator down to the ground floor. While I'm in the car, I remove the hidden pieces from inside the body of my bow and assemble them together into a long dart. I place it onto the bow — as insurance. If there are guards and they have guns, I'm screwed, but if they don't, I might have a chance.

Two of the women who were outside the day before are sitting in chairs by the metal door. They leap up when they see me clomping toward them in my boots, a sharp dart aimed at them.

"Hi again. I'm leaving now. Open up."

They look at one another for a second, then the younger one does what I want.

Once outside, I don't look back. I race north as fast as I can. I'll hide somewhere in Central Park to make sure no one's following me, and then I'll figure out where to go next. One thing's for sure, I need to get off of this island.

3

Seventh Avenue is as empty as every other street in New

York as I keep loping along. I swivel my head from side to side at each cross street just to stay sharp. If someone from King's tower is chasing after me, I need to know. In my seven years on the hunt, I've gotten pretty good at giving unwanted company the slip, but I've never had to use my skills in big city blocks. There are plenty of tall humps of snow in the street — no doubt there are abandoned cars, trucks and buses underneath. But although there is potential cover at hand, the white shapes are making me feel like I'm being herded in a certain direction. I try to pick up my pace.

It's no good, it's hard to run in snow with a heavy pack on your back. I need to slow down for a while.

I'm looking through a partially broken window as I pass by, wondering if it's a good idea to head inside to catch my breath when it happens. A flick of something black in motion reflected in the dirty hanging glass. I whirl around, but see nothing. My heart pounds and I flee the storefront. No way am I going in there now.

An abrupt change of direction seems like a good idea, and I shift over several blocks on a cross street before continuing toward the park. A loud fall of snow a hundred feet or so back startles me. I think it slid off of a large metal awning, but I can't be sure. Did someone dislodge it? Panting now, I cut one block back towards 7th Avenue. I don't want to get too far off course and miss the park.

The next building has mirrored glass. I see my own reflection.

And another moving figure some distance back.

Whoever it is, they're wearing white as camouflage. But my eyes are used to picking out anomalies against the snow. I can't run much further. Where is the park? My breath is coming raggedly now. At last, I glimpse the wide open space up ahead between the buildings. I have to find some place to hide, so I can target him.

Closer behind me now, the white shape comes on. It's given

up stealth and is following directly after me. Past the last building, the park opens up before me. Too late I realize my error. All the tree trunks are gone, cut years ago for someone's fuel.

Two snow covered buildings form a sort of a funnel, so I slip in between them, and then I quickly crouch down on one knee behind a trash can to nock my dart again. Focusing my eyes on the open space, I wait, trying to quiet my breath for the shot. It's a man in a white hood, and he's examining my tracks in the snow.

My breathing is under control now. I've got a clean shot.

But I hesitate. I only have the one dart. Maybe if there's only one person, I can reason with him.

He comes closer, and closer still, panting out a billow of steam with each breath.

I stand up, my bow aimed directly at his heart.

He stops and pulls off the hood. "For God's sake… Greer… don't shoot me," he pants.

Nash.

I should have known.

He stands for a moment with his hands on his knees, trying to catch his breath.

"Why are you following me?"

"Because… I wanted to make sure… you're okay. I saw you go in, and I waited for you to come out."

"Yeah, thanks for that. I'm just fine. You scared the shit out of me."

He crouches down beside me. "I've come to bring you back with me, if you want to come, that is."

"Why would you think I'd want to do that?"

"Because you didn't find your boyfriend — and Glass City isn't for you. You're the type that wants to be out in the wild, not shut up in a greenhouse."

"Very perceptive of you."

"Maybe you deserve a little happiness, instead of searching forever for someone who's probably already dead. Maybe there's someone else who can give you that happiness. I'm hoping that's me."

"Oh, Nash, you don't want to fall for me."

"Too late." His mouth curves upward in his usual wide grin.

I sigh. "I told you, I'm not that nice. I've done some things you wouldn't want to know about."

His face takes on a more serious cast. "We've all had to do things we didn't want to do to survive this long. It's okay, really."

He reaches out one gloved hand for mine, but I knock it away.

A black figure is rushing toward us, so I raise my bow and shoot.

The man in black goes down with a howl.

"What the hell?" says Nash.

"Why'd you shoot me?" says the writhing figure on the ground, clutching his leg.

I take a closer look. "Oh my God! Trent! I'm sorry."

I pull out the dart and we patch him up as best we can.

"Why were you stalking me?" I ask.

"I wasn't stalking you. I couldn't keep up. You run too fast. I wanted to talk to you to get you to help us."

"Us?" I look at Nash. Are they in on this together?

Nash holds his hands up and shakes his head. "Nothing to do with me. I've never seen this guy before."

Trent groans again. "We're slaves, in Glass City. Didn't you notice King didn't show you anything outside of the floors he personally uses in his tower? Weren't you wondering where all the people were who make things run? Everyone's locked up in cages when they're not working. Except for those favorites he keeps around him."

"If everyone is locked up, how come you're not?"

He grimaced. "I'm one of his favorites. I'm careful to make

him feel like royalty. So he gives me little privileges. Extra food. Access to recreation. The chance to *breed* with the women. His favorites get jobs in his tower and can move around more."

"You're a breeding pet? That's sick."

"I agree. It's no kind of a way to live. That's why we need your help. You and these mammoth hunters," he gestures toward Nash. "You're different than us. Not beaten down or desperate. If you came with me, I can guarantee the slaves would rise and follow you."

"My God, slaves. I knew there was something creepy about that place." I take a big breath, and blow it out again. "Yeah, Trent, sounds like a great plan. But that's not my thing, saving people I don't care about."

"You're lying, that's not what you're like at all," says Nash. "You do too care about people."

"Yeah?" I turn on him. "If you think it's such a good idea, why don't you go save them yourself?"

"I plan to, but I'm not exactly the kind of guy people follow. It needs to be someone who stands out."

"Why not Warren? He's a good leader."

"Warren's an old man," says Nash.

"Why not him?" I say, pointing at Trent.

Nash jerks his thumb. "Him? He'll be limping for weeks."

"You have to help," Trent says, fumbling in his pocket. I watch him closely, just in case he tries to pull something. His hand emerges again and he passes something to me, his eyes cast down, his face curiously neutral.

I unfold it. The paper is all creased and worn. It's the kind of thing people used to do with their home linkstation and printer, spitting out a disposable image on cheap paper, just for fun.

I yank the pictures closer to my eyes. It's Boone and me. Two pictures from a day at the beach in 2034. In the first one, we're both wearing bathing suits and holding hands. The second shot is just me, tall, blonde, and golden skinned in the sunlight. A brittle pain surrounds the glass around my heart. Years of yearning and longing explode like fireworks inside my chest.

Boone. Alive. My chin quivers.

"He's inside, in a cage. But you can leave. It's your choice. You have to decide what kind of person you are. Here. Today. What do you believe in?" Trent's eyes still don't meet mine.

Nash watches me closely. "The rest of the guys are hidden on the other side of the park. It won't take me any time to go get them. We can help."

Somehow my mouth still works. "Glass City is locked up tighter than a chastity belt. How would we even get in?"

Trent shifts onto one elbow. "Some of the miners have dug a secret entrance. What we lack is the manpower to overcome the guards and get enough people out of cages so we can rush King's tower and take over."

"Nash, you only have ten men. No way is that enough." But I don't mean it. I will go no matter what. It's Boone.

Nash is shaking his head. "Ten is just what you saw at the camp. There are twenty-seven of us. We don't stay all together — for safety reasons."

The gray clouds scud overhead, as always. I think about those sunny rooms up above, and the man running this place like a spoiled potentate. The man who has Boone locked up. The one who lied to me to get me to stay. I turn back to Trent. "How many guards are there?"

"Twenty men guard the cubicles. And they're spread out on forty floors. Nighttime is best. Some of them sleep on duty."

"A whole population enslaved, and King only has twenty guards to keep them all under control?" It's not making sense.

"I didn't say that. There are more men in King's tower. But only twenty at a time guard the workers. There used to be more, but King has a bad habit of killing anyone who ticks him off, and most of the guards were pretty annoying people. And there aren't that many slaves, either."

"What kind of weapons do the guards have?"

"There are storehouses with guns, but those on guard duty just carry blackjacks. King doesn't want anyone useful to be killed, he just wants them controlled. The guns are mostly to fight off invaders."

"Like us. I don't like this."

"Look, if it starts to go south, we can just cut and run," says Nash. "These are human beings we're talking about. We should at least try to set them loose."

"I'm not going to cut and run. I'm going to get Boone out."

I pull Trent up. Nash takes off across the park, promising to rejoin us with reinforcements. I push up under Trent's arm and slowly we begin heading back down the Island of Manhattan.

9

A ragged hole in the sidewalk shows up darkly in the snow. I stare down at it. The whole Kansas incident comes rushing back to me, and I'm not sure I can make myself go underground. I was raped and beaten and starved for a long time, and it still devastates me that when I found my chance to escape, I left my parents behind to be killed. It's why I have to save Boone. I need to right the wrong I did to my parents. Not that I'm going to tell any of these guys any of that.

We're blocks away from the nearest glass tower, Trent assures us. Nash's men are all gathered close behind us. Some are armed with guns, but most carry spears and hunting knives. Even though some of them are old enough to have served the last time the U.S. went to war before the plague and ice came, to my dismay none have any military experience. What they do have, however, are a bunch of mammoth tranquilizer darts which they can't use to hunt mammoths, since the drug circulating through the bloodstream ruins the meat. We're going to see how they work on men.

I look into the hole, and make out a rough wooden ladder in the shadows. We'll be going in one at a time. To someone who's been through what I have, this has the distinct smell of a trap. I shift from one foot to another.

"Trent, tell me again who made this tunnel?"

Trent's face is pale from loss of blood "I told you. Two miners. They're friends of mine. We'll pass through one of the abandoned mine tunnels to get to the cubicle building."

"Great. Does this sound like a bad idea to anyone else?"

No one answers. The mammoth hunters are all shifting around in the cold, the fog of their combined breath hanging in the freezing air. They're all in. This is what they wanted, a way to get access to the resources of Glass City. They're tired of living in the snow and ice. None seem concerned about the risk. Why am I? Boone is in there.

Nash is watching me closely. "You don't have to do this if you don't want to."

"Yes I do."

I swing my bow down from my back and load up my single dart. I wish I had more ammo, but from what Trent said, we should have a good chance of picking off the unsuspecting guards one or two at a time. The big knife in the leather sheath at my waist comforts me.

Trent is shivering, obviously suffering from exposure. "Get him down the ladder first," I say.

10

The tunnel floor is uneven, its walls are just barely shored up with odds and ends of junk, and to me it looks like it might collapse any moment. It's too narrow to walk abreast, so we go single file. Not far in Trent collapses, so the other men awkwardly carry him along as best they can. Warren is in the lead now, a working flashlight in his hand. Someone behind me wears another light on a strap around his head.

Thoughts of Boone fill my mind, dizzying me. How soon until I find him? What kind of shape is he in? Will he still…?

None of it matters. He's alive.

The tunnel gives way to a wider passage that leads more or less straight in one direction. How much time has gone by since we climbed down that ladder, I don't know. We can't have gone that far, because the buildings of Glass City aren't really that far apart. I try to control the jittery sense of urgency I'm feeling.

Trent is trying to walk with help but is having a hard time. My dart definitely messed his thigh up, and I feel bad about it.

"Stop," he says, "I need to listen."

Everyone comes to a stop, and after a little nervous fidgeting, the mammoth men are all more or less still.

"I think we can go up. Sometimes there's a second crew in the mines with some guards standing watch, but I don't hear anyone. Move that way." Trent jerks his chin towards a steel door set in the wall.

I still have a bad feeling, but I'm having trouble figuring out if I'm just worried about what might go wrong, or if it's some ugly memory bothering me. Everything is perfectly still in the tunnel. There's nothing that I can see or hear that makes me suspicious.

Warren's men heave the door open. There is a wide stairway inside, circling up and up and up. Cement stairs held up by a painted steel framework. There is no way we can avoid making noise. Trent's plan is for two of the mammoth men to help him up using the headlamp. If they run into anyone, Trent will talk his way out of any trouble. The rest of us are supposed to follow a few floors behind, as quietly as possible. We all take off our boots, tie the laces together, and sling them over one shoulder. When Trent is three floors up, he taps to let us know no guards are there, and we start tiptoeing after them.

Up, and up, and up. The flights of stairs go in a squared spiral pattern. I shake my head to clear it, and redouble my efforts to stay quiet. Trent told us the first cubicle farm is twenty floors up, and unless I've lost my count, we'll be there in a few minutes. I hear the sound of a door creaking open up above, and I hold up my hand for everyone to stop.

We listen. I can't hear any voices, only the sound of three pairs of feet, one of them limping. Warren tiptoes up to me with his flashlight, and I nod and wave for everyone to follow us. We climb the last couple of floors, and then we're through the open door.

The smell hits me first. Sweaty bodies, urine and excrement, mildew. It's dark, there are no windows, but in the light Warren grips in his fist, I can see that office cubicles have been covered over with chain link mesh, including the floors and ceilings. These first cages are empty. Maybe the slaves are up ahead. We go around a corner and I can see the beam of the headlight. The man uses his hand to cover the light, then uncover it, cover it, then uncover it. That's the signal.

We pace along the hallway to where Trent and the others wait for us.

Then all hell breaks loose.

Guards all in black swarm onto us from everywhere, grabbing our weapons, clubbing the men over the head. I see two guards go down, one with a spear in his guts, the other with a big hypodermic sticking out of his neck. I fire my bow and the dart buries itself in a huge man's chest, and he drops.

It doesn't matter.

It's all over before we've even freed one slave.

The empty cages. King needed fresh male slaves, and now he has them.

Trent limps past the wire door of my cubicle supported by two of the guards. He doesn't even look my way. He's done his job. Loyal.

I slide to the floor and cradle my face in my hands.

11

The pain of chain link imprinting itself into my hip wakes me.

A lump on my head throbs. One of King's goons must have whacked me with his club.

All the dread and fear I felt the last time I was locked up come rushing back. "I'm an idiot," I mutter to myself.

"No you're not, I am. I wanted this to work. I should have noticed it seemed too easy."

By some twist of fate, they've caged Nash right next to me. I'm hoping he's not looking at me with puppy dog eyes. I'm really not in the mood.

Where is Boone? A fierce longing comes over me.

Almost as if he's read my thoughts, Nash begins telling me something I don't want to hear.

"We've been talking to the other slaves. One of them remembers Boone. He was killed four years ago trying to escape. I'm sorry, Greer."

I curl up on my side into a tight ball of misery, but no tears come. It's like something brittle inside of me — something I've been cradling and protecting for seven long years — has shattered into a million tiny pieces. At some level, I think I've known the truth for a long time.

I can barely make out anything in the one flickering light far above the cages. Sitting is my only option since the roof of the cage is too low to accommodate my height. I'm careful not to kick over the plastic chamber pot in the corner. Judging by the smell, somebody nearby hasn't been as vigilant.

Strangely, I feel lighter inside.

"Nash?"

"Yeah?"

"We have to get out of here."

12

I wait for the summons that I know is bound to come. King said I'd be back, now he'll want to gloat. And then ... I don't want to think about what will come after that.

Footsteps echo along the long passage. It's Amy from the spa. Another pet, like just Trent. She has something large tucked under her arm, and a heavy bag on her back. She stops and leans her head close to my wire cage.

"Greer, I need to talk to you."

"You might as well go tell him I'm not going to play his little game. I'll fight him off. I'll kill him if I can."

"Shh. Listen to me." She stops and turns her head to make sure no one is coming. It's silent all down the row of cubicles. Everyone is listening. "He didn't send me to fetch you. Not yet. He will tomorrow, but I'm not going to take you to him."

"What did you say?"

She kneels down. "People have been talking. They're saying you're the one."

"The one? That's stupid. I can't do anything from inside this shitty cage."

"You won't be in there much longer. I stole the keys," she says, her eyes fierce.

"The keys?"

"All of the keys. To the locked storage, to all the cages, and to the gun rooms. No one notices little Amy, from the spa." Her mouth twists downward bitterly. "Most of the guards are sleeping after all the excitement. It's got to be now. It's our best chance." She fumbles with the key to my cage. Her load is preventing her from getting the rusty padlock open. She places my bow and quiver of arrows on the floor, and resumes working the key into the lock.

I pop out through the door. It feels so good to stand up straight. "Give me some of those."

She hands over half of the keys. "The numbers match the cages."

"How organized."

We make short work of opening all the cages. In spite of the fight, the mammoth men look pretty good, but the slaves obviously have been worked hard and locked up for a long time. Fifteen of them huddle in the hall. Some can barely walk. I'm beginning to doubt this crazy plan.

"Amy, it won't work. These people can't fight."

"There are more. Lots more. There are fourteen floors full of cages in this building alone, and I have all the keys." She dumps the heavy bag she's been carrying on her back. It's full of keyrings. It's only a moment's work to sort them out and assign groups to liberate each floor.

"Warren, take your men and go with Amy to get the guns. I'll work in here until everyone is freed. Kill any guard you come across, and we'll meet you at the bottom of King's tower to get everyone armed."

I look around me, and everyone is nodding resolutely. Whatever happens next, whether it's death or freedom, I'm okay with it. I have a new purpose, and it feels right. Nash is grinning at my right hand, and Amy stands at my left. The shards of glass inside my chest have all melted away.

"Let's go," I say. "It's time to start the revolution."

i

.

SACRIFICE

By
Jessie Campbell

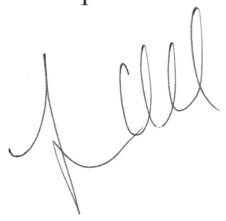

ABOUT

Jessie Campbell's short fiction has appeared in over fifteen indie publications. She is a writer, a freelance editor, and a reader. Her wanderlust led her to sell everything and move to Costa Rica, where she lived for two years. Only a job as an editor in the book business finally drew her back to the US, where she now lives in literary Boston, Massachusetts. One day, her time travel novel will be published — if it doesn't kill her first. She can be found at

www.jessiecampbell.net.

*

A snore escaped my little brother Dex. His rust-colored hair was tangled on his pillow. His pale eyelashes reflected the fluorescent light that seeped through the window. Mother's arms encircled his concave chest. *I must do this thing,* I thought. *For them.*

We lived on the brink of starvation. Mother and I took every job available, but the pittance we earned hardly bought moldy bread at the night market. I couldn't bear to see them suffer anymore. There was only one thing I could do to make sure they didn't waste away — if they could make it six months without me. I hadn't told them my plan; they would never have agreed.

Careful to avoid the squeaky boards of the half-rotten floor, I tiptoed away. Only once did I look back. They were a dark lump in the corner of the bedroom, indiscernible as people.

*

I carried nothing. No food or clothing, for I would not need it where I was going. No identification, for I didn't want my family to be implicated if I got caught after curfew by the Sneaksters. Not even my inhaler, for Dex needed it more than I.

I locked the door from the inside and stepped out into the harsh light of the curfew lamps. They hung like metal skeletons from nooses along the scaffolding of the tin ceiling far above the rooftops. Long ago, no tin ceiling obscured the stars, but these days, Outside was even more polluted than under the Dome. The Council had enclosed us three years ago, when I was thirteen.

Pressed against the side of the building, I crept toward the city center. Soon, I was in an alley that connected two main streets. It was darker here and I breathed easier, though my lack of inhaler made it difficult to gulp down the toxic air. I was just about to run across a brightly-lit street when I heard them. Sneaksters.

I crouched in the gloom, ready to leap away. The Sneaksters guffawed; they had no reason to keep their voices down. But then a hush descended. "Well," said an oily voice, "what's this?"

A small female voice stammered, "I... I was just —"

"It's after curfew. Where d'ye think yer goin'?"

The girl squeaked, "My mama needs a physician." Even without seeing her, I could hear the lie.

"Yer not goin' anywhere but The Cages, little mouse," said the Sneakster.

"Please, sir, I promise —"

There was a sickening sound of flesh slamming against flesh. Something thudded to the ground. I clamped my hands over my mouth to capture my scream.

"Pick 'er up," said the oily voice.

I didn't breathe again for what felt like several minutes, until they were well out of earshot.

Nearly an hour later, I reached my destination. It was the tallest building, with sheer obsidian walls and a peaked roof. Two hulking men with machine guns stood guard. I walked up to the wrought iron gate. "I wish to speak with the Lord of the Dead," I said.

One of the men chuckled. "And what use could he have for a skinny girl like you?"

"Plenty," I said, heat rushing to my cheeks. "And you know it."

They considered me. My heart pounded. If the Sneaksters found me here...

The guard who hadn't spoken lowered his gun and unlocked the gate. "Inside."

I obeyed. They shut the gate behind me. It clanged with

finality. I would not leave this place alive.

*

The Lord of the Dead was coal black. Smoke shivered off his form like a pall. The hood of his heavy robe fell about his shoulders. His eyes glowed like embers. He looked more like the Lord of Fire, had there been such a thing. He smelled of burning flesh.

His whisper hissed and popped like a simmering blaze when he spoke. "You are not the first to answer my summons," he said. "You will join the ranks of my army as an infant."

I stood straight but could not quite meet those eyes.

The Lord of the Dead stood. "Six months," he said. "Six months you will lie in a coffin, and then you shall rise in death and do my bidding for all eternity."

He touched my forehead with one hot finger, and I died.

*

Something was wrong. I stood over my corpse, next to the Lord of the Dead, and he did not sense my presence. My hands were as insubstantial as the dust from a moth's wing. The Lord of the Dead turned his back on both my living spirit and my dead body. Two men—two *living* men—entered the room, their slippered feet a quiet susurrus on the gleaming floor. They lifted my body and carried me away. I felt a tug in my navel and followed. I found I could walk through the door behind them.

The men gossiped in low murmurs, glancing back frequently to ensure their master did not hear. "They get younger and younger," said the one with the bottlebrush mustache.

"He pays," replied his companion, a short, fat man.

Mustache sighed. "She'll go straight to the —"

A door opened. A man with a hooked nose beckoned them across the threshold. We entered a room filled with rows and rows of coffins.

"I heard we got a young 'un," said Beaky.

"Where d'ye want 'er?" asked Shorty.

Beaky pointed to an open coffin. The side was painted with the number four thousand, two hundred and thirteen. Shorty and Mustache dumped me into the coffin. Mustache arranged my limbs and pushed an auburn lock from my deathly pale cheek. They shut the lid. As the hammers came down on the nails I felt my connection to my body sever. I was free. Dead and free.

*

Six months is a long time to live when even breathing the air hurts. When every meal begins with picking fuzzy teal mold off hard bread. When a family member has vanished without a trace and the only explanation is that she has gone to serve the Lord of the Dead.

Six months is nothing when you are dead.

Untethered from my body, I tested my boundaries and discovered I could go anywhere. I wandered the barren palace, its rooms devoid of human life save for the three men I had already seen. I stayed far from the chamber of the Lord of the Dead. I couldn't be sure he would not sense me somehow, even though he had not been in the coffin room. After all, I did not know how this worked.

Back in the coffin room, curiosity overcame me. I held the breath I did not take and plunged into each coffin, my face melting through the wooden tops as if they were made of nothing but light and I nothing but shadow. I could see the faces of my comrades. Some were old, some young. All wore the ragged clothing they had been wearing when they died.

The ones closest to my coffin were filled with fresh corpses. But for the waxy pallor of their skin, the cloudy eyes, the purplish stain of their skin, they could have been sleeping. Were they here in the palace too? Did they stand right next to me, as invisible to me as I was to them?

I dipped beneath the lid of number four thousand, one hundred and ninety-eight… to stare into the face of my best friend. I staggered back into the light. Her brown skin had turned pale and purplish in death, and the swelling of decomposition had disfigured her facial features, but it was her. Her full lips and gentle face. Her wide-set eyes. Her gorgeous halo of black hair in tight corkscrews. Even her ratty tee shirt on which she had printed by hand, "The mind is its own place, and in itself can make a heaven of hell, a hell of heaven." The quote from the ancient text called *Paradise Lost* had never held meaning for me. Until now.

"Oh, Jacinta," I whispered. "I wondered." I had done more than wonder. I had searched for her when she'd gone missing, two weeks ago. Volunteering for service for the Lord of the Dead had been something we talked about the way other teenagers talked about getting into their parents' illicit liquor stashes.

It was one thing to think about in theory, and quite another to realize my best friend was dead and hadn't confided in me. What happened? We'd talked about it for a year, but I'd never thought she was serious. Sadness crowded my thoughts. I had no right to judge her for taking the same path I had chosen. She'd just beaten me by a few days.

Was she here beside me? Was her spirit staring at the face of my own corpse a few rows up? That line of thought was futile. I couldn't shake the sense of absolute solitude. It was nice to imagine her around, but I was just avoiding the inevitable admission: something was wrong with me, and my sacrifice had gone awry.

Sacrifice. Even thinking the word made me angry. The Lord

of the Dead made our lives miserable. The Council enclosed us under the dome to "protect" us, but then the Lord of the Dead ruled with violent Sneaksters and high tithes to make our lives miserable. He offered a payout to surviving family members if we volunteered to die for him, so we did. I was a cog in the system, nothing special about me, blindly following a path that had been set out for me by a dictator who craved power. I didn't even know what I had volunteered for. Maybe I would spend eternity fighting threats on the outside, or maybe I would work on the building projects to expand the Lord of the Dead's collection of scary-looking castles, or maybe I would just mine riches for the elite Council. Or maybe we did nothing, and he only wanted a multitude of mindless followers he could control with a thought—and whom he didn't have to feed—in case the citizens ever wised up and decided to revolt.

What was the point?

I shook my head and moved on, trailing my fingers along the grain of the wood of her casket as if I could impart a trace of my presence to her. The bodies got older — more decomposed — as I made my way down the endlessly long room. Time passed, though it was hard to tell how much. Hours? About halfway along the hall I discovered a closet filled with syringes and scalpels. I assumed it was some kind of mummification supply room, because the oldest corpses at the far end of the room were more like mummies than decomposed human bodies. They were strange, desiccated things barely resembling anything human, their faces stretched over their bones and their sinews popping out from beneath thin layers of flesh. Preserved soldiers ready to do the Lord of the Dead's bidding.

I would look like that, soon. And so would Jacinta.

Walls did not confine me. My spirit cast no shadow under the glare of the overhead lights. My hand passed through objects without disturbing them.

I existed. Yet I did not exist.

I left the obsidian palace. I passed through the iron gate as if it were made of smoke. It had no power to imprison me. The two guards, arguing over identical hats, sensed nothing as I glided between the insults they hurled at one another in gruff undertones.

I went home. The streets stretched out in front of me with a surreal fisheye effect, the farther I got from my body. But I made it into the relative darkness of our flat. Inside, Dex sobbed brokenly in Mother's arms. Mother's face was oddly calm, her eyes flat and dead like two glassy pools of dark water.

Dex, my sweet Dex. His shoulders shook with the tempest of his grief. I reached out to tousle his hair, but my hand passed though him. A shiver racked him. His sobs dissolved into hiccups. Though my heart no longer beat in my chest, I felt it anyway: a sharp pain followed by a deep ache at the knowledge I had caused him to feel such terrible loss.

"It's all right, Dex," I murmured. In six months, my family would receive the standard payout from the Lord of the Dead's coffers for my sacrifice. Then finally, my brother would be able to afford to eat properly. That made *everything* all right.

Neither showed any sign that they heard me. I was right next to them, but farther away than the planet Neptune.

*

I watched over Dex and Mother. They mourned without words. They knew, though I had left no note, where I had gone. Where everyone went sooner or later.

I learned I could whisper to them in their sleep, telling them the best places to find work to make money until my payment came in. I wandered the city, invisible to the Sneaksters, casting no shadow and bound by no walls. I did not see another ghost. This bothered me like a twitchy eyelid.

My time to rise in the Army of the Dead approached. My spirit would reinhabit my corpse to do the bidding of the Lord of the Dead. Forever.

Most of the officials claimed our city was the last bastion of humanity. Supposedly, the city contained the only sane, healthy beings left on the planet after the nuclear winter. There were others left, yes: inhuman mutants and radioactive creatures that mindlessly attacked anything that moved. The voices on the radio frequently alerted us to vague victories against evil-sounding invaders, as if we were supposed to feel safer each time it happened. We never celebrated. Now, as I wandered the city, every announcement I heard made me shiver, thinking of my undead-self fighting off brainless beings with oozing, radioactive sores.

I should have used my awareness as a weapon, to prepare myself, to arm myself with information about the inner workings of the city. But I didn't. Selfishly, I stayed with Dex. Though I could do nothing for him, I wanted to be near him. I watched him grow older, as if each month were a year — and less curious. The light in his eyes dimmed each day.

One day, during the two mandatory hours of public education, his teacher asked him, "What is your dream, Dex?"

"I have no dream," he intoned, eyes fixed on the floor.

Had I a heart, it would have broken. I was responsible for this. But soon they would receive the payout from my sacrifice. That would make this all worth it.

I went back to the obsidian palace, gliding between the guards and through the locked gate unseen. I wound through the labyrinth and found the casket room. At number forty-two thirteen, I stopped, my eyes captivated. There was no attachment to the thing inside. It was only ever a vessel.

After an hour or two, they arrived. The same three men I had seen before — Beaky, Shorty, and Mustache — preceded the Lord of the Dead himself into the room. He was not so frightening after all. His ember eyes were unseeing as he gestured at my coffin. One of the men hefted a black crowbar and pried up the nails. The Lord of the Dead stepped forward and I followed, peering over his shoulder as he shoved the lid aside.

An invisible yet inexorable force pulled me into my body. I whooshed into the corpse like backward steam. I felt the case of my flesh encircle me, but it felt wrong, different. When I tried to open my eyes, nothing happened. Instinctively, I attempted to open my mouth to protest. But my lips did not part, and no sound came from the decrepit corpse. Consternated, I tried to move my arm, clench my fist, shift my legs, even wiggle my toes. Nothing. My corpse was nothing but a mummy now, cleaved from my control for some reason I didn't understand. I couldn't even flutter an eyelash.

I sensed the moment the Lord of the Dead understood what was happening, because his rage was a physical assault. Heat fled the room. Whatever force that pulled me into my body released me. I floated up above my useless corpse to watch what transpired. The three men inched backward from their master. His taut skin contorted into a mask of rage. In this crowded space I was pummeled by the coppery tang of their fear, the sharp notes of their bewilderment, the miasma of his fury.

The moment spiraled out.

And then he spoke; his voice was as I remembered, like the hissing of a fire. "Cremate her with the next batch. She is useless. Her spirit is long gone."

Despite the tension, or perhaps because of it, I almost laughed. How did the all-powerful Lord of the Dead not know I was right there, treading on his robe? Would that I could hear his thoughts. My own whirred, but I did not have the faintest idea of what had happened. One thing was certain: my big death payout wasn't going anywhere. I was stuck in this awful state of nonexistence. Unseen, voiceless, bodiless, and lost. Not even undead, just a ghost.

He stormed from the room. The other men glanced at each other nervously. "That's only the third time that's happened," said Shorty. "What does it mean?"

"Nothing," snapped Beaky. "Just that her spirit is stupid and weak. He should screen them better."

"Hush," said Mustache. He stroked the bushy thing that lived on his upper lip. "I think he can hear through walls. I ain't gonna land in one of these boxes because of yer prattle."

They obeyed him, though it was hard to tell if he was in charge or he just made the most sense. In silence they pulled my coffin down. One of the men lost his grip. The top left corner clattered against the sterile floor. I heard rather than felt the crumpling of my corpse inside and shouted, "*Hey!*"

Of course they didn't hear me.

Two of them picked up the slender wooden box and toted it out of the room. Mustache stayed behind.

I didn't know how, but I had to warn Mother and Dex. They might be in trouble.

Just as I turned to leave, the minion with a bottlebrush mustache returned to the coffin room. He shut the door behind him with such an exaggerated air of secrecy, it caught my interest. I waited to see what he would do next. He laid his ear against the door and listened a long time for sounds from the hallway outside. Eventually, he turned and faced the coffins inside. He stared right at me, but blindly, unseeing. It was a sheer accident that his eyes pointed in my direction, I could tell. He was seeing the rows and rows of empty coffins behind me, not my spirit.

All the same, I eased off to the left a bit, out of the line of his unsettling gaze.

"I don't know if you're still here," he whispered. His eyes darted as nervously as a rat's. "Girl? Hey—girl? I'm sorry, I don't know your name."

I grew still. Was he...? No. He couldn't be talking to *me*.

His voice was barely a whisper. I caught myself leaning forward to catch his words. "Listen, girl, you weren't on the list, or I would'a told ya sooner. I had no idea you were one of us. How was I supposed to know? No one told me. But you *must* be one of the rebels. Only choosing to go without yer inhaler would cripple the Lord of the Dead's control over yer spirit like this." He petered out, muttering about the inhaler.

I was thunderstruck. My *inhaler*? That was all? How could I have been so stupid as to endanger Dex instead of sacrifice for his security? I wondered if Mustache could feel my guilt, so close to me.

He shook himself. "Anyhow, girl, welcome. And sorry. Report to Warehouse Eight in the old garment district and you'll receive yer assignment. And... godspeed."

His eyes swept the coffin room. I shuddered as they passed over me, seeking me, but unseeing. He nodded and left the room in a hurry.

"What am I supposed to do?" I muttered. I didn't receive an answer. It would be folly to ignore the only words that had been spoken directly to me in six months, though; I had to find out what this meant. Mother and Dex could wait a few hours.

*

I didn't know the layout of the city very well. Even in my wanderings to find jobs for Dex and Mother, I had stuck to the market, the neighborhood around my flat, and the old school where the two-hour education sessions still carried on.

The old garment district was a place to be avoided. Mother had always mentioned it in hushed tones—they all did, the adults. Before I was born, she had worked in a textile factory making pants. She had lost three fingers on her left hand in an accident, but she still talked of her job with fondness and a certain glimmer in her eye, if she mentioned it at all. But once the factory shut down, gangs moved in, drug addicts and killers. *You go there, you're as good as dead,* she had told me.

Well, I was dead already.

I headed out of the palace, barely noticing my surroundings. Questions crowded my thoughts. I was already in the street and making my way down unfamiliar, deserted alleys before it occurred to me that I should go see my body, say goodbye before it was cremated. What if I ceased to exist once my flesh was reduced to ash? This thought made me pause. Longingly, I looked back to the sleek obsidian walls that loomed over the ramshackle buildings behind me. But if that were true, I couldn't afford to waste precious time looking at a body that no longer even accepted me.

I moved on.

What did he mean, "assignment"? And who were the rebels he talked about? No one rebelled against the Lord of the Dead. Not only did he defeat anyone stupid enough to stand up to him, and brutally murder them and their loved ones, he went on to control their spirits for eternity.

We volunteered for service because he paid. But no sane person would risk being his *enemy* while dead.

I saw two Sneaksters leaning against a wall in an alleyway. They smoked and laughed raucously. Sneaksters enforced curfew and perpetually terrorized the citizens of the city. The Lord of the Dead was smart to employ living humans, ones who were happy to serve because they were just as soulless as he, to keep the rest of the city in line. I hated them for their audacity, built on a foundation of brutality. I hated their greasy locks of hair and their comfortable government-issued shoes. I hated their full bellies. My anger rose and I soared through them. They both screamed, dropped their pipes, and gasped as they felt the icy shock of a spirit passing through them. Without words, they scattered. Their pipes remained abandoned in oil spots on the cracked pavement, forgotten in their haste to escape the haunting.

It was nothing, but it felt like I had accomplished something. Bastards.

The garment district wasn't hard to find. I knew the general direction, of course, because I had always been forbidden to go there. All but two of the fluorescent bulbs on the scaffolding under the dome had burned out. One of the remaining lights flickered erratically. Debris — clothes, mostly — littered the streets. Even the air tasted stale, though being dead, I did not know how thin or polluted it was. I passed two tenement buildings that had collapsed in on themselves. Had anyone been inside when it went down? Worry. It consumed every bit of me. I still had a thousand things to worry about. I wished the world could be different. For Dex.

Ahead of me, loomed a long row of huge, boxy buildings, their corrugated tin roofs in varying states of disrepair. I floated along shadowy streets past them. A different kind of ghost occupied this space: that of harsh chemicals. The pungent odors lingered even after all this time—bleach, dyes, solvents, and acids. Even though I did not breathe them in, I felt the urge to cough. No wonder so many people from Mother's generation were sick with lung rot.

The third building had the numeral three on it. It clung to the wall by a single loose bolt, upside down and backward.

The next building had no number, but the one after that had a numeral five affixed to the front, almost obscured by an illegible graffiti tag. I sped up, anticipation and dread mounting in equal measures. Who would be waiting for me? This place seemed like it had not seen a living inhabitant for at least a decade.

Warehouse Eight lurked on the left. I hesitated at the outside wall, straining to hear any sounds from within. Nothing. I plunged through the wall. Inside, the gloom was even deeper. Only a trace of light filtered through the grimy windows and the occasional gaping hole in the walls to lay on the haphazard items strewn about the factory floor. A veritable city of wooden crates teetered in crooked stacks to the ceiling. Bottles of dried-up dyes, in innumerable colors, waited on their shelves forgotten for eternity. Metal contraptions crouched like giant spiders with their venomous stingers poised to strike.

Uneasily, I moved through the room. There was no one here. I was stupid to have come. That man was crazy, and I should not have listened to him.

However, just as I turned to go, I noticed one of the offices that lined the far wall. It was shuttered tight and the windows were covered with something heavy and dark. Underneath the door, there was a seam of light, weak but sure. As I watched, a shadow shivered across that line of light. Someone was inside that office.

I went over and listened hard outside the door, but heard nothing. I poked my head through and was greeted by a girl my age with thick, smudged glasses, a halo of black, corkscrew hair, and a clear plastic gas mask covering her mouth, leaving her lips still visible beneath the surface.

She blinked. "Hey! Don't you knock?"

Shock stilled me. It was almost as if she was talking to *me*. She seemed to be looking right at me. I recognized her from Jacinta's tenement; I had never quite liked her because she was always talking to Jacinta. Max, I thought her name was. With her slightly bucktoothed grin and spray of freckles across plump cheeks, this girl was cute and quirky—two things I always wanted to be myself, but was too worried and tired to be. Jealousy shot through me, hot and unexpected.

"Well?" she demanded. "Ain't ya going to answer me?"

Still thrown off by the sudden rush of emotion, I stammered, "M—me?"

She rolled her big brown eyes. "Yes, you! You're being kinda rude, ya know."

Stupefied, I stared at her for a few seconds. She was the first person who had seen me in six lonely months.

With a miffed little sigh, she turned her back on me. It was only then that I realized she was missing an arm. The sleeve hung loose over a short stump just past her shoulder. "Might as well come in," she said, unaware. "You're not on the list, but you're… well…"

"Dead?"

To my surprise, she didn't even pause. "Exactly. Deader than I am handicapped, that's for sure."

I frowned at her back. It was almost as if she had heard what I was thinking. I shook my head and floated after her. That was just silly.

"You're Jacinta's friend, aren't you? I've seen you around." A beautiful idea occurred to me. "Is she here, too?"

Max made a negative sound in the back of her throat. "Of course not. She's joined the Lord of the Dead's service. She's undead now. Not like you. You're *dead* dead."

"How can you see me? What is the rebellion? How do you know about Jacinta? What's going on?" Once they started pouring out of me, I couldn't stop the stream of questions until she whirled and interrupted me.

"Wait, you don't know about the rebellion?"

I stopped short. "Um, no."

Her eyes narrowed, suspicious. "How did you know not to take your inhaler?"

"Accident, I guess."

She sighed and led me through a small doorway — being alive, she actually opened it — and down a rickety staircase to a hidden basement. She shut a heavy steel door behind us while I gazed with interest at what I could only assume was the rebellion.

Fifty, maybe a hundred, ragtag citizens stood staring back at me. No, not at me. They stared toward me, like they knew I was there but could not see me. It was even more disquieting than

Mustache had been. Their eyes were like marbles, their faces hard, their bodies lean and sinewy, and their clothing patched. Some sported faded neck tattoos of a red grinning skull: escaped convicts and personal slaves of the Lord of the Dead, or so the legend went. I had grown up to fear that symbol as a sign of a desperate person willing to kill you as soon as look at you. But I had never seen them this close. Only once did I ever glimpse of one of those tattoos, before Mother whisked me away to safety.

These people looked dangerous, but not for the same reasons as Mother told to scare her little girl. No, they were frightening because they were hard, and hopeless, and angry. The bareness of the room, the lack of warmth, the silence, the irritation of chemicals that necessitated gas masks... these people lived for nothing but—

"Vengeance," Max said, coming to stand beside me.

I gaped at her. She grinned and tapped her temple. "I have some gifts. I can't read minds, not exactly, but I can weave threads. A textile factory is a perfect place for that kind of work, don't you think?"

"Who *are* you?" I demanded, incredulous. "Are you seriously planning on overthrowing the Lord of the Dead?"

The grin disappeared. "Yes." Her voice had a hard edge to it.

I waved my invisible arm. "With them?"

"Yeah," she said. "Now it's my turn for questions." She pointed to the middle of the room, where the people had been sitting on the rough concrete. They were all occupied, some with food more meager than my family had, some with mending, some with sharpening makeshift weapons, no doubt pulled from the machinery upstairs. We went right in the center of the dark room. It was so large I couldn't see the far corners.

She settled down and gestured to the floor in front of me as if she were a queen and I merely a visitor in her mansion. My grip on my patience and my sanity began to unravel. I pretended to sit down cross-legged, though I couldn't actually touch the floor.

She nodded curtly at me like a woman much older than her years. "What happened to you?"

"I tried to make the sacrifice," I said. I glanced around at all the people who watched me. "Can they hear me?"

She nodded. "Only when I amplify your presence, like I am now."

I frowned. "I just wanted my family to be safe." My voice dropped to a whisper. I was uncomfortable being heard again. Unused to the idea. "I couldn't reanimate my body. I couldn't even do that for them. And now they'll starve, or worse."

Max's expression softened. The long blade of her finger lifted as if she meant to touch me, but then she withdrew. "Maybe not."

Hope flickered like one of those dying fluorescent bulbs outside. "What do you mean? Who are you?"

She chuckled. "I am the daughter of the Lord of the Dead."

Revulsion overcame me. I scrambled back away from her, hurtling through the bodies of several other followers in my haste. They gasped and shuddered as if doused with icy water. I blubbered incoherently. "You! You're—"

"Calm down," she said. She was more serene than I'd ever been. I envied her for it. "I want him gone, just like you."

I didn't bother telling her that wasn't my goal. I didn't care if he was dead or alive, in power or not. Maybe I was a coward, but all I cared about was Mother and Dex. I wanted Dex to be happy, and healthy, and protected. The rest of the city, and the world for that matter, could go to hell for all I cared.

She tapped her temple knowingly. "Look, you may not think of yourself as a revolutionary, but your kid brother can't be safe in this world while my father still reigns."

I floated like a caged animal between her followers, who looked wary for another outburst from the ghost in their midst. I scoffed at her. "So what, we're supposed to believe you — his *daughter* — would be any better? Give me a break. I'm not that dumb."

She rolled her eyes as if exhausted, beleaguered. As if she had said it a hundred times before, she said, "He mistreated me as well. He murdered my mother before my eyes. He hurt me in ways..." She trailed off. The stump of her arm shrugged to punctuate her point.

I drifted toward her, this time weaving among her followers in the gloom, trying not to notice their unwashed body odor as I passed them. I watched her face, her body language, the quiver of her full lower lip, the defiance in her eyes.

Begging on the streets between the jobs I worked and the night market, I'd learned how to read people. I'd gotten good at it. Which ones thought it would be funny to be cruel to me, and which ones would be still as a snake unless I bothered them but then explode into violence. Which ones weren't worth my breath. Which ones were telling the truth when they said they didn't have anything to spare. And which ones weren't.

She was telling the truth.

But still, I shook my head. "I don't even know why I'm here," I muttered. "I can't help you and you can't help me. I don't wish you ill or anything, but —"

"I ain't so sure about that," she said. "The helping each other part."

Her followers leaned in a fraction. I felt the air around the room squeeze, the pressure of their anticipation. They wanted to hope.

"What do you mean?"

She leaned forward. The guarded, wounded look vanished from her features, making way for something equal parts excitable and businesslike. "Is your corpse still in the palace somewhere?"

I pursed my non-lips and raised my non-eyebrows. "I dunno. Your father—"

"*Don't call him that!*" she hissed.

I backpedaled. "The Lord of the Dead, then — happy? — he

gave the order to destroy it. It's going to be cremated soon, if it hasn't already happened. He said I was useless, and…" I paused. The weight of my impotence threatened to crush my soul to oblivion. "And he's right. I am useless."

Max didn't contradict me, though her honest face imparted her pity. She looked over at a man behind me and nodded once. He got up and walked away.

"Listen," she told me. "The Lord of the Dead didn't know I existed until two years ago. He raped my mother and left her for dead. She died nine months later. In labor with me."

I winced. It was my turn to feel sorry for her.

"He always kills his accidental offspring because we're a threat. We inherit his *abilities*."

Rolling my eyes, I said, "Well, I guess that is a pretty big daddy issue?"

A flicker of impatience marred her composure. "When he found out about me, he came to kill me — I barely escaped."

Cold penetrated me, the same way I imagined the living felt when I touched them with my ghostly spirit. "You have his powers, you say?"

"I can communicate with the dead, for starters." She jutted her chin at me in acknowledgment.

"Can you raise me from the dead so I can go back to helping Mother and Dex?"

Her excited face fell. "No. I'm sorry, but no. That's not how it works."

Disappointment flooded me as quickly as hope had risen. "Oh."

"But," she hurried on, "I can spirit walk. I can separate myself from my own body and—theoretically — occupy other people's bodies. If a body were vacant, like yours, and the spirit already claimed for the Lord of the Dead's servitude, I could take it over and lead the rebellion from the inside. He would have no idea it wasn't you in there."

I frowned. "There are hundreds of bodies there already. Maybe thousands. Why don't you take any of those?"

The man returned, carrying a small box. He handed it to Max and settled down, looking through me but not seeing me. "We tried that, of course," he murmured. "But she needs the previous owner of the body to relinquish its claim or she can only hold onto the body for a few minutes at a time."

Silence ballooned in the room. It was so much to process. A rebel army, led by the illegitimate daughter of the Lord of the Dead, a girl I'd spent been jealous of over my best friend's attention. No hope existed of taking back the choice I had made. Mother and Dex faced likely punishment for my failure—the Lord of the Dead was sure to send someone to harass them since he invested so much in me only to have to cremate my useless corpse. And this army wanted me to give up my body to serve as a vessel for this their leader.

It was incredible. But as many times as I turned it over in my head, I believed it was true. The pieces, though jagged and new, fit.

With graceful deftness that made me almost forget that she only had one arm, she opened the box the rebel had given her. It contained a matchbook, an antique brass lantern, and a clear glass sphere. She fussed with these things and lit the lantern without speaking. Giving me my time to think. And —belatedly I recalled—listening to my thoughts.

Creepy. Her lips quirked behind the gas mask.

"No," I said. "I have no reason to help you. I don't care about overthrowing the Lord of the Dead. Things are fine the way they are. You play at war like a kid kicking an anthill. You're only going to make things worse."

Max gently polished the sphere on her loose shirtsleeve. "I'll take care of your family," she promised. "Bring them here. Feed them. Protect them."

I looked around. "Ha! You think this would be a good home

for Dex?"

"No," she said, "but it's the best chance he's got until we make things right."

The entire rebel army chorused, "Hear, hear!"

I jumped. "I'm not a martyr. I only sacrificed myself because I knew it would help my little brother. We would have all starved to death by now."

"I can make that happen," she said.

Tentatively, I allowed the idea to take root. How I wanted to believe her.

"Jacinta is already in place," she added. "As well as about two dozen or more undead soldiers biding their time in the Lord of the Dead's service. Awaiting my orders. They can help the transition go unnoticed, so he doesn't catch on before it's too late. So he doesn't send men after your family."

Betrayal pierced me. *Jacinta*, I thought. *Why didn't you tell me all this?*

"She loved you," Max said. She reached out to touch my shoulder, but her hand swiped through nothing but air. "She loved you more than anyone. When you decided to join his service, did *you* tell the people you loved what you were about to do for them?"

I closed my eyes. No, I had not. Of course I hadn't — they would have tried to stop me, and I was determined to help them at the expense of my life and freedom. Anger was replaced by a soft pillow of grief and love for Jacinta in the place where my heart used to be.

"All right," I said. My resolve hardened as I opened my eyes and met Max's intense stare. "I'll do it."

The men and women of the rebellion erupted in a cheer. "We finally have a chance!" cried one nearby. "We can defeat him once and for all!"

Max moved the lantern to the halfway point between us. A smile played at her mouth as her people celebrated. She knew how to love, too. Maybe she had never deserved my jealousy.

I had been a terrible provider for Dex. A terrible protector. Even in death I had been too weak to do what it took to take care of him. Not everyone was strong enough to make the world better, but maybe Max was.

Shy of haunting the occasional Sneakster in the street, what could I really do? This. I could do this.

As they quieted down, I asked, "How does it work? What do I have to do?"

She was very still. "We need to test it and see if it works. With luck, they haven't cremated you yet. They're kinda slow to act in there, I've heard. My hope is that you can stay here while I inhabit your body, but I don't really know if that'll work."

Resigned, I nodded. "It might destroy me?"

Her brown eyes were wide and serious, the meager flame of the lantern an orange glint reflected in the pupils. "Yeah, it might."

My non-hands trembled. "Okay. Let's try it."

The army fell perfectly silent. Max said, "Look at the flame's reflection in the sphere. You will feel me intruding on your spirit. Don't fight me. You have to be the bridge to your body. It will feel like I'm walking on you, maybe, or stabbing you, or burning you. I have to use your energy and it might hurt."

She didn't know what she was doing, I realized. Not entirely. To stave off the fear this ignited, I conjured the image of Dex, sweet little ginger Dex with his head bowed saying he had no dream. I stored up this image and let it expand and fill every part of me. Dex deserved not just to eat, but to dream.

"Ready," I whispered.

Pain exploded. Everywhere. I burned. Fire. Screaming.

Then... nothing.

*

Awareness flickered like an old bulb. Snatches of harsh electric light and sound came first, a jumble I couldn't make sense of. Then smells. Sterile smells, not the chemicals from Warehouse Eight. My non-eyes snapped open. I floated like a cloud near the ceiling in a brightly-lit room. Five mummified corpses lay on the spotless black floor.

Light, yellow and incredibly hot, poured through a door that was ajar. Fire. I shuddered at the memory of my spirit being burned to bridge Max into my body.

I dropped down to look more closely at the bodies. The middle one was me. I reached out and caressed my own face. I barely recognized it. Even when I was alive, I rarely saw my reflection. But the muddy auburn hair spread in a tangled cloud beneath my head, the taut cheek, the skinny arm, the pale eyelashes, and the twine friendship bracelet that matched Jacinta's — all mine.

Once, anyway.

The body was unoccupied. This must be the staging room for cremation. Where was Max? Like with all my plans, something had gone wrong.

I settled down into the body, relishing the feeling of its familiarity around my damaged soul. Out of habit I tried opening my eyes — and it worked.

I reanimated my corpse!

With effort, as my muscles were dead and tight, my sinews like tanned leather, I sat up. All of me, body and spirit united. It felt so good. I touched my arms, my face, my belly. Wiggled every digit. Reveled in the sensation of my hair against my stiff fingers.

This was my chance. I could get up, walk out, apologize for my earlier weakness, and finish what I had started. I could join the infantry, earn the payout for Mother and Dex, do as I was told, perpetuate the system. I could do the sure thing.

But...

How long would that payment last, really? Prices kept going up in the Lord of the Dead's regime. There were stories of undead slaves being forced to terrify their own family members to extort tithes from them. My sacrifice was only ever a bandage, a temporary abatement of a permanent problem.

Max had gotten into my head, and I couldn't shake her. Her offer was scarier, less certain, and a lot more dangerous. But if she succeeded, then maybe she could wreak permanent change. A new world, a less cruel world, for Dex to grow up in. Instinct told me I probably wouldn't survive another attempt by her to use my spirit as a conduit to my body. I would likely cease to exist altogether. The thought terrified me to my core.

I was too weak to do anything useful myself, and too cowardly to fight the system. But I was selfless enough to sacrifice. Maybe it was my low self-value that gave me the highest worth. Other people like Jacinta and Max would go on to change the world, fight the good fight. Other people like Dex would make the world a brighter place.

Still, they needed me to take the first big step. It was selfish to want to stay in this body. Selfish to give up this opportunity to do the one tiny thing I was capable of doing because I was scared, because I didn't want to stop existing.

Was I willing to give up everything for the hope of a better world for others?

I was on my feet without thinking about it.

The decision was clear. Yes, I was.

I opened the other door — the one that didn't lead to a fiery chamber of destruction—and looked out on a brightly lit hallway. I knew this hall from my time exploring the Lord of the Dead's palace. I walked as quietly as I could down its length. My body creaked and groaned from time to time. I tried not to be disgusted by it but to love it for its endurance in spite of the hardships I had put it through. The place was empty as before and there was no one to hear the small sounds I emitted.

I went back to the coffin room I knew so well. The long, dry room contained wooden boxes stuffed with the most hopeless, destitute, broken people in the city. I found the freshest ones at the front and picked a casket that had already been nailed shut. I pried it open using my dead fingernails. They snapped off one by one, but I felt no pain: an advantage of being undead. With great effort, I eased the lid off. Inside reposed a young boy, younger than me. I didn't know him.

Tenderly, I pushed him against one side of his coffin. It was tight, but there was room. Both of us were so skinny and frail. "I'm sorry," I whispered. "Whoever you are, you deserved undisturbed rest." My voice sounded like a dry scrap of parchment scraping along the unmoving air. I pulled myself up and into the coffin, settling into the cramped space with this stranger. I imagined he was Jacinta. With a grunt, I pulled the lid up to seal the coffin tight over us both. My head rested against his shoulder, and my arm came to embrace his torso. Selfishly, I took another minute to relish the sensation of being part of the physical world.

I relinquished my body. I simply let go of it, and it allowed me to leave. Something about Max's power had allowed me to connect and disconnect from it at will. I hoped when I returned to her, I could use this knowledge to bridge her to it completely. If it took every bit of energy I had, I would make it happen. The pathways had been forged. I knew how they felt now. They were familiar to me. Maybe, just maybe, I had the strength to guide her along them now.

Leaving the blackness of the coffin, I checked my handiwork from the outside. I'd been careful to put the nails inside, so as long as no one looked too closely to see they weren't in the holes, there was no evidence the box had been tampered with. I hoped no one would notice.

Time to go.

*

Selfishly, I went to visit Mother and Dex first. Every delayed minute potentially cost them; the Lord of the Dead would surely think to seek them out and punish them for my futility. But I couldn't resist the urge to see them once more, even though they couldn't see me.

I passed through the door to find them both inside. They did not speak to one another. Darkness pervaded; the electricity had gone out again. Dex stared at the wall, his expression blank, and Mother stared at him, her face filled with sadness. A cabinet door stood open, revealing nothing but an empty wrapper with half a crust of green-blue bread inside.

"I'm sorry," I whispered. "I love you."

Life entered Dex's eyes and he looked around. Had he heard me? Hope rose in that place where I carried my feelings. I resisted the urge to touch him, knowing it would only bring him discomfort.

"I miss her," he muttered to Mother.

"Me, too, baby," she said, tears in her eyes. "Me, too."

The moment was shattered by a pounding on the door. "Dex? Anna? Open up. Now."

The fear and terror I felt was reflected in their faces. Dex got up and hid behind Mother as she approached the door. The boards squealed ominously beneath their combined weight and I wanted to scream at them to be careful. Was it the Lord of the Dead's men, here to punish them for my weakness? Had they already discovered my missing corpse? Cowardice prevented me from peeking through the door to find out for myself.

"Who is it?" Mother asked. She seemed so small. Not nearly powerful enough to protect the precious boy who relied on her.

"Get back!" I cried. "Hide!"

"Open up, quick," boomed a male voice outside.

Mother's hand shook as the unbolted the lock. The door swung open.

I gasped. It was the man from the rebellion, the one who had brought the box with the lantern and the glass sphere that allowed Max to bridge to my corpse. He carried a similar wooden box in his arms. He pushed his way in despite weak protests from Mother, and he shut and barred the door behind him.

"I'm from the rebellion," he said. "Your daughter tried to help us. We're going to take care of you now."

Relief poured through my spirit and warmed the room. Dex stepped out, his eyes wide with childlike wonder. "You saw my sister?"

The man shook his head. "Nah, didn't see 'er. She's dead, kid, make no mistake. She's on our side, or was. We take care of our own." He opened the box. Inside rested two gas masks, an entire loaf of fresh bread, and a good-sized hunk of salty, cured meat. A feast.

Had I tears I would have wept a river of happiness to see Mother and Dex tear into the food. They ate their fill hungrily, and still there was more to eat.

They were going to be okay. At least for now.

*

I went to Warehouse Eight feeling lighter than I had in my entire existence. Without announcing myself, I went in the office, down the secret stairs, and into the gloomy, ill-lit basement where the rebels gathered. Max's eyes shot up and she exclaimed, "You survived!"

I grinned. It was the first time I could remember smiling in a long time. "It surprised me, too," I replied.

"I thought the strain had killed you," she said. "I made it almost to your body but then your energy just disappeared. I think it was too much for you to handle."

The men and women of the rebellion had gathered, clutching each other with hope written all over their visages. Their excitement buoyed up my strength even more. "Thank you for taking care of them," I said. "You kept your promise."

She nodded. "Of course we did. You kept your end of the bargain, or at least you tried."

Quickly, I recounted what had happened. She told me that two days had passed. "You ceased to exist, I think," she said. "But you're stronger than you think. You found your way back to finish what you started."

Pride sparked in me at the approving sounds the rebels made around me. Acceptance and approval filled the room. "I'm ready. I know where to take you now."

"Let's do it fast, while you still feel strong," she said. "This will likely take every ounce of energy you have. You realize you may not survive it if we make the connection?"

I nodded solemnly. "I'm prepared to make that sacrifice."

"You're braver than you think, you know," she said. "Your kind of strength is not as obvious, maybe, but it's the best of all, the strength to love the way you love."

The praise fell on my non-shoulders like a cozy blanket. "Fight well," I said. "Take him out. And the Sneaksters, too. Give the city a chance again."

"I promise we will," she said. The rebels cheered. "This won't be in vain."

She led me to the center of the room and I gathered every shred of myself. Every bit of energy I had. Every glimmer of willpower. Every feeling and emotion I owned. When I was ready, I nodded.

I felt her spirit leave her body and join mine. I felt her

unraveling my spirit, making a bridge to my body, so far away. I gave her more and more of myself, willingly. It burned. So hot. My energy was a fire, a current of wild electricity. It consumed me, and I still gave her more. I showed her the path to my body and I gave her the energy she needed to find it.

The pain became too much to bear, and I screamed with effort as I gave her the very last of me.

The tiniest remaining crumb of me watched as she opened the eyes of my corpse and pushed off the lid of the coffin.

Perhaps I only imagined it, but the last thing I was aware of was the distant scream of the Lord of the Dead as he sensed her nearby.

He was going down.

A NOTE FROM
LITTLE BIRD PUBLISHING HOUSE

By KATIE M JOHN

In 2015, after years of watching it unfold on social media, I attended UTOPiA. Being London based, and UTOPiA being in Nashville, Tennessee USA, it didn't only feel a long way away in terms of dreams but in distance and finances too.

Despite all the barriers to me attending, I booked a ticket knowing somehow, I would make it happen.

The experience was transforming. It is not hyperbole when I say that UTOPiA, and the work Janet does, changed my life.

The journey I have undertaken both as an indie author and the founder of the small press house, Little Bird Publishing, has often been lonely and full of doubts. UTOPiA vanquished all of that negativity; it filled my life with incredibly clever, funny, kind friends, and it equipped me with specific skills and knowledge to flourish – both the author and the publisher.

As such, I wanted to pay something back into the UTOPiA community, and it occurred to me that organizing and publishing a celebratory anthology was the gift I could give back – not only would if offer the opportunity for several UTOPiAN authors to showcase their work, but it would also raise money along the way.

Janet Wallace, being Janet, immediately suggested that the money made after publication costs went into a charitable project founded by another dear UTOPiAN, Carlyle Labuschagne.

Carlyle, similarly inspired by the UTOPiAN community is the founder of the 'Help Build A Library In South Africa Foundation' It seemed a natural synergy that our community should extend the hand of friendship and enablement into another community.

It has been an absolute privilege to work alongside everybody involved in the project. Each and every author has demonstrated not only the most amazing talent, but utmost professionalism, making the anthology an absolute joy to work on. THANK YOU for that.

LITTLE BIRD PUBLISHING HOUSE

www.littlebirdpublishinghouse.com
&
www.thelittlebirdbookstore.com

Founded in 2013, Little Bird Publishing House was established as an antidote to some of the commercial self-publishing houses that were targeting the indie author community.

Little Bird was established on the model of a co-operative artistic community, in which authors became part of a family, supporting one another, cheerleading and being responsible for one another, and offering authors the chance to engage with high end services of editing, cover art and publication with none of the fees.

Little Bird Publishing is about celebrating diversity of voice and celebrating the individual right to creative expression.
We are currently a community of thirteen authors, and take on five to six authors a year.

As part of our house, we also established the Dark Heart & Night Shade Anthology project as a way of new writers gaining publishing experience and platform.

It has been a delight and a privilege to work on the UTOPiA Anthology, REVOLUTION and pay back into the community that is so dear to us.

57203020R00202

Made in the USA
Charleston, SC
07 June 2016